the

Bookshop

girl

and the

billionaire

THE BRISBANE BACHELORS SERIES

THE BOOK SHOP GIRL AND THE BILLIONAIRE

ISBN: 978-0-6451076-3-0

Copyright © 2022 by Jennie Kew
Published by Wooden Key Press
Edited by Wooden Key Press
Cover by Mayhem Cover Creations

PREVIOUSLY PUBLISHED AS
REVENGE AND REDEMPTION (2018)

www.jenniekew.com

Praise for Jennie Kew

The Viking Blues – Heart Award 2021 (2022)
Erotic Romance – Winner

The Viking Blues – Passionate Plume Award 2022
Short Contemporary Romance – Finalist

The Viking Blues – Stiletto Award 2022
Erotic Romance – Finalist

His Own Heaven – Passionate Plume Award 2021
BDSM Romance – Winner

His Own Heaven – Stiletto Award 2021
Long Romance – Finalist

This Time Around – Koru Award of Excellence 2020
Short Romance – 2nd Place

This Time Around – Stiletto Award 2020
Mid-length Romance – Finalist

Third Time Lucky – Passionate Plume Award 2019
BDSM Romance – Finalist

Third Time Lucky – Stiletto Award 2019
Erotic/BDSM Romance – Finalist

"Be prepared to be taken along on a wonderful,

sexy, heartwarming, sometimes tear
inducing, slightly kinky joy ride!"
Review for *Third Time Lucky*

"The story is heartwarming and empowering.
The plot is gripping and keeps you turning
pages. Definitely one click worthy."
Review for *Third Time Lucky*

"This novel was so romantic!
I'm in love, love, love with Rafe!
I will read this book again it was so good!"
Review for *This Time Around*

"...Toby was my perfect book boyfriend."
Review for *His Own Heaven*

"It's a sexy, sleek and highly addictive story."
Review for *His Own Heaven*

"Their story is heartfelt, sweet, deliciously
hot and sexy, romantic and more."
Review for *The Viking Blues*

Where there's tea, there's hope.
ARTHUR WING PINERO

Chapter One

"That bloke has been staring at you forever."

Claire Morse followed her assistant manager's gaze to the man sitting in the back of her tearoom. The man conspicuously engrossed in the month-old gardening magazine clutched in his big, strong hands.

She frowned. "Trust me, I am the last woman in the world *that* man would be interested in. Well, second last," she corrected herself as she slid a non-fat chai-latte across the benchtop and thanked her customer.

"Nonsense," Karen said, an irritated scowl decorating her pretty face. "Why do you always put yourself down like that?"

Ignoring the question, Claire nodded at their topic of conversation, a man who still had the power to make her knees wobble and her pulse race at the mere sight of him. "Do you know who that is?"

Her frown quickly replaced by a dreamy stare, Karen sighed. "He's tall, dark and sinfully delicious. Who cares who he is?"

"His name is Luke Hardcastle."

1

"You know him?" Karen said, her voice dropping to a conspiratorial whisper as she cleaned the benchtop.

"Mostly by reputation."

Karen's eyebrow winged up. "Mostly?"

Claire sighed softly. "You know those overbearing, self-absorbed, stupidly wealthy playboys with the endless string of model girlfriends and the holier-than-thou attitude that you hate *so* much?"

"Yeah," Karen said, her tone cautious as she drew the word out.

"Meet their leader."

"Fuck."

Claire chuckled at her assistant manager's crestfallen expression. "If it makes you any feel better, he wasn't always an arsehole, not really."

"What changed?"

"Not sure, but a couple of years ago his women started getting thinner, blonder and more frequent."

"Typical," Karen said with a derisive snort. "I tell you what though, he's looking at you again."

Claire shifted her gaze to Luke's and got caught in his potent stare.

"Are you *blushing*?" Karen whispered, her voice suddenly filled with amusement.

Claire turned away and cleared her throat. "I'm going to do the rosters. I'll be in the office if you need me," she called over her shoulder, then took off downstairs, wincing at the thunderous sound of her footfalls on the ancient timber staircase.

Located at the rear of the bookstore, her office was roughly the size of a largish toilet. Not the ideal workspace by any stretch of the imagination, but at least it was hers. Sucking in her stomach, she squeezed past the boxes of newly arrived bestsellers then slumped into the cheap plastic garden chair at her desk. She wriggled in her seat as she tried to find a comfortable position and cursed herself again for breaking her office chair.

Still amazed the chair was the only thing that had been broken, Claire frowned as she remembered the night she'd tripped over in the dark and landed awkwardly on the stupid thing. The fact she'd been drunk at the time hadn't helped relieve the guilt of breaking something she'd spent almost half a week's wages on.

Of course, the only reason she'd been drunk in the first place was because her so called date that evening had been a total wanker. He'd actually admitted during the entrées that he'd only asked her out because she was Amanda Morse's niece, and he'd been hoping for an introduction, a shortcut into the corporate shark tank that was Morse Industries, her aunt's blood sucking corporate demolition company. Shortly after that little revelation she'd stopped paying attention, to both her date and how much wine she'd consumed.

When it came down to a choice between talking about her aunt with forced civility or suffering a blinding hangover, the hangover was definitely the lesser of two evils.

Claire huffed out a sigh. Why did every man who asked her out want to talk about her aunt? How did every one of them buy into the lie that was Amanda Morse? Of course, she knew how. Because Amanda was an expert at hiding her true colours until it was too late. She was the spider, they were the fly and eventually everyone got caught in her web.

But Claire still thought it might be nice if just one man actually wanted to date her for, well, *her*. Surely there had to be someone out there who didn't see her surname and salivate at the career potential. There must be someone who appreciated smart chicks with fat bums and a penchant for chocolate cake and antiquing.

Of course not, Claire. Don't be daft.

Staring vacantly at the spreadsheet open on her laptop, she wondered if Luke Hardcastle had ever dated someone like her. Probably not. Not "Love 'em and leave 'em Hardcastle". Claire knew his preferred type well enough. Models. Tall, blonde, snap-in-half-in-a-stiff-breeze-willowy, butter-wouldn't-melt-in-their-mouths models. Women who oozed sophistication and grace. Not a tall, overweight, brunette klutz who'd opened a tearoom above her bookstore because she appreciated the sheer indulgence of pretty china tea settings, miniature cakes and finger sandwiches, and thought skim milk was a crime against nature.

Luke wouldn't be caught dead dating someone like her.

What is he doing in Novelteas?

Claire hadn't laid eyes on the man in eighteen months, not since the unpleasantness that got her sacked from Morse Industries. It didn't make any sense for him to be in her shop—surely he had people who could fetch him a cup of tea when he wanted one. She guessed it was possible he didn't know who owned the place. He probably didn't even remember her. Officially, they'd only met twice before and the second of those times had basically entailed her trying not to burst into tears while he hurled obscenities at her for twenty minutes straight. Or maybe he did remember her and that's why he'd tried hiding behind the magazine.

Either way, speculating about Luke's agenda wasn't getting the rosters done. But just as she refocussed her attention, someone knocked on her open door.

"Come in if you dare," Claire said, thinking it was

Karen with a Luke update, but when she glanced up, she was surprised to see the man himself.

Oh crap!

In a moment of panic, she shot to her feet and knocked her chair backwards, then in typical Claire form, as she tried to step over the protruding chair legs, she tripped. The only thing stopping her from face-planting into a pile of boxes was a strong, warm hand gripping her forearm.

An equally strong, warm voice accompanied the action. "Do be careful, Miss Morse. We wouldn't want you to have a fall in the workplace. The paperwork alone is a nightmare."

Claire stared, wide-eyed and slack jawed as his deep, rich voice filled her tiny office and wrapped itself around her like a lover's arms.

Oh no, not again.

She'd had the same fanciful reaction the first time they'd met face to face, ten years ago when she was a shy, nervous nineteen-year-old interning for her aunt. And again, eighteen months ago when he'd stormed Amanda's office demanding retribution.

But it wasn't just his voice that made her insides quiver with awareness.

Ten years of unrequited yearning surged through her body at the feel of his flesh against hers, at the fantastic sensation of scorching heat flowing from his fingertips and into her arm. She pressed her thighs together as her body flushed with wanting.

Goddammit!

All he'd done was touch her arm and she was behaving like an idiotic schoolgirl, staring at the man like a deer caught in headlights.

Claire groaned inwardly. *Why him?* Why couldn't she

crush on some nice normal bloke with a regular job and a boring little life? She knew why. Because no man like that had ever made her feel the way this man had. No nice normal man had ever made her heart thump out of her chest just by touching her arm.

Did it matter that he had a reputation for being a womanising pig, or that he made more money in a day than she did in a year? Apparently, it didn't make a lick of difference to her libido.

Nope.

Not a single lick.

Chapter Two

Claire's posture softened as she let her gaze drift over the man standing in her office doorway—a man tall enough to hold her the way she'd always imagined a man should hold a woman, and strong enough to lift her large body effortlessly in his perfectly sculptured arms.

Not that she'd seen those arms firsthand, but photos of him shirtless appeared on the cover of enough supermarket tabloids to give her a pretty good idea. That coupled with a fairly decent imagination meant she had some very nice arm porn tucked away in her spank bank. But it was his face that really did her in.

Luke Hardcastle was a disturbingly handsome man with a wide, sensuous mouth that she just knew could satisfy her every carnal fantasy, and golden amber eyes that sparkled with the promise of mischief. Eyes that were... narrowed under a stern brow as he stared at her, no doubt waiting for her to snap out of her lust induced fugue state.

Snapping her mouth shut, Claire managed to pull herself together long enough to free her arm from Luke's strong grip. "Thank you," she muttered as her cheeks flamed with heat.

Shoving his hands in his pockets and leaning against the doorjamb, Luke said, "Quaint little office you have here. Cosy."

Body stiffening again as Luke's words hit a nerve, Claire folded her arms across her chest and gritted her teeth. "Do you need something?" she said as politely as possible, which truthfully wasn't very polite at all.

"As a matter of fact, I do," Luke said, his voice and manners all practiced charm as if she hadn't just snarled at him. "I wish to speak with you about a personal matter and I'd like you to come by my office so we can discuss it. My car is waiting," he said, nodding towards the street.

"A personal matter?" Claire repeated, her brow pulling down in confusion.

"Yes."

What personal matter could Luke Hardcastle possibly wish to discuss with me?

As soon as she finished the thought, she was struck by another. The realisation Luke thought she would simply drop everything to accommodate him. *His car was waiting?* And that pissed her off even more than his snide remark about the size of her office.

"I have a business to run, Mr Hardcastle. Getting across town in the middle of the day for no good reason is a waste of time I don't have. If you wish to speak with me about anything, you're welcome to step inside *my* office. Cosy as it may be."

Luke's perfect mouth twisted and his eyes narrowed. "Fine," he said, then stepped inside and struggled to shut the door, shoving it past the same stack of boxes she'd squeezed past earlier.

"I'd offer you a seat but...." Claire said, leaving the statement hanging as she gestured at the lack of available space. Turning away from him, she righted the garden chair, sat down and waited for Luke to speak.

As he leaned against the boxes, he sniffed the air. "What is that smell?"

Breathing deeply, Claire smiled. *Best smell ever.* "Knowledge."

"Excuse me?"

"Technically it's the degradation of the chemical compounds used to make paper, ink and the polymers used to bind them together into books. But 'knowledge' sounds nicer."

For a fleeting moment Claire could have sworn she saw a genuine smile grace Luke's handsome face.

And for a moment she forgot to breathe.

Recovering her senses, she cleared her throat. "What did you wish to say to me?"

With his implacable mask back in place, Luke said, "I own you."

Claire folded her arms again. "That's funny. I don't remember being for sale."

Luke inclined his head. "I misspoke. I meant I own your shop. I've bought up all the property in this section of Merthyr Road."

"I see," Claire said slowly, her voice cautious. "And you're telling *me* this because...?"

"The previous owner told me some of the other retailers look to your business acumen and expertise when dealing with the landlord, so consider this a courtesy call. I'm your new landlord, and I wish to discuss the parameters of the new lease agreements. I thought you might like to take a look at them before I speak with the other retailers."

Frowning, she said, "I thought you said you wanted to discuss a personal matter?"

"I would have thought the future of your business *was* a personal matter, Miss Morse. We wouldn't want anyone going out of business unnecessarily now, would we?"

Claire felt the heat drain from her face and ice skittered over her skin. "I don't suppose you happen to have one of these new agreements on you?"

The bastard smirked. "Not at present, no. But if you would just come with me to my office...."

"I told you, I can't just up and leave in the middle of the day. Unlike some people, I don't have the luxury of swanning off whenever I feel like it."

The bastard's smirk slipped into a look of impatience. "What time do you close?"

"Five o'clock."

"Can you be at Hardcastle Tower by five-thirty?"

Claire pasted on a smile and tightened her arms across her ample chest. She didn't miss Luke's gaze darting to her breasts, lingering. "I don't drive, so, probably not." Even on its best days, public transport was notoriously unreliable.

Flicking his gaze back to hers, Luke said, "I'll send a car for you." Then he was reaching for the doorknob as though everything was done and settled, but before he opened the door, he looked back at the boxes of books and shook his head.

Slipping his suit jacket off, he handed it to Claire. "Hold this." Then he leaned into the stack and shifted it back just far enough that the door could swing freely again.

Claire stared at his body as he moved, watched his back flex and his biceps bulge with the effort of shoving 200 hardcover novels out of his way. He made it look so easy, as if the boxes weighed next to nothing instead of the 150 kilograms she knew them to be. She half expected his muscles to burst through the stitching of his business shirt, Incredible Hulk style.

Luke smash!

She tried not to stare when he took his jacket back and slipped those strong arms inside the sleeves, hiding them from view.

She did, however, bite her lip.

And maybe squeeze her thighs together. Tightly.

Luke didn't seem to notice. "A car will be here at five o'clock sharp to collect you. I suggest you don't keep me waiting, Miss Morse."

And just like that, her interest waned as the urge to tell Luke to get the fuck out of her *quaint little office* bubbled up inside her, but she bit her tongue instead. Changes to her lease meant possible changes to her income, and Claire had a mortgage to pay, and wages, and insurance premiums, and electricity bills and a hundred and one other day to day expenses that sucked her bank accounts dry every month.

She couldn't afford to be rude and the arsehole knew it.

Afraid of what she'd say if she dared to open her mouth, Claire nodded sharply.

"Good. I'll see you this afternoon, then." Then he shut the door behind him and disappeared into her bookstore.

Claire wanted to scream. She wanted to rail and hit and scratch Luke's golden-boy eyes out. For a moment there, when she was ogling the live-action arm porn, she'd forgotten who he was. Who he *really* was.

He wasn't someone to be admired and he certainly wasn't someone she should be drooling over.

Luke Hardcastle was the man who'd gotten her sacked.

"You're going to be late."

Luke shuffled the deck then dealt the cards. "She can wait."

"Luke."

Luke matched his younger sister's warning tone. "Lottie." Then asked, "What's with the purple wig?"

Picking up her cards, she said, "I've been helping out in the children's ward, reading to them, playing games, that sort of thing. Purple hair makes them smile. It helps distract them. And distracting them distracts me. But don't change the subject. What's wrong? You don't seem as enthusiastic about our plan as you did last week. Did something happen?"

Raking his hand through his hair he eyed his sister with caution. After eighteen months of nagging her to fight back she'd finally relented and agreed to join him in his quest for vengeance against Morse Industries.

Only now he was having second thoughts.

Because of Claire.

It had been so long since he'd last seen her, he'd forgotten the effect she had on him.

"Are you really sure you want to do this, Lottie?"

She raised a brow at him. "A bit late to be asking that now, don't you think? Are you having second thoughts?"

Luke stared at his cards. "Honestly? Yes."

Lottie smirked. "Is this because you still have a thing for Claire Morse?"

"I do not have a *thing* for Claire Morse."

I might have a thing for Claire Morse.

He'd preened in her office, for fuck's sake.

He'd flexed his muscles and moved a huge stack of boxes out of her way then gloried in her open sexual response to him. He hadn't missed her perfect white teeth sinking into the pillow of her bottom lip, or the way she'd pressed her thighs together as her gaze raked over his chest and arms.

The speed of his erection under her unfettered stare had also caught his attention.

"Uh-huh." His sister grinned. "You're thinking about her right now, aren't you?"

"I admit to nothing," Luke said, rearranging the cards in his hand. Then he pinned her with a serious stare. "Lottie, you're my baby sister and you know I would do *anything* for you. But I need to know you're comfortable with what we're doing, and not just doing it to appease me. This is some serious shit and it could get very nasty. I don't want you to have any regrets."

"I'm not a child, Luke. I know exactly what we're doing. And if everything goes according to plan, I won't have any regrets. I know it's the right thing to do," she said, and Luke's heart sank. But he smiled at her anyway. "I don't know how much time I have left but I want to accomplish something worthwhile before I die. Taking Morse Industries down and making sure that evil company can't hurt anyone else seems like a pretty freaking noble endeavour, if you ask me. So no, Luke, I'm not doing this to appease you. I'm doing it because it needs to be done."

Luke stared at his sister for a long moment then nodded. He would proceed with the plan. He would ignore the lust he felt screaming through his body every time he saw Claire Morse and he would take Morse Industries down from the inside. Luke would seek vengeance on his sister's behalf, and he would shove aside his misgivings and focus on the goal.

Destroy Morse Industries.

Destroy Amanda Morse.

Rid himself of Claire Morse once and for all and forget she ever existed.

Easier said than done.

"Do you have any nines," Lottie said, pulling him from his thoughts.

"Go fish."

Chapter Three

Five o'clock rolled around and as expected, Luke's car pulled up outside Novelteas. A young man jumped out of the sleek black car and opened the rear passenger door.

Claire ignored the twinge of disappointment that Luke himself wasn't picking her up.

What the fuck is wrong with me?

"Miss Morse?"

Claire met the driver's gaze. "Yes?"

"My name is Edward. Mr Hardcastle asked me to pick you up this afternoon and take you to HQ."

"Oh. Well it's nice to meet you, Edward."

"Please." Edward gestured for her to climb in the back seat then shut the door behind her.

"There's bottled water in the centre console if you're thirsty," Edward said as he buckled his seatbelt. "Or Tim Tams if you'd like a snack."

Claire adjusted her belt strap so it wasn't cutting her in half. *His last passenger must have been a swizzle-stick. Or a model.* "You keep the car stocked with Tim Tams?"

She caught Edward's grin in the rear-view mirror. "Don't tell him I told you, but they're Mr Hardcastle's favourite."

"Good to know," Claire said, and filed the information away for future use.

Just like her aunt had trained her to do.

And how she now trained her staff to do.

The difference being, when Amanda filed information away you never knew how she'd use it later. Could be to send a personalised gift basket to someone she wanted to do business with. Could be to crush her enemies into street pizza before they'd even realised they had enemies.

After years of feeling physically ill every time she reported something to her aunt, Claire now preferred to use her powers of observation for good. Discover one of your regular customers is a published author? Offer to hold a book signing. Overhear a patron lament the lack of gluten free goodies in your cake cabinet? Add a gluten free selection to your menu.

It wasn't rocket science, it was just good business—something her aunt had forgotten somewhere along the way.

The drive to Hardcastle Tower only took fifteen minutes, even with peak hour traffic. Edward dropped Claire off at the Market Street entrance, waved goodbye and then pulled away from the curb and quickly disappeared around the corner.

Standing on the footpath, Claire stared up at the building across the street and shook the nervous tension from her hands.

Morse Industries.

She'd not been within cooee of the place for eighteen months, not since the day her aunt fired her and had security escort her out of the building. Just the thought of going anywhere near the place sent a shiver down her spine, and yet here she was.

A sucker for punishment.

The tall concrete and glass building was as cold and uninviting as it'd ever been, much like its owner. Amanda was in there somewhere, barking orders at her simpering cronies, making millions from other people's misery, and that old familiar feeling of self-loathing began crawling over Claire's flesh, chilling her blood and sucking the air from her lungs. She felt unclean, knowing the things she knew, the things she'd seen... things she'd done.

Rubbing at the sudden ache in her chest, she turned away from her past, and then with her head held high, she entered the lobby of Hardcastle Tower and went to meet her future.

Or my doom.

With Luke it could go either way.

When the lift reached the top floor and the doors opened with a ping, Claire was greeted by Luke's assistant—a thin, leggy blonde in a skirt-suit so short it bordered on obscene, and heels so high it was a wonder she could walk at all.

Feeling quite rumpled by comparison, Claire smoothed her hands over her hair then tugged at the hem of her T-shirt. "Shit," she muttered to herself as she spotted a smear of strawberry jam on her shirt, right near her left breast. She licked her thumb and rubbed at the offending stain to no avail.

When she looked up, the leggy blonde was smirking at her. "Ms Morse? I'm Sandra," she said, and indicated for Claire to follow her. "I'm Mr Hardcastle's personal assistant. He's running late and requests that you wait for him in here."

"*Miss* Morse," Claire corrected. "Not Ms."

"Of course." Sandra pushed open the stylish timber door that led to Luke's expansive corner office and gestured to a black leather couch against the wall. "Sit," she ordered, as though Claire were a trained poodle. "Would you like a coffee or tea while you wait?"

"Tea, please," Claire said, using her best underestimate-me-at-your-own-peril voice, the one she reserved for dealing with people who thought they were better than her, as this chick obviously did. Then she smiled with practised politeness and tilted her chin up so she could look down her nose at her opponent. Even in five-inch stilettos, Sandra still stood three inches shorter than Claire.

The smaller woman straightened her jacket, her gaze slid down and away. *Gotcha.* "Mr Hardcastle won't be long," she said, then she turned and left to fetch the tea.

Not that Claire actually wanted tea, she just wanted Luke's assistant to bugger off so she could gather her thoughts in private before he arrived.

No sooner had Sandra closed the door before Claire began pacing out the room.

Nothing quaint *about this office.*

Stopping by the wall of glass that served for a window, Claire marvelled at the magnificent view. She saw clear across the Eagle Street Pier to Kangaroo Point, and could even see the southern entrance to the Story Bridge. Late afternoon traffic crowded it in both directions as people made their way home from work.

To their families.

Not allowing herself to get bogged down by things beyond her control, Claire turned her attention to the Bris-

bane River and watched the City Cats ferry people back
and forth from one jetty to another.

"Great view, isn't it?"

Luke's deep voice boomed in the silence of his office
and made Claire jump. She turned around to see him stride
into the room, his long legs eating up the distance to his desk
with ease. A moment later his assistant reappeared carrying
a basic tea service, a glass of ice and two bottles of water on
a tray. She assumed the ice and water were Luke's.

"Thank you, Sandra," Luke said after blondie set the
tray down on his desk. "You can go home now."

Luke waited until they were alone again before speaking. "Sorry I'm late," he said as he slipped his jacket off and
tossed it on the couch. His tie quickly followed. "My
meeting ran over time. Please, have a seat."

He gestured to a stylish black leather chair in front of
his desk. Claire watched his every movement as he loosened
his shirt collar with long, lean fingers and rolled up his shirt-
sleeves, revealing the toned muscle of his forearms, the
strength of a man who knew the value of hard work.

"Now, I suppose you'd like to see the new lease agreement," he said, making himself comfortable in his own
chair.

The way he spoke made Claire hesitate. "That's why
I'm here," she said. "Isn't it?"

Leaning back in his chair, Luke smiled, smug. "Not
exactly."

Chapter Four

"What do you mean 'not exactly'? Why am I here?"

Claire didn't sit down and Luke couldn't be happier. Standing in front of his desk, she slapped her hands against the timber surface and leaned forward so she could look him in the eye. Only with her leaning over, and the way her pale pink T-shirt hugged her huge rack, Luke's eyes were otherwise occupied.

She made a growling noise and rolled her eyes. "They're called tits, Mr Hardcastle."

Yes they are.

And he had a perfect view of them.

"Please," he said, dragging his gaze up to hers. "Call me Luke. And you're here because I want your help with a small... side project I'm working on."

Frowning at him, Claire eased herself into the chair behind her. "What sort of project?" she asked, her tone wary.

Luke smiled his most charming smile. "The destruction of Morse Industries."

Claire didn't even blink. "I thought you said this was a *small* project."

Not knowing what to make of Claire's indifference, Luke reached for the tea tray and set about making her a cup. "Milk? Sugar?" he asked.

"Half a spoon of sugar and just a dash of milk," she replied.

Luke handed her the tea and watched as she lifted the cup to her full lips, then tried very hard *not* to imagine how'd those lips would feel wrapped around his—

"This... *pig swill* is the tea you serve your guests?"

Pig swill? His daydream eviscerated by Claire's disdain, Luke straightened in his seat, the insult cutting more deeply than it should have. Why the fuck did he even care what she thought of his tea? But his words still came out snippy. "What's wrong, Miss Morse? Not fancy enough for your discerning palate?"

"Tea doesn't need to be fancy, Luke. It needs to be good."

The sound of his name slipping off her tongue softened his mood immediately. And hardened his dick. *Fuck.* "And that's not good tea?" he said, imagining all the ways he wanted to hear her say his name.

Moaning.

Screaming.

Begging....

Claire put the teacup and saucer back on the tray and scrunched up her nose in disgust. "I'd rather drink hot cat piss. And don't change the subject."

Unable to contain his surprise at her use of foul language, he said, "I don't remember you being this feisty."

"Considering our limited interaction, I'm surprised you remember me at all."

Yeah, right. Like he'd ever forget the woman who'd set his blood on fire with little more than a shy smile and a body so curvy she should come with a road map.

Of course, the moment he'd learned who she was his blood had frozen solid.

It had been ten years since that fateful meeting. Ten years of wanting a woman he loathed. And it didn't matter how many anti-Claires he banged in his attempts to rid himself of his infatuation, every time he caught even a glimpse of her rounded arse, or big breasts, or her lovely face with those intelligent steel-blue eyes he just wanted to pin her down to whatever hard surface was handy and fuck his way into her.

But she was right. He'd changed the subject.

Time to change it back.

"You don't seem surprised by my request."

Claire licked her thumb and rubbed at a reddish smudge on her T-shirt. "I'm not."

Distracted by her disinterest—and the way her tit bounced as she attacked her stained shirt—Luke frowned. "Why not?"

Abandoning her task, she returned her focus to him. "Because every time a man wishes to discuss *anything* with me the conversation invariably turns to Amanda." She sighed quietly. "I'm kinda used to it."

Then Luke saw it. Claire lowered her eyes and pursed her lips for just a moment before lifting her chin and squaring her shoulders. *"I'm kinda used to it."* She was disappointed, hurt even.

Interesting.

"In that case let me get straight to the point. Eighteen months ago, Morse Industries bought out Cassidy Holdings, broke it up and sold it off bit by bit, making your aunt a tidy fortune in the process. Amanda acquired the shares at a fraction of their value because information was leaked to the business community at large that caused prices to plummet. It's my belief that Amanda leaked that information knowing it would cause a panic and give her the opportunity to strike."

He watched Claire shift in her seat as she crossed one long leg over the other and wondered for the umpteenth time that day what they'd feel like wrapped around his hips as he drove himself into her.

"Okay," she said, lifting one shoulder in a half-shrug. "So go to the Department of Fair Trading or the ACCC. Why come to me?"

"Because all I have is hearsay. I need proof, and you're going to get it for me."

Claire started laughing. Not giggling, not chuckling, but pure, unadulterated *laughing*. At him. But worse was the fact her laughter sounded so fantastic. It was raucous and vibrant and shook her whole body with the effort. She even grabbed her belly to stop it from jiggling.

Luke clenched his jaw and forced himself to focus.

Can't let her affect me. "This isn't a joke, Claire. I'm serious."

Wiping actual tears of mirth from her cheeks, she said, "I know you are."

He scowled. "Then what's so funny?"

"That you need me for something like this. *Me!* I sell books and tea for fuck's sake. I'm a klutz who spills jam on my shirt with alarming regularity. I'm not a corporate spy. I wouldn't even know where to begin. Besides," she said. "I'd have thought a man like you would have people to do that for you. People who actually know what they're doing."

"I do have people like that. How do you think I know

about Amanda leaking the information? But I need actual proof if I want to take her down."

"So tell your people to find you 'actual proof'."

Luke's mouth pulled down in frustration. "They tried. They couldn't get past her security."

"And what makes you think I'll be of any help to you?"

"Because you worked for her, with her. You know how she thinks, how she conducts business." Luke leaned back in his chair. "And I know what she did to *you*, Claire. She not only fired you, she kicked you out on the street. You're her niece, her only family, and she stripped you of everything and left you with nothing." He cocked his head to one side. "Exactly how long did you have to stay in that shelter?"

The laughter died from Claire's face and he felt a twinge of regret. His words had killed her lovely smile and dulled her brilliant eyes.

She sat very still, rigid. "Mr Hardcastle—"

"Luke," he reminded her.

Getting to her feet, she stood before him, tall and proud. "Mr Hardcastle," she said, enunciating his name with the superior tone of voice he remembered from their last encounter. "I'm going to say something I should have said to you this morning. Go to hell." Then she turned and headed purposefully towards the door.

"Not so fast, Claire," Luke said, smiling grimly. "There is another reason I thought you'd help me that I think you might be forgetting."

Her hand on the doorknob, she said, "And that would be?"

"I own you." Claire's hand fell to her side. "You'll help me destroy Amanda or I'll destroy you instead."

"Why?" she said, the shake in her voice barely audible as she spoke to the door.

"Why not? Amanda ruined my sister's life and you helped, and you know it. I simply want to return the favour as Lottie can no longer do it for herself."

Luke leaned forward and steepled his fingers under his chin. Watching Claire as she slowly turned to face him was harder than he'd anticipated. Her pretty face was devoid of all colour, all emotion, but her eyes shone with unshed tears and her chest heaved with every breath she took, even as her body crumpled in on itself. She looked miserable, like a woman defeated.

And Luke felt like a right bastard.

He curled his toes in his boots until it hurt, until the urge to get up and go to her, to hold her, to tell her he didn't mean a word of what he'd just said to her, passed.

She hurt Lottie. She deserves to feel miserable.

Distracted by his wayward thoughts, Luke almost missed the part where Claire pulled herself together, determination overriding her misery, and took a set of keys from her pocket. She plonked the *Anne Of Green Gables* key ring down in front of him and pointed to each key as she spoke.

"The blue one opens the door to the shop, the red one is my house key, and the green one opens the laundry door. It sticks sometimes, but if you jiggle it, it'll come good."

What the fuck?

"What are you doing?"

"You said you'd destroy me if I didn't help you. Amanda will destroy me if I do. Oddly enough if I have to lose to someone, I'd rather it be you than her." Then she flipped him off and walked away. "Goodbye, Luke."

Luke stared, dumbfounded, as Claire walked out of his office. When he'd gone over every possible scenario in his mind as to how this meeting would play out, he certainly hadn't pictured this. He raced after her just in time to catch her at the lift, wiping tears from her face with one hand while repeatedly jabbing her finger into the call button with the other, as if she could will it to appear any faster.

He grabbed her shoulder. "Claire, stop. We're not finished."

"Back off," she snapped, knocking his hand away. "We have nothing further to discuss."

Luke growled his frustration. He'd definitely underestimated this woman. It wasn't something that happened often and as much as he loathed to admit it, his level of respect for Claire Morse was rising.

The doors to the lift opened and Claire stepped inside. Luke was desperate. He hadn't wanted to do this, the tactic so far below where he'd wanted to go, but she was leaving him no choice. Bracing his arms against the doors of the lift, he held them open, filling the cavity with his large body. He stared at Claire, keeping his face blank and his voice from betraying his hesitation. "What if I didn't destroy you? What if I went after your fellow retailers instead?"

He stepped back and waited with his arms folded neatly across his chest. The lift doors began to close... until Claire's hand shot out between them and made them open again.

Luke had been glared at by his fair share of women, but something in Claire's steel-coloured eyes chilled him to the bone, and when she stepped from the lift, she slapped his face.

Hard.

"Jesus Christ!" Luke cradled his cheek.

One corner of Claire's mouth lifted in a sneer, then she turned on her heel and marched straight back into his office.

Adjusting his jaw as he followed her, Luke closed the door behind them, then sought out the glass of ice on his desk. He almost laughed as he sat down in his chair, holding the glass to his cheek. "I've been slapped before but, bloody hell that hurt."

Claire raised one brow at him. "Be thankful that was all you got."

Seeing her with new eyes, Luke chuckled as he said, "You really aren't what I was expecting."

"Didn't your people investigate me?"

"Of course they did." That's how he knew about her aunt kicking her out and cutting her off, how he knew about her sleeping rough. How he'd known the time was right to kick off his plans. "But we've met before. I thought I had you pegged."

She looked away and stared out the window towards the river. "You met a different person."

"So I see. Never judge a book by its cover, eh?"

She looked back and smiled tightly. "Cute."

Luke rolled the glass of ice across his cheek. "I admit I find it intriguing you will quite literally fight for the rights of your business associates but don't even bat an eyelid for your aunt."

"Your point?"

"She's family."

"Families come in all shapes and sizes, Luke. Amanda may be my relative, but she is not my family."

Luke put the glass down but kept his fingers wrapped around it, the cool of the ice helping his brain stay anchored in the here and now instead of indulging in one of his Claire fantasies. "Then why won't you help me? You *know* she's crooked."

"What I *know* is that I never witnessed anything illegal

in all my time at Morse Industries. Morally reprehensible, yes. Illegal, no. And the reason I won't help you is not because of some misplaced sense of loyalty to Amanda." Sighing heavily, she ploughed on. "All outgoing employees are made to sign non-disclosure agreements forbidding them from discussing any and all information gleaned while working at Morse Industries. I'm sorry, Luke, but the agreement is binding for three years. I can't help you."

There was a moment of silence, then a *crack*.

The glass in Luke's hand shattered.

Glass and ice spilled across his desk, blood dripped from his palm. Remotely, he was aware of Claire speaking to him, saying... something. Her voice was soft, her words precise and to the point, but he had no idea what she was talking about.

"What?"

"I asked where the first aid kit is," she said again.

Luke stared at his hand. "Behind Sandra's desk."

A moment later she was by his side, tweezing shards of glass from his palm and cleaning the cut with iodine.

Burning, stinging iodine.

Luke gritted his teeth against the searing pain. "Sadist," he growled.

"It's not that bad," Claire said, then gently applied a Band-Aid to the cut. "You'll live."

Luke met her gaze dead on. "But Lottie won't."

Chapter Five

"I thought she was in remission?" Claire said quietly, pushing the words past the lump in her throat.

Luke closed his eyes. "It came back."

Luke's half-sister, Charlotte Cassidy, had taken over Cassidy Holdings after her father passed away, and in little less than a year in the top job, she'd turned the company around. Where once there had been a flailing financial nightmare, there now stood a prosperous and worthwhile venture.

Claire's aunt had been furious.

She'd been watching the decline of Cassidy Holdings with glee, just biding her time until the shares bottomed out and she could scoop them up for a steal. But Lottie had proved a more competent businesswoman than many had given her credit for, and Amanda had missed her chance.

It was soon after that the rumours began. And after the rumours came the news articles.

Cassidy Holdings Health Crisis.

The Cassidy Curse Strikes Again!

Does Charlotte Cassidy Have Cancer?

Nobody seemed to know what type she had or how long she'd had it, but the mere mention of The Big C put people in a panic and crashed Cassidy's share prices faster than she could say, "No comment." In a bid to stem the bleed of profits, the board of directors ousted Lottie. And when that didn't work, they decided to cut their losses, voting to sell the company off to Morse Industries.

For far less than it was worth.

Claire had always suspected Amanda had something to do with the rumours—the timing was simply too convenient —but she'd never found any proof of wrongdoing. And she wasn't lying to Luke when she'd said she never saw anything illegal take place at Morse Industries. Amanda had some of the best lawyers on retainer to ensure she never crossed *that* line.

Staring down at Luke, Claire considered his proposal.

What did she have to lose if she helped him wage war against Amanda?

The answer was simple. And terrifying.

Everything.

She had everything to lose.

And it didn't matter how devastatingly handsome Luke was, or how vulnerable he looked in that exact moment, or how desperately she wanted to wrap her arms around him and cradle his head against the pillow of her breasts and tell him everything would be okay. He was still the man attempting to blackmail her into doing his dirty work. And if Amanda found out what they were up to, she wouldn't just cut Claire off, she'd crush her.

Novelteas? Gone.

Her house? Gone.

Her life...? Not worth living.

Realising she was still holding his hand, Claire pulled

away. When Luke opened his eyes and stared at her, she busied herself with cleaning up the used iodine swabs and Band-Aid wrappers. She couldn't look him in the eye. "I'm sorry, Luke. Really, I am."

"Are you?"

Claire couldn't blame him for his hard tone of voice, or that he was directing it at her. He was right when he'd accused her of helping Amanda. She had. And when she'd learned of their success, the black stain that had marked her soul for so many years had almost consumed her.

"Yes. I know better than anyone what Amanda is capable of. She—" Claire cut off the thought before she spilled too many of her own secrets. "I don't blame you for wanting to cut her down to size."

"Then let me take a look at that agreement."

Claire blinked in surprise. "What?"

"The non-disclosure agreement. I'll have my lawyers go over it, see if they find any loopholes. If they can, will you help me?"

Wait. Was Luke giving her an out...?

"And if they can't?"

He frowned. "Then I'll just have to think of some other way to bring that bitch to her knees."

Claire shoved her hands in her pockets to stop from fidgeting and betraying her nerves. "And until then, are you still going to hold the Merthyr Road leases over my head?"

"Yes."

She almost growled her disappointment. *Of course he is.*

"I can't take the chance you'll go telling tales to Aunty Amanda in the meantime, can I? I wouldn't want you trying to curry her favour."

Claire almost laughed out loud. If only Luke knew how bloody unlikely—or impossible—that statement was.

"Fine," she said, leaning on the desk again and giving Luke another eyeful of her ample cleavage. On purpose this time. "But if you want to hold a lease over my head, then hold *my* lease over my head. Leave my friends alone. They're honest, hard-working people. They deserve better than getting caught in the middle of our bullshit."

Luke didn't even bother pretending not to look down her top. "Fair enough."

"And I'll be taking a look at those new lease agreements you mentioned," she said, easing herself back in her chair again and staring Luke down, daring him to refuse. "I don't care if we have to sit here all night."

He surprised her when he picked up his phone. "I'm hungry," he said. "Do you like Chinese?"

She nodded then listened to him rattle off a dinner order large enough to feed a football team. And while they waited for the food to arrive, Luke produced the new agreements and began explaining the changes he'd made. For the most part, the evening was a positive and productive interaction, but Claire couldn't help the feeling of unease that niggled at the back of her mind.

Waiting for the other shoe to drop.

As she stabbed a piece of lemon chicken with her chopstick, she voiced her concerns. "You know, I used to think you were one of the good guys, and not just because of the way we met."

With a pen sticking out of his mouth, Luke lifted his gaze from the pages in his hand. "Been keeping tabs on me, huh?"

Claire's cheeks heated. She stabbed the chicken harder. "Professionally speaking, yes. I've always found your work ethics something to be celebrated. Hardcastle Construction is a progressive company that champions renewable resources, practices sustainable building techniques and advocates equal pay for equal work. I'd never have thought you would lower yourself to Amanda's standards," she said quietly. "You're better than this."

Luke laid aside the pen and paper and reached for the plum duck. "It's called fighting fire with fire," he said, then shovelled the food in his mouth.

"Nice theory," Claire said, desperately trying to ignore the way Luke's tongue flicked out to lick plum sauce from the corner of his sensual mouth. "But do you know what happens when you fight fire with fire?"

"What?"

"Everyone gets burned."

Chapter Six

"Claire? We're here."

Luke cut the engine and turned to face the woman fast asleep in the car seat beside him. Her hair had fallen over her face and the urge to push it back, to reveal her pretty mouth and the stubborn jut of her strong chin had him lifting his hand before he could think better of it. The long, dark strands felt silky against his fingers as he tucked them behind her ear, and when he turned his hand over and gently stroked her cheek, he found her skin to be soft and warm.

Luke licked his lips and swallowed hard. He wanted to kiss her. No. *Kiss* was too simple a word.

Luke wanted to *devour* Claire.

All evening as he'd sat opposite her, as they'd worked and talked and gone over the tenant leases line by line, all he'd thought about was how good it would feel to hold her in his arms after making love to her. How he'd hold her against his naked body and they'd snuggle together for warmth. And then he'd imagined how she'd taste between those lovely, thick thighs and his trousers had grown uncomfortably tight.

More than once he found himself walking around the office in a bid to put some distance between them and relieve his discomfort. He'd even removed himself from her presence completely, at one point, and jerked off in the bathroom. It was either that or actually proposition her and risk another slap. Not that he'd minded the sting of her palm.

Strong women excited him.

Stroking her cheek again, Luke smiled. Claire was beautiful. Even in jeans and a T-shirt. Especially in jeans and a T-shirt.

That morning when he'd entered the tearoom above her shop, he hadn't recognised her. Gone were the hideous grey, ill-fitting pantsuits she wore at Morse Industries, and *Hello!* skinny jeans and pale pink nerd-shirt. It was also the first time in ten years he'd seen her with her hair down, the dark waves cascading over her shoulders and caressing her breasts.

Luke had always thought Claire to be an attractive woman, but he'd forgotten exactly how pretty she was when she wasn't dressed like a younger, less aggressive clone of her aunt.

Taking a seat at the back of the room, he'd simultaneously hoped she'd be the one to serve him and prayed she wouldn't. He'd wanted to smirk as she was forced to serve him, but he also wanted to watch this fascinating new version of her as she moved about the room, smiling and laughing with her customers, unencumbered by the weight of his stare. When she'd finally looked his way, he'd panicked and shoved his face in a magazine, but when he'd glanced up again... *wow!*

Daylight had streamed through the window behind her and bathed her in a halo of sunshine. Her bountiful curves had taunted him, and her hair had shone like the richest mahogany.

Then she'd blushed like a schoolgirl and run away.

And it had taken every ounce of his self-will to stop himself from chasing after her.

When he did finally follow her to the broom cupboard she called an office and watched her bend over to retrieve her chair....

Holy fucking hell!

Every fantasy he'd ever had about the woman reached inside his trousers, grabbed his dick and went to town. He'd wanted to grab her sexy arse—perfectly packaged in tight blue denim—and smack it. Bite it. Caress it....

Claire shifted in her seat and murmured something unintelligible.

Luke snapped out of his reverie and pulled away.

What the fuck am I doing?

That same thought had rolled through his mind on a never-ending loop ever since Claire had said, *"You're better than this."*

Four little words and he was second-guessing his entire plan. Well, maybe not the *entire* plan.

Reaching for her knee, he gave her a gentle shake. "Claire."

Sleepy, steel-blue eyes blinked at him, and she drew in a deep breath as she opened her mouth to yawn. "Hi," she said, her voice roughened by sleep.

Luke couldn't help smiling at her. *Fuck, she's cute.* "Hi." She returned his smile and blinked at him again. "Uh, you're home."

Swivelling her head to stare out the passenger window,

Claire yawned again. "Groovy. Thanks." Then she looked down at his hand spread across her leg, the hand Luke hadn't realised he'd been caressing her with, gently circling his palm against her thigh, the action feeling as natural to him as breathing.

The fact she didn't shy away from his touch didn't go unnoticed. "No problem."

She reached for the door handle. "Um, why don't you come inside and I'll get those papers for you?"

Swallowing hard, Luke thought of all the reasons following Claire inside her house was a really bad idea, then fought the urge to ignore them. "It can wait until tomorrow."

"What time is it?" Claire rubbed at her eyes.

Luke checked his watch. "Around two."

"Then it already is tomorrow," Claire said, opening her door. "Come on. They're in my safe. It won't take a minute."

Luke's resolve weakened. "Okay," he said, then followed Claire up the short path to her little house.

The old worker's cottage was standard fare for this area of Brisbane. A tiny timber box on short wooden stumps, half a dozen steps leading up to a deep veranda and the whole thing capped off with a corrugated iron roof. The paint was peeling off the weatherboards, the veranda decking was warped and the railing was loose, but at least the roof looked new.

Following her through the front door he found himself in her lounge room.

"Excuse the mess," she muttered, hurrying to grab an overfull laundry basket off the couch and kicking a pile of shoes under the coffee table. "Why don't you wait here? I won't be a sec."

"Don't want me to see your safe combination, huh?"

Her lips quirked in a half-smile. "No, I just don't want you to see how messy the rest of the house is." She disappeared down the hallway.

Luke sat on the couch to wait and immediately flinched as what felt like a loose spring jabbed the back of his thigh. Shifting to a more comfortable position, he took in his surroundings.

The small house was the same type he'd cut his teeth on when he left high school to work for his father, when Hardcastle Construction was in its infancy. Claire's house was a dump, but as he took in the timber casement windows, VJ walls, wide timber floorboards and cast-iron fireplace surrounded by an elegant yet simple mantle, his builder's brain realised it had a world of potential.

Her furnishings on the other hand.... The only potential they possessed involved setting them on fire. The couch, especially, had to go.

On either side of the decrepit couch sat what Luke assumed were side tables, made from upside-down milk crates and timber off-cuts. Each was stacked high with books. More books and a china mug with the Novelteas shop logo on it sat atop the mantle. But there were no photos hanging on the walls. No art. No pictures of any kind. Not even a clock. Just a few swatches of grey paint on the far wall.

It all felt so... cold.

Lonely.

Claire's shop had only been open for six months, and Luke knew from his investigations that it was turning a consistently tidy profit, but aside from the shiny new roof it was obvious she wasn't spending the money on herself. At least, not in the showy way he'd expected.

Amanda Morse had never hidden her wealth. Quite the opposite. Claire's aunt couldn't wait to tell people how rich and successful she was. Taking another look around the sparsely furnished lounge room, Luke decided Claire lived more like a broke university student than an up-and-coming business owner.

Getting to his feet, he rubbed the back of his leg and wondered what was taking Claire so long.

It *was* late. Maybe she'd fallen asleep? *Annnd* that had him thinking about her bedroom. And her bed. And her naked in her bed....

Dragging a hand over his face, he groaned, "Get a grip before you do something stupid."

"Are you all right to drive?"

Luke turned around to find Claire frowning up at him, concern lacing her expression.

He cocked a brow. "You're not worried about me, are you?"

"No," she said quickly, then shifted her weight from one foot to the other. "Just being a decent human being. I don't want to turn on the news later and find out you drowned because you fell asleep at the wheel and drove your car into the river."

Luke bit back a grin. "Of course."

She shoved a Manilla envelope at him. "Here, I made a copy of the original. You can keep it."

His hand brushed hers as he took the envelope. It was such an innocent gesture, but the result was always the same. The first time they'd met, and the last. And again in her office when he'd grabbed her arm. *Heat.* Blinding, scorching heat blazed through every nerve in his body and set his lust aflame.

He knew what he wanted to do.

And knew he shouldn't do it.

But.... "Fuck it."

Letting the envelope fall to the floor, Luke hauled Claire against him and wrapped his arms around her. Holding her firmly, he kissed her, his lips bruising, demanding. He'd wanted to taste her perfect mouth for ten years—even if she was a Morse—and tonight as he'd worked alongside her, his body had ached for her.

Half expecting her to pull away and slap him, he almost sagged in relief when she slid her hands through his hair and returned the kiss with equal fervour. Surrendering to the moment, he snaked his hands over her hips and down to cup the ample rounds of her arse, then pulled her closer, tighter. Pressed the full length of his erection against the softness of her belly.

Claire gasped but Luke swallowed it down as his tongue lashed against hers, searing her with the passion he'd long denied. He wanted to claim this woman. Claim her and keep her. Take her to bed and bury himself deep inside her voluptuous warmth.

But he couldn't.

He wouldn't.

As abruptly as the kiss had begun, it ended. Luke put Claire at arm's length and slowly shook his head. He stared at the ceiling as he dragged air into his lungs and exhaled his frustration. When he faced her again, her eyes swam with confusion.

I'm an arsehole.

"I'm sorry," he said. "I shouldn't have done that. It's been a long day." He knew the excuse was weak but what else could he say? Even if he told her the truth, she'd never believe him. He hardly believed it himself. He picked the envelope up off the floor. "Is this everything?"

Claire touched her lips with trembling fingers. She nodded. "Yes."

"Right then. I'll be off." He cleared his throat. "Goodnight, Miss Morse."

"Goodnight," Claire whispered, her sweet voice barely audible over the blood pounding in his ears.

Luke walked back to his car in a daze then slumped into the driver's seat and head-butted the steering wheel. "You bloody, fucking idiot."

Chapter Seven

Shoving her way into her shop, Claire made a mental note to report the sticking front door to her new lord and master. The previous landlord had been less than useless when it came to property maintenance and she held little hope Luke would be any better. He'd made his interest in purchasing the building quite clear. It was nothing more than a means to an end, a way of controlling her and forcing her to do his bidding.

Arsehole.

She slammed the door behind her, the bang of timber against timber so loud it drowned out the sound of the tinkle bell above the door.

Five hours had passed since he'd kissed her.

Five hours of confusion and anger and hoping and longing before circling back to anger. Five hours of tossing and turning in bed as her overactive brain recalled that bloody kiss in excruciating detail, of wondering if it was just a kiss or if it was maybe something more.

She shook her head as she made her way to her office. *Daft.* She was completely daft if she thought for even a moment Luke wanted her for anything other than a weapon to use against her aunt.

Claire groaned. It was bad enough that yet again a man was using her to get to Amanda, but why did it have to be Luke-fucking-Hardcastle?

And why did he have to kiss her?

He'd obviously seen her staring at him, watching him walk around his office showing off his powerful legs and perfect arse and—wait. Was that why he'd had to *stretch his legs* so much? Because he knew she'd watch him, knew she'd want what she couldn't have? Was she really that obvious? But of course she was.

Much to her aunt's never-ending frustration and disappointment, Claire had never mastered the act of indifference. Of course where Amanda was concerned it wasn't an act.

"It's called fighting fire with fire, Claire," she said, childishly imitating Luke as she spat the words out. "Probably laughing his bloody head off." She slumped in her chair. "Well, to hell with him. It wasn't even that good a kiss."

Liar.

Okay, it was an amazing kiss and at one point she'd actually forgotten to breathe, but if Luke thought he could get the best of her, he had another thing coming. You didn't grow up in the shadow of the great Amanda Morse without developing a thick skin.

Amanda.

Claire sighed wearily. She should have known something cataclysmic was headed her way. Her business was turning a profit, she was finally beginning the renovations on her house and for the first time in she didn't even know how long, she felt at peace with herself. Being out from under Amanda's thumb had given Claire the freedom to breathe, to be her own woman. To grow.

And heal.

She should have known better. People like Claire didn't get happy endings. Pain begot pain. That's just how things were. And now here was Luke Hardcastle throwing her back in the path of the one person who could crush her dreams with less effort than it took to brush her teeth.

And it royally pissed her off.

Claire hadn't spoken to Amanda in eighteen months— not since she'd confronted her aunt over the Cassidy Holdings deal and been summarily dismissed for her efforts.

Luke was right about one thing. Amanda had used the news of Lottie's illness to her advantage. That was what she did. Taking advantage of other people's shitty situations was literally her job. But how did the story get out? And if it was Amanda who spread the rumours, how did *she* find out?

Claire rubbed her temples. She was missing something, she just didn't know what. But she'd better figure it out quickly if she ever wanted this nightmare to end. The fact she had free arm-porn on tap would only soften the blow for so long.

Speaking of which....

Yawning loudly, Claire leaned back in her chair and wrote a mental to-do list, then calculated how much time she needed to complete it before opening the shop.

Yeah. I've got time.

Five hours had passed since the man of her dreams had kissed the ever-loving life out of her and stirred up the aching need between her thighs. A need that refused to go away no matter how much she tried to ignore it.

She closed her eyes and called up her favourite fantasy. "Spank bank don't fail me now."

Unable to stop the smile that always accompanied Luke when he entered her daydreams, Claire pictured his tanned, muscled body smeared with sawdust and sweat. He was dressed in ratty denim shorts slung low on his hips, a leather tool belt and scuffed leather work boots. A sensual smile played around his wide, kissable mouth.

"Miss Morse," Luke said, handing her a hardhat. "Shall we begin?"

Claire Morse, building inspector, followed Luke Hardcastle, local builder, around the half-finished house, her clipboard in hand as he rattled off the build's progress. She followed him down the hallway and through the kitchen, absently ticking boxes on her checklist as she ogled his body and the way he moved. Biting her lip, she watched his biceps flex as he pointed out the work he'd completed and tried desperately to ignore the rivulet of sweat trickling down the centre of his back. It disappeared under the waistband of his shorts. Leaning closer, she inhaled. The scent of freshly cut timber and healthy male filled her nostrils.

She moaned.

Loudly.

"How long are we going to play this game, Miss Morse?"

Claire looked up into Luke's grinning face. "What game?"

He shook his head and sighed. "Every inspection, it's the same thing. I pose. You stare. But we never do anything about it."

"About what?"

"This itch we never scratch."

Claire straightened and lifted her chin. "I have no idea what you're talking about." She knew exactly what he was talking about but didn't want to admit it.

He stalked forward, forcing her back against a wall. "Really? So you weren't undressing me with your eyes just now?"

"It's a little hard to undress you when you're already half naked," she snapped. "Now, let's get on with the inspection."

"Miss Morse, the only inspection I'm interested in continuing," he said, tossing her clipboard away and pinning her hands to her sides, "Is of your lips."

"My—no! Let me go."

"I'll let you go if you let me kiss you." His smile was all seduction and his golden eyes shimmered with lust. Hypnotic and beautiful.

Claire bit her lip. "That's all? Just one kiss?"

"On your lips."

With a roll of her eyes she let loose an exasperated sigh. The sooner they got this over with the sooner she could complete her inspection. "Fine. One kiss on my lips then you let me— Wait, what are you doing?"

Luke knelt before her, slid her skirt up her thighs.

"Stop that! You said a kiss on my *lips*."

His grin broadened. "I never said which lips...."

In a matter of seconds, Luke had Claire's skirt around her waist, her panties around her knees and he was blowing warm breath across her exposed pussy. Her knees shook and her thighs trembled and she grabbed his shoulders to steady herself.

Luke stroked his hands over her thighs and used his long fingers to part her wet folds.

And then he kissed her.

Claire felt the heat of his mouth as he pressed his lips against hers, as he explored her pussy with his tongue. She felt him lick and suck and nibble and probe, and she writhed against his face like some demented belly dancer, grinding her hips back and forth as she tried to reach that seemingly unreachable state of bliss.

Closer and closer, she was almost... there.... "Luke. Oh, God.... Just a little more... please."

Luke grabbed her arse in both hands, pulling her forward, forcing his tongue deeper and deeper, greedily lapping at her sweet liqueur. Claire grabbed his head in both hands, her fingernails scoring his scalp, and held him against her as she finally came.

"Fuck!"

The chair shook as Claire's orgasm shuddered through her. Her legs twitched and her stomach spasmed and then she was clamping her thighs together and slowly but surely sucking air back into her lungs.

Eventually she opened her eyes and pulled her fingers from her panties.

Fantasising about the man who's blackmailing me. "I am pathetic."

Forcing herself to her feet, Claire began her morning routine. She flicked on the shop lights and put up the new book display, counted the tills, sanitised the benchtops and mopped the floors for good measure, all with the memory of Luke's hot lips and strong arms keeping her company while she worked.

Why couldn't she shake the thought of that kiss? Maybe it wasn't the kiss that bothered her. Maybe it was the rather sizeable erection that had gone along with it that had Claire's brain in a tizzy.

Had she done that, given Luke Hardcastle—a man renowned for his rather particular appetites where women were concerned—an erection?

A heady thought indeed.

She couldn't deny the feeling of being wrapped in his arms as he kissed her socks off had been fucking amazing.

And not.

It wasn't that Claire hadn't enjoyed the kiss—she had—but at the age of twenty-nine she'd essentially given up where men were concerned. She'd already decided she was fated to become a lonely old spinster who would never go anywhere or do anything and would only be missed when the junk mail started spilling from her letterbox and caused some sort of safety hazard on the footpath outside her house.

Being kissed by her fantasy man had never come into the equation.

And she still had no bloody clue as to why he'd kissed her in the first place. Except for the whole fighting fire with fire revenge thing, and she had to admit, using someone's desires against them was something Amanda Morse would do if there was an edge to be gained by doing it.

Claire shook her head. She was being silly. They were both tired and angsty and it was *just* a kiss. It wasn't like he wanted to fuck her, for pity's sake.

Still....

It was probably best she knew his intentions for certain, and better yet that she made her position known as soon as possible. He might be able to blackmail her into doing his dirty work, but under no circumstances would she allow Luke Hardcastle to blackmail her into bed.

No matter how tempting the possibilities might be.

It was almost opening time when Karen bounded up the stairs and found her staring vacantly out the window at one of Luke's enormous construction cranes, the giant phallus just one of many that dotted the ever-expanding cityscape. This one had a Hardcastle Construction banner flapping from it, a larger than life reminder of her doom.

"Thanks for coming in early," she said as Karen made herself a cuppa.

"No probs," she said, then frowned. "You look like shit. Is everything all right?"

Claire forced a smile. "I'm fine. I was up all night with Luke."

"Oh, really?" The bubbly blonde pulled up a chair and propped her chin in her hands. "Tell me everything. No detail is too sordid—I mean small."

Claire pushed her hair over her shoulder and scowled. "It was nothing like that. We were discussing new lease agreements."

"All night?" Karen asked, one brow cocked in disbelief.

"Yes, all night. He wants me to call a proprietor's meeting so he can be introduced to everyone along the row and assure them their businesses are safe and blah, blah, blah." She made a hand gesture like a sock-puppet.

Karen shook her head. "Same shit, different landlord."

Claire chuckled. "You know it."

"When's this meeting supposed to take place?"

"Tomorrow evening."

"Good. Go home and get some sleep. I can hold down the fort."

"I know you can, and I would love to go home." Claire smiled sleepily. "But I can't just yet. I have to see Angie about booking a table at the restaurant, then call everyone about the meeting, plus some... other stuff. But then, yes. I will go home and leave the shop in your very capable hands."

Chapter Eight

Standing outside Luke's office, Claire stifled a yawn behind her hand and waited patiently for his annoying receptionist to finish her phone call. Her very personal, long-winded phone call.

Itching to lean over, grab the rude girl's phone and throw it against a wall, Claire realised her patience was about to expire. "I have better things to do with my time today," she muttered and made a move for Luke's door.

It was almost amusing how quickly Sandra threw her phone down. "You can't go in there, Ms Morse," she said, angling herself between Claire and the door.

"*Miss,*" Claire hissed through gritted teeth. *Why was that so hard to remember?* "And why can't I go in there?"

"Mr Hardcastle is in meetings all day. He said he wasn't to be disturbed."

Claire forced herself not to snap at blondie. She was only doing her job. "I only need a moment of his time, Sandra," she said and grabbed for the doorknob.

Blondie got there first and fisted her hand around the

shiny knob. "I can't allow it. He's with a very important client."

"Look, you bottle-blonde bimbo—"

Sandra gasped then stumbled as the door was yanked open and a very crumpled-looking Luke filled the doorway.

Claire's eyes widened. Unshaven and half-dressed, he looked like he'd just rolled out of bed after a night of hot sex. Only she knew he hadn't slept with her. Her gaze slid sideways to blondie and she hated herself for the spear of jealousy she wished she could wrench from her chest and stab through his assistant's.

"Sandra, continue holding my calls. Claire, come in." Luke stepped back and let Claire into his office then shut the door behind her. "Apologies for my appearance," he said, his voice deeper, gruffer than it had been the previous night. "I haven't been home yet."

Claire opened her mouth to say something but the words vanished from her brain before they could pass her lips. Luke's unbuttoned business shirt afforded her a tantalising glimpse of his finely muscled chest and abdomen, and again he'd rolled his sleeves up to expose his strong forearms.

Arms that had crushed her to his body when his mouth had crashed into hers and he'd given her a taste of something she'd never experienced before.

True passion.

A sudden heat swept through her, she pressed her thighs together and just like that, she'd forgotten why she was there.

Oh, yeah, that's why.

To tell Luke her body was off limits.

Because sleeping with him would be bad.

Very, very bad....

"What can I do for you, Claire?"

As she continued staring at Luke's chest, Claire cleared her throat. "I've set up the meeting you wanted with your new tenants," she said, dragging her gaze up to meet his only to be greeted by a thinly veiled smirk. Her cheeks heated with embarrassment and she quickly looked away. "Tomorrow at seven at Mama's Kitchen."

"Good," he said, and folded his arms across his chest. "Anything else?"

"Yes, actually. There is," she said. Luke raised a questioning brow. Claire took a fortifying breath. "I'm not having sex with you."

Luke's other brow joined the first as they reached for his hairline. "Okay," he said, drawing the word out. "And you felt the need to tell me that because...?"

"You kissed me."

He propped his arse against the edge of his desk. "Ah."

"And I think we both know it wasn't just a kiss."

"Do we?"

"Yes, we do." Claire twisted her hands together as her anxiety ate away at her insides, but she had to say this now or she never would. "I understand you want revenge against me for my part in the Cassidy Holdings deal. I get it, really, I do. But not like this. Not with sex. I'd like to get through this—whatever *this* is—" she said, waving her hand between them, "With at least some of my dignity intact."

"Dignity," Luke repeated, smirking again. "This coming from the woman who has spent the last five minutes ogling my body?"

Claire stiffened as she realised it was her spank bank daydream all over again. *Greaaat....* Then bit her lip to stifle a moan and wondered if he'd go down on her in reality too.

Daft. She really was daft.

Or possibly just in dire need of sleep.

"I—" she started.

Luke held up a silencing hand. "Don't get me wrong, Claire. I don't mind you looking," he said, pushing away from his desk. "As long as you don't mind a little tit for tat." His gaze fell immediately to her tits.

Claire scowled at him and crossed her arms over her chest.

His smirk broadening into a grin, Luke said, "Yeah, that's really not helping."

Looking down, Claire saw her folded arms had only pushed her boobs closer together and created more cleavage for him to perv at. She anchored her hands on her hips instead. "You're a pig."

"Why, because I find you attractive and I'm too tired to be bothered hiding it?"

Attractive? Claire's frown deepened. Who was he trying to kid?

But before she could respond, he moved away to the couch and flopped down on it. Stretching out on his back, he tucked his hands behind his head and crossed his feet at the ankles. His shirt fell open and revealed more hard, gloriously tanned muscle, but Claire also noticed he wasn't wearing any shoes or socks, and although she couldn't put her finger on why, she found the whole ensemble incredibly sexy.

Stepping closer, she said, "What are you doing?"

"It's commonly known as sleeping," he said, then he turned his head towards her with his eyelids lowered and his soft, sensual lips parted slightly, ready to be kissed. "Care to join me?"

Indignant rage caused a spluttering sound to come out of her mouth even as her body warmed to the idea. At some point she was going to have to sit herself down and give herself a stern talking to, because hell if she wasn't tempted to join him.

Dignity be damned!

But then he said, "Relax, I'm kidding. I just meant you look tired, like you didn't get much sleep last night either." He grinned again. "I wonder if the reason for your lack of sleep is the same as mine."

Was he playing with her? *"I'm kidding."* Of course he was.

Every spark of lust left her with the speed of light, replaced by hurt and anger. "Fuck you, Hardcastle. I'm leaving."

Looking even more amused than before, he said, "Suit yourself," and went back to staring at the ceiling.

Claire marched towards the door, determined to get some sleep and put this whole conversation out of her head, but as she grabbed the doorknob, she remembered something else.

"Why didn't you go home last night?"

Luke yawned. "What?"

"You said you haven't been home yet. Why not?"

"I wanted to go over those papers you gave me as soon as possible," he said, sitting up again, "And I don't like taking work home with me. By the time I finished reading, the sun was up. Figured I may as well sleep here. Unlike some people, I can't just swan off whenever I feel like it."

Claire rolled her eyes as he threw her own words back at her. "And? So? What did you find?"

"That Amanda has very good lawyers." Luke rubbed the back of his neck. "I couldn't find anything that would allow you to freely share information with me." He sighed. "I've sent the agreement to my legal department for a fine combing, see if they can find something I missed, but I'm not hopeful."

"So... does that mean I'm off the hook? No more blackmail?"

"No."

"No?"

"You give me a level of access to Amanda I can't get anywhere else. I need you, Claire, and if I have to blackmail you to keep you close then I will."

"Oh, for fuck's sake," she muttered, throwing her hands in the air. "Did it ever occur to you to simply *ask* for my help?"

Luke stared at her for a moment, silently frowning, then said, "Will you help me?"

Claire snorted. "After you've already blackmailed me, are you kidding?"

"I realise this is probably just my exhaustion talking," Luke said, his lips twitching into that all too familiar smirk. "But you're in very real danger of earning my respect, Miss Morse."

"Oh, goodie," she drawled.

"And I love how you mock the situation, as though it were nothing out of the ordinary."

"Because this isn't out of the ordinary for me," she said with a sigh. "And maybe this is just my exhaustion talking, but to tell you the truth, Mr Hardcastle, it almost feels like I'm back at Morse Industries."

The look on Luke's face was disturbing, as though she couldn't have insulted him more completely if she'd tried.

Reaching for the doorknob again, Claire said, "Get some sleep, Luke. You're going to need it. I have a feeling you're about to head into uncharted territory."

Chapter Nine

Checking her watch for the hundredth time in as many seconds, Claire drummed her fingers on the table and smiled tightly at her fellow shop owners. Seven o'clock had come and gone and Luke was nowhere to be seen.

"He's not impressing me so far, my darling."

Angie Campioni, proprietor of Mama's Kitchen, took her seat next to Claire and huffed impatiently. To a woman who ran her restaurant like clockwork, tardiness was a punishable offence.

"I'm sure he won't long," Claire said, as much for her own peace of mind as anyone else's. "And let's not forget, the last landlord didn't bother meeting us at all until he wanted to jack up our rent. At least Luke wants to be on good terms with his tenants."

"I suppose," Angie grumbled. "Or he wants to lull us into a false sense of security for when *he* wants to jack up our rents."

"I don't think you need to worry about that, Angie."

Claire was under strict instructions not to say anything, but during their negotiations Luke had actually agreed to lower their rent. He might be out to make her life hell, but she firmly believed he would do right by the rest of the Merthyr Road tenants. "I trust him," she said, looking at her watch again. "Even if he can't tell time."

Leaning closer, Angie lowered her voice. "I hope you're not being swayed by the fact he's so handsome."

Annoyed by her friend's observation—and more than a little hangry—Claire snapped, "Of course not. What do you take me for?"

"I take you for a woman who's only been on three dates in the whole eighteen months I've known her."

"I trust him because of his track record in business," Claire said. "Not because he's pretty to look at."

"I'm glad to hear it."

Busted.

Biting back a curse, Claire peered over her shoulder at Luke. "Hi," she said.

He smiled down at her. "Hi."

Standing to greet him properly, her dress caught on the chair, but before she could fall on her arse and make a fool of herself in front of a restaurant full of people, Luke's large hand settled at her waist and steadied her.

She shivered at the contact despite the heat of his palm seeping through her dress. "Thank you," she said, suddenly breathless.

His voice lowered so only she could hear him, Luke asked, "Are you always this clumsy?"

"Only when I'm trying to impress someone," Claire said, trying desperately not to lean into his hold.

Luke grinned. "Consider me impressed."

Realising they had an audience, Claire stepped away and Luke's hand fell to his side.

Taking the hint, he addressed the table. "I apologise for running late, folks," he said. "There was a delay getting the paperwork finalised and I didn't want to arrive empty-handed."

Murmurs of, "That was thoughtful," mingled with grumbles of, "Could've called."

Claire stepped forward again and silence fell. "Why don't we have dinner first and then everyone can be introduced more formally afterwards?"

"Excellent idea, my darling," Angie said, then clapped her hands loudly. "*Marcos, servirà la cena ora, grazie.*"

Angie's son, Marcos, appeared moments later followed by three other waiters. The table was quickly laden with several pasta dishes and risottos, salads and slow-cooked meats, and Claire's favourite dish—veal scaloppini in mushroom sauce.

"*Buon appetito.*"

Luke moved to an empty chair on the opposite side of the table, introducing himself to the men either side of him as he sat down, and Claire kept a watchful eye on him throughout the evening. She told herself she was looking after the interests of her friends and fellow vendors, but even after she felt assured of Luke's good intentions, she couldn't drag her gaze away from him. Everything he did fascinated her, every movement of his body, every word out of his mouth.

She felt like a teenager with a crush.

Sooo pathetic.

During dessert, Angie leaned in and whispered, "I take it back, my darling. He's not handsome."

"No?" Claire said, her brow raised.

"No. Handsome doesn't do him justice. That man is *sexy*," she growled, making Claire laugh. "He would make a good match for you, I think."

"Don't even go there, Ang," she said, reaching for a cannoli. "I'm not his type."

"Not his type? Bah."

"He only dates models. Thin, waifish models." Claire sighed. "Not fat chicks like me."

"Firstly, my darling, you're not fat. You're voluptuous, like a goddess. And secondly, if he cannot see how beautiful you are, inside and out, then he is a fool. A big man like him needs a real woman, not some skinny little thing who parades around in her underwear."

"All women are real women, Angie."

"Bah."

"And what makes you think I even want to date Luke Hardcastle?"

"I'm not blind. I can see well enough how you look at him," Angie said, grinning. "And how he looks at you."

Wait, what?

Luke was looking at her? Chancing a glance at him, Claire saw he was in the midst of an animated discussion about... something. She listened harder. Dry rot. He was talking to Craig, the artisan butcher, about dry rot. And that's when she remembered she'd asked everyone to provide Luke with a list of building complaints.

So he could get busy fixing them.

Not so she could make him wish he'd never bought the place.

No, no, no. Claire would *never* do something so petty....

Well, maybe just this once.

Chuckling quietly to herself, she reached for another cannoli, and at the precise moment she took a bite and chocolate cream spilled out of the shell, Luke looked right at her. And frowned. Refusing to be intimidated by his disapproving stare, she made a point of shoving the whole pastry in her mouth and chewing it as noisily as possible.

She was surprised when Luke grinned, then embarrassed as he pointed to the corner of his mouth and then at her. Quickly swiping her finger across her lips, she discovered a glob of chocolate cream clinging on for dear life, then stuck that finger in her mouth and sucked it clean.

The simple action felt almost... *provocative*. Especially when Luke's grin vanished and his eyes darkened, the gold almost swallowed up completely by the black of his pupils.

Heart racing, she sucked on the pad of her thumb next and watched excitedly as Luke's eyes tracked the movement. But a moment later his attention was commanded elsewhere as he was drawn into another conversation with another vendor.

While Luke was distracted, Claire slipped away from the table to gather her thoughts. She'd always sucked at seduction. Amanda had tried to teach her the finer points of using sex and suggestion to get a man to do her bidding, but she'd always thought it dishonest. She'd never understood why she should have to lie to someone to make them like her.

That wasn't the type of person she wanted to be.

When she returned to the dining room, Luke pulled her aside and whispered in her ear. "I need to speak with you privately. Can we go to your shop when we're done here?"

His breath was warm, his voice alluring and her heart skittered with excitement. She might suck at seduction, but Luke Hardcastle was the leading authority on the subject.

"Of course," Claire said, once again reminding herself that he was not her secret lover, he was blackmailing her for personal vengeance, and wondering why it so damned easy to forget that one annoying little fact.

Chapter Ten

The dinner meet and greet only ended when the restaurant started to close, and Luke was more than ready to make his escape.

For three hours he'd been trapped, forced to make small talk with his new tenants when all he really wanted to do was drag Claire somewhere private and shove his tongue down her throat. Watching the woman eat had been the most erotic exhibition of unbridled passion he'd ever seen. She ate food the way some people made love.

With wild and boundless joy.

"Did you enjoy your evening, Mr Hardcastle?"

Angie Campioni, the short, plump and very intimidating Italian woman who owned Mama's Kitchen, sidled up to him and—pinched his arse?

What the fuck?

"The food was superb, thank you," he said, moving out of arm's reach. "I'll have to bring my sister here one night. Lottie loves Italian food."

The older woman shot him an appraising look. "You

should bring Claire. There is a nice, private spot in the corner. Perfect for lovers, *si*?"

Lovers?

"Mrs Campioni, I don't know what Claire has told you but—"

"I saw how you watched her all evening'" she said with a knowing smile. "She watched you too."

What was he supposed to say to that? "I, uh...."

Angie held up her hand to silence him. "Yes, yes she has already told me you don't date women who look like her."

"Well, I—"

"But I tell her, any man who cannot see her beauty is *stupido*, an idiot." She arched one thin brow at him. "Are you an idiot, Mr Hardcastle?"

Luke was saved the trouble of answering when Claire walked up to them and bent to kiss Angie's cheek.

"Good night, Angie."

"*Buonasera*, my darling." Angie nodded at Luke. "Mr Hardcastle."

Once outside the restaurant, they walked up the street to Claire's bookstore. He smiled at the name: Novelteas. It evoked a warmth and sense of fun he'd never expected to find hiding inside the niece of an iron maiden like Amanda Morse. It really was exceptional what Claire had achieved in the last eighteen months, and although he'd had her investigated and knew of her circumstances, lines on a page couldn't tell him everything. And as Luke watched Claire unlock the front door and shove it open, he realised something.

He wanted to know *everything* about her.

"The Campioni family. Tell me about them."

"What do you want to know?" Claire said, navigating her way through the dark shop with practised ease.

Luke must have kicked, tripped over or bumped into every display on the floor.

When the office light finally flickered into being, Claire stood in the doorway, smirking at him. "Are you quite finished trashing my shop?"

"That remains to be seen," he said, immediately regretting his words when her smirk fell and her eyes narrowed. "The Campioni family. They're the ones who took you in, aren't they?"

Claire pulled out her chair and sat down, folded her hands in her lap. "Did your investigator tell you that?"

"Yes."

"Then why ask me?"

Luke kept his distance and leaned against the doorjamb. "Because I'd like to hear the story from your point of view."

Smoothing out the skirt of her dress and avoiding his gaze, she said, "Yeah, well, too bad. Now, what did you really want to see me about?"

Knowing she wasn't going to like what he was about to say, he braced himself for a storm and told her his plan.

Claire was on her feet in an instant. "I'd rather give you my shop!"

Folding his arms over his chest and standing tall, Luke stared her down. "No, you wouldn't. I know how much you love this old place. Why do you think I bought it?"

All the venom left her expression, replaced with caution. "How long have been planning this?"

"Since Cassidy Holdings went under. It took a while for an opportunity to present itself, but just because you disappeared from Morse Industries doesn't mean you dropped off my radar."

"You've been watching me?"

"Yes."

Her brow furrowed. "For eighteen months?"

For ten years.... "Yes."

"Then you should know why I can't do it."

"You can and you will," he said. "This is non-negotiable."

Misery laced her voice when she spoke. "Don't make me do this. Please."

The look on Claire's face almost made Luke change his mind.

Almost.

But he'd waited too long for this. He needed revenge. He needed to know the people who hurt his family had suffered, and Luke could think of no better way to accomplish that goal where Claire was concerned than by making her do something she *really* didn't want to do.

Reconcile with Amanda.

"I want you back in her good graces so you can spy on her for me."

"Yes, I get that thank you," she snapped. "I'm not an idiot. But don't you have people who can plant listening devices in her office or something? Why the hell do I have talk to her?"

"For starters, what you're suggesting is illegal, but more to the point, a listening device can't direct a conversation, which is what I'll need you to do if you're going to make Amanda confess her crimes."

"This is too much, Luke," she said, flopping back into the ugly plastic chair at her desk. "I'm not doing it."

He stepped closer. "Yes, you are," he said softly.

"No."

"You want some added incentive?" Luke asked, coolly. "How about your house?"

Glaring up at him, she said, "What about my house?"

"Do this for me and I'll pay it off."

Claire's jaw literally dropped. "What?"

"You heard me. I know you mortgaged your house to get the money to start this place. Just imagine what you could do if you didn't have that weight resting on your shoulders."

He could see she was thinking about it. He'd noticed the other night when they'd gone over the leases that her eyes would dance back and forth while she was thinking, as though she was reading some invisible document right in front of her face. He'd found it fascinating to watch.

Mesmerising.

But then her eyes stopped dancing. "No," she said, shaking her head. "I can't."

He raised a brow. "Can't or won't?"

She lifted her chin. "Take your pick."

"Okay, then let's try this on for size. Instead of paying off your house, I'll buy out your mortgage. I'll own your shop *and* your home."

Her hands scrunched into fists in her lap. "You're a bastard, Hardcastle."

"Is that a yes?" he asked as calmly as possible. Which, truth be told, was harder than he'd like.

Claire glared at him again then nodded sharply. "Yes."

"Good. I'll leave the details of your reunion up to you. You know best how to go about luring Amanda out from under her rock. Just keep me informed. I want you to make contact with her by the end of the week. Agreed?"

"Yes."

Luke sighed quietly. "Do you need a lift home?"

"Not from you," Claire growled.

He held out his hand. "I'm not letting you take the bus at this time of night and everyone else has gone home. Come on, my car's out front."

She didn't fight him as he led her back through the shop and out to the footpath, nor did she protest when he draped his suit jacket around her shoulders and helped her into his car. It was almost as though she'd just shut down, retreated in on herself. Maybe he *was* asking too much of her. Maybe forcing her back into Amanda's world wasn't the right move here. But how else was he supposed to get the evidence he needed to take that bitch down?

He knew something had happened between Claire and her aunt. Hell, everyone knew *something* had happened. But no one knew the specifics and not even his investigator had been able to dig them up. It was a mystery to all.

All except Claire and Amanda.

Silence reigned on the drive back to Claire's house. Luke wasn't sure what to say now he had her compliance, and Claire offered nothing to ease the tension, just stared straight ahead with her hands folded neatly in her lap, just as she had in her office.

Christ, I've broken her.

"Claire? Are you all right?"

"Fuck you, Hardcastle."

Okay. He hadn't broken her quite yet.

The roads were quiet at this time of night, more so since it was a Wednesday. Luke looked over at Claire, searching for something to talk about. She turned her back on him. *All righty.* Talking was out. Focusing on the road, he let his mind wander instead.

And damn if it didn't wander all the way back to the day they'd met.

The first day she'd made him burn.

Luke was twenty-seven years old and had just taken over Hardcastle Construction from his father. Claire was nineteen and interning at Morse Industries. Not that he'd known that when he first saw her, standing in line for coffee at the mobile café parked across the street from their work. All he'd seen was a pretty girl with curves for days in a dress that was equal parts modest, quirky and sexy as hell. The quirky came from the pattern on the fabric—a rainbow of tiny origami cranes. The sexy part was the way the fabric unashamedly clung to her gorgeous body then flared out over the swell of her hips. And the modesty?

That was all Claire.

Taking her tray of coffees from the barista, she'd turned and narrowly avoided running into him. He'd grabbed her upper arms to stop her from dropping her coffees and he'd felt a spark under his palms where his skin connected with hers.

Looking up at him with those big blue eyes, she'd said, "Thanks," then blushed as red as a beetroot, smiled shyly and glanced away.

"My pleasure," he'd said with a smile, the first genuine smile he'd felt cross his face since swapping out his King Gees and work boots for tailored suits and grown-up shoes.

The barista called out, "Next," and Luke had reluctantly let her go.

"Don't go anywhere," he'd told her, still smiling like a fool, and gave his order.

When he'd turned back to face her, she was chewing her bottom lip and fidgeting with the lids on the take-away coffee cups. She was so fucking adorable, this pretty girl in her sexy dress with her amazing eyes and shy demeanour. Out of nowhere a protectiveness had risen up in him, a possessiveness he couldn't explain, so when some wanker had shoved his way past her and sent her sprawling to the footpath, his first instinct hadn't been to grab the dumb fuck and shake some sense into him.

He'd leapt to her aid instead. "Are you hurt?" Luke had helped her to her feet, then dusted his hand over her skirt, brushing off dirt and skimming his palm over her plush arse. The move had been unintentional, but she hadn't seemed to mind him touching her. "Are you okay, miss...?"

Picking up the ruined coffees and dumping them in the bin, she'd said, "Claire. My name is Claire. And I'm all right." Then she'd sighed, grabbed a handful of napkins and dabbed at the coffee stain on her dress. "Nothing a little Sard Wonder Soap won't get out."

Impressed by her nonchalance, he'd ordered more coffees for her, then said, "I'm Luke."

"I know," she'd said with a shy smile. "You're Luke Hardcastle. You just took over Hardcastle Construction."

No one had known who Luke was. Not back then. But the fact Claire knew had stirred something inside him. Excited him. *She'd noticed me too.* "How do you know who I am?" he'd asked. "Do you work in the building?"

Her smile dissolved, she'd swallowed hard and looked away, nervous again. "No. I'm an intern at Morse Industries," she'd offered.

And the puzzle pieces had clicked into place.

He'd dropped his smile. "Claire. Morse. You're Amanda Morse's niece, aren't you?"

Claire nodded, and just like that all the warmth, all the possessiveness had rushed out of him and their whole interaction felt like a lie.

"Did Amanda tell you to do this? To flirt with me?" he'd accused. "Nice touch, by the way, getting that guy to knock you down. Jesus *fucking* Christ." He'd handed the barista a twenty then passed the tray of fresh coffees to Claire. "Enjoy your coffee. And tell Amanda that's the only thing she's ever getting from me."

Then ignoring the look of devastation that had blanketed her pretty face, he'd stalked away without a backwards glance and spent the next ten years wishing Claire was anyone other than who she was.

A Morse.

He glanced at her again. The Claire sitting next to him was a very different woman. This Claire had confidence. She walked tall and proud and wasn't afraid to speak her mind. But she still blushed when he caught her staring at him, she still had a certain vulnerability about her. And he still felt that spark whenever he touched her, still found her presence intoxicating.

But that was the problem, wasn't it?

Chapter Eleven

P utting her phone down for the third time, Claire jumped up and down on the spot, waving her fists in the air and silently screaming at the ceiling as if that would magically make dialling Amanda's phone number any easier.

"Tea. I need tea."

Upstairs, the tearoom was still fairly quiet, but come lunchtime the place would be packed with patrons, people who appreciated the subtle intricacies of flavour when you matched a particular cup of tea with its perfect cake mate. Like a lightly spiced yoghurt cupcake with a chai latte, or apple teacake with a cup of white Ceylon.

Settling on a cup of Lady Grey and a slice of salted caramel brownie, Claire managed to avoid calling Amanda for another fifteen minutes. Tea drunk and treat eaten, she then strolled around the room, talking with the early morning customers, clearing tables, double-checking the tearoom bookings for the next month... procrastinating like a pro.

Eventually she made her way back to her office,

forced herself to sit her arse down and picked up her phone. She had to make contact by the end of the week. Today was Thursday, and if she stuck to form, Amanda would be in meetings all day Friday, so it was now or never.

Why can't it be never?

Claire called up the keypad on her mobile phone and dialled Amanda's office, the numbers flying forward from her subconscious more easily than she liked.

Anxiously, she waited for an answer.

Silently, she prayed she didn't get one.

The call connected. "Good morning. You've reached Amanda Morse's office. Is she expecting your call?"

Shit. "Uh, no. She's not. My name is Claire Morse and I would like to—"

She was put on hold.

Heaving an impatient sigh, Claire listened to the classical music wafting through the phone, biding her time as her aunt played The Waiting Game. Amanda loved making people wait to talk to her. It agitated them, put them on edge while giving her time to strategise and gain the upper hand. Minutes ticked by and Claire began to hope that Amanda wouldn't take her call, that maybe her aunt wanted to speak to Claire almost as much as Claire wanted to speak to her aunt.

Not at all.

Beyond "hello", Claire hadn't given much thought to what she would say. After all, what was she supposed say to the woman who'd taken her in against her will then packed her off to boarding school the second she was old enough to go? A woman who'd picked at and demeaned and belittled her and everything she did for as long as she could remember, and the one time Claire had stood up to her, Amanda had disowned her, cut her off financially and rendered her homeless.

Mother of the Year, she was not.

"Claire, is that really you?" Amanda's smoky voice sounded in her ear and made her jump. Her mouth ran dry and for what seemed like an age she lacked the ability to speak. "Hello? Are you ther—"

"Hello," Claire croaked, finding her voice. "I'm here, Aunty Amanda."

"Well, I must say this is... unexpected," Amanda said. "I hadn't thought to be hearing from *you* anytime soon."

"Yes, I know, but I, um.... Well, I was over your way the other day, outside Morse Industries, and I got to thinking maybe I should call you. So I am... calling you." Claire winced at her unease. She hated feeling so unsure, but that was what Amanda did to her.

Made her doubt everything.

"Yes, I heard you took a meeting at Hardcastle Tower. I don't suppose you'd care to explain what you were doing there?"

How did she know about that? It really didn't matter how she knew because there it was, the opportunity she needed to bait her aunt. Didn't take long, much less time than she'd expected.

"Oh, that? It was nothing. I met with Luke Hardcastle to discuss a business issue."

Amanda's voice had a saccharine edge to it when she asked, "What sort of business issue?" *Said the spider to the fly.*

"Nothing that would interest you, I'm sure, Aunty," Claire said, spoon-feeding the older woman breadcrumbs. "It's small fry, really." She sighed, but not too dramatically. *I should win a bloody Oscar for this.* "Luke bought the row of shops along Merthyr Road, near the Brunswick intersection. He's my new landlord."

"Is he now?" Amanda said, and Claire could hear the calculation in her voice. "And what would someone like Luke Hardcastle want with a bunch of second-rate restaurants, knick-knack sellers and a bookstore?"

Bristling at her aunt's derision, Claire forced herself not to snap. "I don't know. He only met with me to discuss lease terms."

"Did he?" Amanda paused, then said, "Have lunch with me tomorrow. We'll catch up, discuss what's new."

"Won't you be in meetings all day?"

"I do stop to eat occasionally."

Yeah, the souls of newborn babes.

Unsure if what she was feeling was relief, dread or a sickening combination of both, Claire agreed to meet Amanda for lunch the following day at midday sharp, then hung up and released the breath she hadn't realised she'd been holding. She felt light-headed.

And she still had to call Luke.

As soon as she finished filling him in on her conversation with Amanda, he said, "I'll pick you up after work so we can come up with a strategy, figure out what you're going to say."

Claire hated how much she wanted to see him. After the way they'd left things the previous night the last thing she should want was to be in the same room as him. But again, her libido didn't care. As soon as she'd heard his dark velvet voice, her nipples had tightened, her pussy had grown wet and she'd had the overwhelming urge to lock her office door and rub one out.

Much safer to keep her distance.

"You don't need to do that. I'll just call you when I get home and we can discuss it then."

Yes. That was a much better idea. A disconnected voice was a lot easier to deal with. Especially when the man in question had the power to make her knees go weak at the slightest provocation. One of those impish smirks usually did the trick.

"It's no trouble. Besides, I have to get my jacket back. I'll swing by the shop around five o'clock. Do you want some dinner? I was thinking Indian."

Scrunching her brow at the unexpected gesture, Claire said, "Uh, sure, I guess. As long as you're buying. And I love Indian food. The spicier the better. And something with goat in it. Korma is always good with goat."

Luke snorted. "Goat? Seriously?"

Claire smiled, relaxed a little. But not too much. "Hey, don't knock it until you try it."

"Let me write this down so I don't forget," he said, his voice still light with humour. "Goat for the crazy lady."

"Just for that you can get me some veggie pakoras too. And raita. Don't forget the raita. Oh, and a mango lassi. A big one. Make it two."

Luke was outright laughing now. "Anything else?"

Should I...? Fuck it. "Kashmiri naan."

"What the hell is that?"

"Naan bread stuffed with dried fruit, spice and crushed nuts. It's great served warm with a scoop of vanilla ice cream. Oh, and buy ice cream!"

"Got it," he said, still chuckling. "You weren't kidding when you said you love Indian food, were you?"

"I never kid about food."

"I'll try to remember that." Then his laugh trailed off and his voice deepened. "I'll see you this afternoon, Claire."

Her breath hitched as she realised his words sounded more like a seductive promise between lovers than a business appointment between blackmailer and blackmailee.

Claire's pulse thrilled at the idea.

There was no denying she found Luke insanely attractive. What woman wouldn't? He was tall and broad and practically filled any doorway he stood in, but there was so much more to him than his physical presence. Luke was confident, sure of every move he made, decisive and bold. His whole demeanour commanded one's attention, captured it.

Since taking over his father's company he'd truly made it his own. And Luke's special blend of industry knowledge, dedication and confidence had seen Hardcastle Construction win bid after bid until it grew into the corporate giant it was today.

Around the time he'd succeeded his father, Amanda had tasked Claire with studying Luke. By the time she was done, she thought she'd known almost everything there was to know about him, but it wasn't until she met the man in person—and almost spilled five cups of coffee on his suit—that Claire had learned something not in the file: Luke Hardcastle could be a really nice guy. Or a real jerk. Oh, and he hated her aunt for some reason.

So, they had that in common at least.

But the other thing that had stuck out in her mind was how much he loved his family, his stepfather and half-sister included. Lottie was five years younger than Luke, his baby sister, and Claire had felt keenly the envy she always felt when she read about happy families. Then wondered for the umpteenth time what she'd done to deserve the relatives she'd been stuck with.

Ten years later and Luke's family had dwindled considerably. His dad had died from a sudden heart attack and his mum passed less than a year later. And his stepdad, the man Lottie had taken over from as CEO of Cassidy Holdings, had finally succumb to the lung cancer that had seen him step down as chief in the first place. Lottie was Luke's last living relative. And she was sick too. In the not too distant future Luke would be all alone.

Just like Claire.

Chapter Twelve

Luke strolled into Novelteas just before five and spotted Claire helping a customer. She looked up and smiled when she saw him, and he had to consciously stop himself from going to her, driving his hands through her hair and pulling her soft mouth to his.

Fuck.

He had to get this infatuation under control. Before he did something really stupid.

Claire held up a finger, silently asking for more time. Luke nodded in response then picked up the nearest book and started flicking through the pages.

"Back again, Mr Hardcastle?"

Luke looked up from *Cricket Through the Ages* to find a blonde woman staring up at him. It took him a few seconds to place her. "You served me tea on Monday," he said, setting the book aside, then looked at her name tag. "Karen." He grinned. The words *Assistant Book Nerd* were printed under her name.

"Sure did. So... what did you do to my boss?"

Luke frowned. "What do you mean?"

"She's been distracted all week," she said, then held up her hand to silence him before he could get a single word out. "Not that that's necessarily a bad thing. The woman needs a good *distracting*, if you know what I mean."

Luke knew *exactly* what she meant. But.... "I'm going to stop you there. I think you may have the wrong impression. My meetings with Claire are purely professional."

Karen folded her arms over her chest and raised a brow at him. "*Riiight*. So, when you were staring at her the other day like you could just eat her up with a spoon, that was you being 'purely professional'?"

Shit. Letting the damage control part of his brain take over, he smiled seductively and let his gaze travel the length of her slender body. "Maybe it wasn't Claire I was watching," he said, but he felt... *nothing*.

Karen snorted. "Yeah. You keep telling yourself that." Then she turned on her heel and walked away.

Luke barely had time to process Karen's parting volley before Claire was standing beside him, shrugging into a pink leather biker jacket. *So fucking cute.*

"You ready to go?" she asked. Her voice seemed off, distant.

Dropping his voice, Luke murmured, "Are you all right?"

"Fine."

Fuck. If having a sister had taught Luke anything, it was when a woman said 'fine' you knew you were screwed.

He lightened his tone. "Okay. Let's get going," he said, then led her outside to his car. "I got ice cream on the way here, and I've ordered the Indian food. It should be ready to pick up by the time we get to the restaurant."

Claire fastened her seatbelt. "Okay."

Greaaat. Single word answers. Oh yeah, tonight was going to be awesome.

"So, why a bookstore?"

After a near silent thirty-minute drive back to Claire's house, Luke attempted once more to draw her into conversation. He'd already set the dining table—if a folding card table could be called a dining table—and was watching her serve out the take-away.

Tossing the empty containers in the rubbish, she said, "I thought you wanted to talk about Amanda."

Screwing up his face, Luke replied, "Not while I'm eating."

Claire approached the table juggling two plates of curry, a plate of plain naan and a bowl overflowing with the vegetable pakoras she'd told him to buy. He may have gone a bit overboard with the pakoras, but he'd never tried them before and ordered four serves, thinking they'd eat two each. How was he to know a single 'serve' actually contained four of the small, spicy misshapen patties?

After helping her set everything down, he held her chair out for her. She looked wary as she sat in the ugly plastic garden chair, as though she expected him to yank it out from under her. He shouldn't have been offended by her reaction. But he was.

Taking his seat, he asked again, "Why the bookstore?"

Claire tore off a chunk of naan bread, scooped it through her food then bit into it, korma dribbled over her hand and down her wrist. Luke watched with bated breath and a hardening cock as Claire followed the path of the mess with her tongue, licking and sucking until her skin was free of all saucy goodness.

Christ, I need to get laid.

Once she'd finished torturing him, Claire shrugged and said, "Business 101. Make your passion your profession and you'll never work a day in your life." She grabbed more naan. "I've always loved books, so a bookstore seemed the logical choice."

Now they were getting somewhere. "And the tearoom?"

"I like tea."

Annnd they were back to square one.

Luke frowned at Claire as she continued eating and not talking. After their animated discussion on the phone, he'd hoped to keep the momentum going, to maybe find a more amicable way of resolving their issues. Preferably something that involved getting naked, having lots of wild monkey sex and possibly chocolate cannoli.

"I know we're not friends, Claire, but there's no reason we can't keep this friendly."

Very friendly if he got his way.

Which he usually did.

She didn't even spare him a glance as she grabbed a pakora and dipped it in the raita. "I am being friendly."

"No, you're not," he said around a mouthful of korma.

Lifting her gaze to his, she said, "I didn't spit in your food. What more do you want?"

"All right," Luke said, laying aside his fork and resting his arms on the table. "What have I done."

"Hmm, besides the blackmail and the threats of making me homeless again...? Gee. Let me think."

"You seemed happy enough to see me when I arrived this afternoon. I'm assuming that's why you smiled at me."

"I work in retail," she said. "Smiling at people we don't like is ninety percent of the job."

Right. Picking up his fork, Luke conceded defeat—for now—and ate the rest of his meal in silence. Even after dinner, when she was preparing dessert, Claire kept the chatter to a bare minimum. Whatever game she was playing, it was beginning to piss him off. Mostly because he seemed to be losing. And sitting through the spectacle of watching her eat hot fruity naan bread covered in French vanilla ice cream with her fingers—without flipping the table over, tackling her to the ground and fucking her senseless—was just about the hardest thing he'd done all week.

Speaking of hard....

He needed a distraction. *Now.*

Discreetly adjusting himself, he said. "About tomorrow, what's your plan of attack?"

Claire sprung out of her chair and started clearing the dishes, her back ramrod straight and her face pinched, contorted by an odd look conveying both horror and hostility. "Amanda wants to meet at Aria, that place on the Pier."

"I know it," Luke said. "It's very nice."

"And way outside my budget, so she'd better be buying."

"I'll give you some money," he said, pulling out his mobile phone. "What are your account details?"

"I'm not telling you that. And I don't need your charity."

"Claire, I've already bought you dinner three times this week so what's a lunch on top of that?" Before Claire could answer he sighed and said, "Consider it a slush fund, then. Something to help you keep Amanda interested, keep her guessing. Make her wonder just how well you're doing for yourself."

"I don't want your money," she said, enunciating each word as though she were speaking to a moron. And maybe she was considering he had no idea how to react to the intensity of her declaration. How long had it been since a woman wanted nothing from him?

Too long.

Luke grabbed the last few dishes and joined Claire on the other side of the kitchen bench. She'd already filled the sink with soap and water and was scrubbing a plate with way more force than was warranted. Her back was still too straight, her face still pinched, and when she spoke her voice sounded brittle, raw.

"Money doesn't fix everything."

"But it doesn't hurt," Luke said, grabbing a tea towel and drying the plate she'd finished torturing.

"Yes it does," she whispered, then turned her face away from him and swiped her hand across her cheek.

Shit. Luke loathed the sound of crying women. Usually because if they were crying in front of him in was in the hopes he'd buy them something to shut them up, which was usually when he found himself walking out the front door without a so much as a backwards glance. Claire's tears were silent and punched him in the gut so hard he almost couldn't breathe. He didn't want to walk away, he wanted to drag her into his arms. And if he thought he could without earning another slap across his face, he would.

He tried talking to her instead. "You were right about the goat by the way. About all of it, actually. It was very good." He could see the pakoras becoming a regular treat.

When she turned back towards him, her face was slightly blotchy, and her eyes rimmed in red but otherwise dry. "Are you actually trying to make me feel better?"

"Depends. Is it working?"

A watery smile curved her lips and she nodded, then she blew out a breath and turned serious again. "Are you sure you want to do this?" she said quietly.

Luke knew what she was asking. "Quite sure. Why?"

"Because Amanda's been at this for a long, long time and she's very good at what she does. She isn't going to admit any wrongdoing any time soon. "

"Your point?"

"I just hope you realise what you're going to have to do to beat her at her own game, what you will have to become. Despite everything that's happened this week, I still believe you're a good man. But to beat Amanda you're going to have to become something you're not."

"Really?" Luke said, ignoring the seriousness in Claire's voice. "And what's that?"

"A prick."

Luke laughed out loud at the sincerity on Claire's face. "I can be a prick."

"I know," she said, handing him a bowl to dry. "I remember."

Luke sobered, the memory of berating her in front of a roomful of Morse Industries employees quick to fill his mind.

Claire continued. "But you're nowhere near her level. If you're serious about taking Amanda down then you are going to have to be ruthless, merciless, and I'm sorry but your reputation leaves a lot to be desired in that regard."

"I've already resorted to blackmail, Claire, what else would you like me to do, sacrifice a small child?"

Throwing the dishcloth down, she turned to face him, leaned her hip against the sink and folded her arms across her chest. "If you really wanted to make sure you could keep me in line you would never have conceded to my demands over the other leases, you would have held them over my head too in case I had any ideas of, oh I don't know, say, changing premises to a building *not* owned by Hardcastle Construction? If I move my shop, you'll have no hold over me. No bargaining chip."

Luke tossed the tea towel on the bench and match Claire's stance. His agitation bleeding through his words. "You think I'm weak because I conduct myself with integrity."

"I've never thought that," Claire said so vehemently he had to bite back a smile. "But Amanda does, and she will use your integrity against you." She sighed and rubbed her forehead. "But I guess we won't really know how to play the game until I see her tomorrow."

"I suppose not," he agreed as they resumed their task.

Claire handed Luke a glass and their fingers touched. A shock of sensation sizzled along his skin and he almost dropped the damned thing. Grabbing on to it with both hands, he somehow managed to imprison her fingers under his.

Setting the glass aside, Luke kept hold of Claire's fingers and lifted them to his mouth. She trembled against his lips as he kissed a path from her fingertips to her wrist, gasped when he sucked and nipped her flesh.

Moving swiftly, he pinned her against the kitchen bench and dropped his gaze to her breasts. They rose and fell with every staggered breath she took, threatening to pop the buttons on her pretty blouse.

"Luke."

Claire's sultry voice drew his gaze up the smooth column of her neck, over the jut of her chin, the swell of her lips, the gentle slope of her nose. He took her all in, committed every inch of her to memory. The thick fall of her dark hair, the roundness of her cheeks, those incredible steel-blue eyes, the three pale freckles adorning the shell of her ear.

"You're so beautiful," he whispered, then moulded his lips to hers and kissed her long and deep.

Chapter Thirteen

The flavour of fruit and spice and vanilla exploded across Claire's tongue as it lashed against Luke's, waging war on her common sense as her libido said, *Fuck it! What's the worst that could happen?*

Fisting her hands in his hair, she threw caution to the wind and kissed Luke like her life depended on it. A masculine growl met her ears then strong hands were grabbing her arse and hauling her closer until she was practically humping his leg.

No. Not a leg.

An *erection*.

A long, thick, iron hard, Hardcastle Construction sized erection.

Halle-freaking-lujah!

So, she hadn't imagined it the other night. And maybe she wasn't destined to die alone. Because if she, Claire Morse, the anti-thesis of a professional coat-hanger, had the power to give Luke Hardcastle an erection, then anything was possible.

Curiosity getting the better of her, she slid her hand

between them and cupped the front of his trousers. *Holy crap!* The size of him terrified her, but it was a wonderful kind of fear, exciting, seductive.

She felt him smile against her mouth, heard his soft chuckle. "Do I meet with your approval, Miss Morse?"

Snatching her hand back, Claire felt her cheeks heat and she stammered for something to say. Thankfully Luke came to the rescue, hooking his hands under her thighs and hoisting her onto the kitchen bench.

Grabbing his shoulders to steady herself, she gasped, "Don't do that."

Luke grinned. "Why?"

"Because," she said. "I'm heavy." Feeling very uncomfortable as she stated the obvious, she mumbled, "You'll hurt your back."

A burst of laughter escaped him multiplying her unease tenfold. She struggled to free herself and get off the damn bench, but he held her fast, his hands firm on her upper thighs, his thumbs stroking back and forth. Teasing her with possibility.

"How much do you weigh?"

Mortified, Claire doubled her efforts to free herself. "You can't ask a woman that!"

"How much, Claire?" Luke said, pushing himself between her legs and spreading her knees wide, unashamedly pushing that magnificent erection against her clit. *Oh God.* Struggling against him only made it worse. She bit the inside of her cheek to stop from moaning out loud. He didn't notice. "Less than a hundred kilos, I'm guessing."

Nodding sharply and with eyes narrowed to slits, she spoke through gritted teeth. "Ninety-three kilos."

Luke's grin returned. "Sweetness, I bench-press more than you weigh." Claire was suddenly very aware of his hands sliding over her blouse. "So stop fretting about my back, and let's get you on yours."

His head descended to the patch of bare skin visible in the V of her blouse, his lips hot and wet kissed a path up her throat, along her jaw, distracted her from his clever fingers and the buttons they were popping open, one after another.

Claire sucked in an excited breath as Luke parted the halves of her blouse. It was her favourite blouse too. Off-white cotton with a lace trim, pearl buttons and a short puff sleeve, perfect with a skirt or jeans. It made her feel pretty.

Luke called me beautiful.

Unfortunately, the only way she could wear her favourite blouse without the buttons flying off and taking someone's eye out, was to encase her enormous breasts in a minimiser bra, the clothing equivalent of a dam wall, constructed to restrain a tidal wave of flesh. Designed to be practical more than pretty, the one Claire wore, while not ugly, was also not the sexiest item of clothing she owned. It certainly wasn't what she would have worn had she known Luke Hardcastle would be taking it off her. You needed an engineering degree to get that sucker off.

Luke has an engineering degree, her libido whispered in her ear.

Even so, he was frowning at it like it was a puzzle to be solved. "How do I...? Is there a password or a magic spell or something? It's like a chastity belt for your boobs."

Claire surprised herself by laughing and Luke peered over her shoulder to look down her back, peeling her blouse the rest of the way off.

"Does it come with instructions?" he asked, tilting his head to the side as though looking at abstract art. Then shrugged and cupped her breasts.

Even through the thick fabric of the bra she could feel

the heat of his palms. She wondered if he could feel her hardened nipples. "Since when do men read the instructions?"

A look of pure mischief spread over his face as he massaged her breasts with a firm yet languid movement. "Good point," he whispered, then stole her breath with another all-consuming kiss.

The way he gently nibbled at her lips, first the top then the bottom, before sucking them between his own and teasing them with his tongue, gently prying them apart and sliding inside her welcoming mouth, wrestling her will into submission.

She'd never been kissed so well in all her life and her whole body buzzed with need and heat, with longing and lust. A lust she'd never felt for anyone but him.

And he didn't even like her.

The realisation punched her in the gut and stole the air from her lungs.

The man doing these wondrous things to her body, kissing and touching and telling her she was beautiful, doing all the things she said she wouldn't let him do, didn't like her.

Anxiety gripped her throat and squeezed, choking off her oxygen and making her gasp. She pushed against his chest. He barely moved. "Stop."

He stroked his fingers along her jaw, gentle, reverent. "What's wrong, sweetness? Am I going too fast?" His voice was as breathless as hers, his golden eyes heavy-lidded with lust.

Fighting the urge to lean into his touch, she said, "We shouldn't be doing this."

"Yes, we should," he said, sliding his hands through her

hair and gripping the back of her head. "We really, really should."

Tilting her head, he ravished her lips and her heart kicked in her chest. A jolt of pure desire shot straight to her core, she moaned.

She needed more.

"That's it, sweetness," Luke groaned as she nibbled her way along his jaw, licked and bit and sucked his flesh, tasted the salt on his skin, breathed in his rich masculine scent.

Pulling away she stared into his eyes, stared at a desire that rivalled her own then she kissed him again, harder, dropped her defences lower....

Until she felt his hands at her waist, popping the button on her jeans.

"Christ, Claire," Luke murmured against her lips. "I need to be inside you."

Before he could unzip her, she shoved him away and blurted, "No!"

Luke stared at her, concern and confusion blanketing his handsome face. "Claire?"

"I can't do this," she whispered, shivering at the sudden loss of his body heat. Sliding off the kitchen bench, she snatched her blouse from where it lay discarded on the floor and slipped it back on.

"Why?" Luke growled the word at her, frustration heavy in his tone.

She shook her head, her fingers trembled as she fumbled with the buttons. "You know why."

Luke raked his hand through his hair and swore. "Yeah, I know why," he said, his voice dripping with sarcasm as he tucked his shirt tails back in his trousers. "Because I'm blackmailing you and you're not that kind of girl." Turning to face her, he added, "Sorry, was that not *dignified*?"

Her dignity a distant memory at this point, she lifted her chin and glared at him. "About as dignified as you flirting with my assistant manager then shoving your tongue down my throat."

Luke jolted back, surprise clearly painted across his features. "Wait, is that why you were pissed at me earlier? Because you think I was flirting with Karen?"

Claire folded her arms over her chest and raised one brow in silent challenge.

Luke growled, as though having to explain himself was so incredibly tedious. "I was talking to her, not flirting."

Riiight. She saw him staring at her breasts. Smiling at her. "And what were you talking about? Her cup size?"

Luke laughed, but it was not a happy sound. "No. You know what," he said, "I'm not going to tell you." His eyes narrowed and his lip lifted in a sneer. "It'll be far more amusing watching you twist yourself up in knots imagining me with another woman."

Claire felt the burn of tears prick behind her eyes, in her nose. "You need to leave."

Yanking his suit jacket on in quick, efficient movements, Luke said, "Yes I do." His voice was tight, his eyes stormy as he stared at her.

Coward that she was, she couldn't hold his gaze.

Walking Luke to the front door felt like walking to the gallows, every step fraught with tension as she waited for the final blow. But as she reached for the door, he took her hand and pressed something small and cold into her palm.

"Take this."

Claire stared at the elegant silver locket gracing the palm of her hand. An antique, judging by the scroll work, and shaped like a shield. Victorian, if she wasn't mistaken. Her penchant for antiques lay more in furniture than shiny baubles, but if she'd had her pick of every locket ever made, that was exactly the one she would've chosen.

How did he know?

And why was he giving her jewellery?

Her hand fluttered to her chest, confusion reigned in her head. "It's beautiful," she said quietly.

Luke grunted. "It's a digital voice recorder."

"What?" Incredulity soured her voice.

"You will record all conversations with Amanda, after which I will debrief you and download the recordings."

Claire cradled the locket in her hands like an injured bird, stared at it in horror. "You destroyed an antique for the sake of a listening device? You're like one of those monsters who rips the guts out of books, shoves an engagement ring inside and thinks it's romantic!"

"Relax, sweetness," he drawled. "It's a replica. I had it made this week."

Claire turned the locket over in her hand, inspecting every facet of it. No one would ever know it was more than it seemed just by looking at it. "So quickly?"

"Amazing how fast problems can be resolved if you throw enough money at them." Luke took the device and quickly showed her how to operate it.

"Is that what I am to you?" she said, cocking her head to one side, staring up at him. "A problem to be solved."

"I'm not sure what you are yet, but I doubt throwing money at you would help."

"Then whatever I am I should be a refreshing change for you," she said and pocketed the locket. Luke almost smiled. Claire frowned. "Anyway, I thought you said listening devices were illegal."

"No, I said your idea of planting them in her office was illegal. Using one in public to record a conversation you're a party to, is not." When Claire continued frowning at him, he added, "I have very good lawyers too." Luke opened the door but stopped halfway out. "One last question before I go. Why haven't you started looking for new premises? Someplace I don't own."

Claire's eyes narrowed as she studied Luke's inscrutable face. "Why?"

"Humour me."

Heaving an irritated sigh, she said, "Because I don't have the funds to move anywhere else. But you already know that."

Luke smiled. Like a shark. "Yes, I already know that. I just wanted to hear *you* say it out loud."

"Why?"

"To remind you of our deal in case you're thinking of changing your mind. I know how fickle women can be."

Hands balling into fists at her sides, she said, "I know the consequences if I don't do what you want, Luke."

"Maybe you should remember that. For the next time you feel like changing your mind."

Fury licked along her veins and her nostrils flared. So that was it, huh? He was pissed because he didn't get laid, because she'd come to her senses and made him pack up his bat and balls. "You need to leave before I slap you again."

Smirking, he stepped closer. "Try it and see what happens." Then he very deliberately slid his scorching hot gaze down her body and back up again.

And she felt it sizzle along every nerve she owned.

Sizzle and burn.

Fuming with indignation—and more turned on than she wanted to admit—she growled, "Get out."

Luke's smile turned smug. "Goodnight, Miss Morse. Don't forget to call me when you're done with Amanda."

And then he was gone.

Claire slammed the front door. The wall shook and the windows rattled in protest. Why did Luke Hardcastle have to be so infuriatingly handsome? He had absolutely no physical flaws she could exploit as turn offs.

Not a single hair out of place or wart on his chin.

Turning towards the kitchen, Claire listed every nasty trait she could think of. "Rude, arrogant, snide, malicious—"

There was a knock on the door. When she turned around, she jumped in fright, hand to chest, then huffed out an angry breath. Luke was peering through the window. Scowling at her.

"Open the door, Claire."

As always, the man's rich voice did things to her. Strange, wonderful, inconvenient things she really wished it wouldn't do, like call up the memory of his hands on her breasts, his firm touch, his endless heat. Her nipples pebbled under her bra.

She groaned and bent her head in shame.

Opening the door just a crack, she snapped at him. "What?"

"You still have my jacket from last night."

Opening the door the rest of the way, she pointed at his feet where they threatened to cross the threshold into her home. "Wait there," she demanded. When he cocked a you've-got-to-be-kidding brow at her, she added, "Not a toe, Hardcastle." Then she strolled down the hall to her bedroom and took her time collecting his jacket.

Slung over the foot of her bed, the navy-blue suit jacket looked like it belonged there. In another life, Claire could well imagine Luke coming home after work and discarding his clothes left and right, like he had in his office the other night. His tie would land on the dresser, his trousers on the floor. His underwear would dangle from the ceiling fan.

She'd wear his shirt....

Claire draped the jacket over her arm. The fabric felt fine and soft and made a *shhh* sound when she ran her hand along the sleeve, as though willing her to be quiet and simply bask in its tailored magnificence. She remembered its weight when Luke had draped it around her shoulders, remembered its warmth—*his* warmth—as it sunk into her cold flesh and stopping her from nosediving into full-on shock.

Lifting the collar to her face, she inhaled his scent. While not as strong as it was tonight with her face buried in the crook of his neck, she could still smell the last few lingering notes of his cologne—rich leather, aged timber and something she couldn't quite put her finger on. Something purely male. Primal.

Sensual.

Floorboards creaked behind her and she spun just in time to see Luke loom into view. He stood outside her bedroom and frowned at her.

"I told you to wait out there," Claire said, thrusting the jacket at him.

Luke took it from her outstretched hand, careful to avoid touching her again. "You were taking forever," he complained. "I thought you might be trying to set it on fire or something."

"Playing with fire is your kink, not mine. I was just wiping my nose on the sleeve." She shrugged. "I couldn't find a tissue."

His lips pressed together in a thin line and his eyes darkened dangerously. But instead of threats or insults or kissing, he turned on his heel and marched out of the house, shutting the door behind him.

Suddenly feeling very tired, Claire locked and bolted the door. She needed her head examined for making out with Luke. But more importantly, she needed to finish the dishes.

With a heavy sigh she returned to the kitchen and finished cleaning up while very cleverly avoiding looking at the kitchen bench. Because if she looked, she knew what she'd see. Luke between her thighs, playful and teasing and gorgeous, her blouse falling from his fingertips, his eyes burnished to copper, darkened with lust, her gut-curdling panic when she'd realised she was about to have sex with the man of her dreams....

Going through her night-time routine, that panic resurfaced. Why did he have to tell her she was beautiful? Why did he have to give her that faint glimmer of hope that she could mean more to him than a means to an end? She'd told him "no sex" and he'd crushed her defences with just three little words. *"You're so beautiful."*

I'm so pathetic.

If she was going to get through this then she had to hold on to the facts, to what she knew to be true.

1. Luke was using her.
2. Luke only dated models. Thin, blonde models.
3. Claire was neither thin, blonde nor a model.

Slipping into bed, she stared at the ceiling and wondered how Luke would've reacted to the knowledge she would have helped him knock Amanda off her perch—if he'd bothered to ask her first—simply because he'd been kind to her once.

Like he needs any more ammunition against me.

The second he was in his car, Luke burst out laughing.

"I was just wiping my nose on the sleeve."

Claire Morse was a pill. A bittersweet pill he'd happily swallow any day of the week. He couldn't remember the last time a woman had delighted him and frustrated him so much at the same time.

Had there ever been such a woman in his life?

Making it home in record time, he quickly found himself on his couch, his face pressed inside his navy-blue jacket and his hand fisted around his cock.

He could smell her.

Claire's perfume lingered in the lining of his jacket and her scent was intoxicating. Floral and spice and heat and so overtly feminine. So... *Claire.* She mingled with the faded scents of his own cologne, a perfect blend.

His cock ached with need.

He wondered again how she would have felt laid out beneath him, naked and glorious, her skin glowing and slicked with sweat. He wondered how she'd taste. Sweet. He knew she'd taste sweet. Like honey.

Fuck. What was it about this woman? How the hell had she wormed her way under his skin in the first place, and how the fuck did he get her out? Minutes. He'd literally spent only minutes in her company before this week, and yet he'd spent ten years wanting her.

Maybe it was just a case of wanting what he couldn't have, the salacious allure of the forbidden.

But that didn't explain the all-consuming need he felt to be near her, to talk to her, to listen to and kiss her.

And when he'd seen her standing in her bedroom, he'd never wanted to fuck a woman so much in all his life. The warmth of the pale-yellow light overhead had cast an ethereal glow over the whole room, and Claire had stood there defiant and proud, her lips still swollen from his kisses, her eyes heavy-lidded and stormy, her bed only two feet away....

And then she'd made him want to laugh out loud. He'd had to leave or he would have kissed her again and their lusty tug-o-war would have started anew.

"This is all your fault," he said, glaring at his cock.

Slumping back against the cushions, he closed his eyes and inhaled again, drank in the raw sensuality that was Claire Morse. She'd been so open to him, so willing. He remembered her hands on him, searching, exploring, feeling him up with such wondrous curiosity. Her fingers had traced the hard ridges of his stomach, her fingernails had raked over the cotton of his shirt, torturing him with a pleasure/pain that had heightened his awareness of her. Made him crave her even more.

His hands had shaken as he'd tried to rid her of that monstrosity of a bra, not that she'd noticed. She'd been too busy licking his throat and nibbling his earlobe. Gently tugging open his shirt collar and biting the cord of muscle connecting his neck to his shoulder. She'd attacked his most erogenous of zones like a pro. Then freaked out like a virgin when his fingers had travelled below her belt.

His frustration had brought out his anger and he'd been cruel to her. Luke was never cruel. An arsehole yes, but never cruel. Her expression had twisted with pain—silent yet deafening—and he'd wished he could take it back.

Then he'd given her the locket. The locket he'd chosen because it looked like something she would wear. Pretty, understated and otherworldly. Just like her shop. And she'd looked at him like a monster for daring to defile it with something as sordid as a listening device. Thank God Lottie had convinced him to get the replica made. Luke wasn't sure he'd ever hear the end of it otherwise.

Shaking his head, he knew he couldn't keep fantasising about a woman he was blackmailing. It was absurd. It was obscene.

It was all he could do not to jump in his car and drive back over there. Christ, he'd only wanted his jacket back because he knew her perfume would be on it. Breathing deep, he sucked her scent into his lungs and imagined his hands on her breasts, imagined their softness, their weight, pictured her nipples forming hard little peaks just perfect for biting and sucking and—

"Oh, *faaark*." Luke's body jolted and spasmed as he came in his hand.

He had to get this under control. Fast.

Chapter Fourteen

Claire sat in Aria and waited for Amanda.

Her aunt was late, as usual, so she took the time to fiddle with the locket around her neck, double checking it was on and recording, then sipped her drink and ignored the urge to chew her fingernails off.

When Amanda did finally arrive, almost twenty minutes late, it was with a grand entrance and an outpouring of affection for her niece so obviously fake it was sickening.

But that was Amanda Morse for you. Entrepreneur. Aunty. Colossal fucking fake-arse bitch.

Claire stood and embraced her aunt as warmly as she was able. Not an easy task when her insides were in knots. "Hello, Aunty."

Amanda's eyes—so very like her own—raked over Claire. "You're looking... well," she said, sitting down and snapping her fingers at the waitress. "Certainly very well fed."

Which was Amanda-speak for, "You're fat."

A petite, smiling redhead brought them menus. "I'll have my usual," Amanda said, her lips pinched together in their usual moue of displeasure. "Claire?"

Quickly reading the options, Claire settled on the trevally and clams with parsnip. Mostly because she was too nervous to eat anything more substantial than fish. The juicy steak she'd envisioned devouring just to piss Amanda off had turned to ash in her mouth the moment her aunt had appeared.

"Look at me, girl," Amanda said, then smiled with satisfaction as Claire obeyed, obviously glad her niece still knew her place in the world.

Under Amanda's heel.

"So, how's business?" Amanda asked.

Claire was sure the question formed from habit more than actual interest. It wasn't as if she'd asked, "So, how's life?" Her aunt had never taken much of an interest in Claire's life before. No reason to start now.

"Fine," she said. But her ego pushed for more. "Better than fine actually. It's really taken off in this last quarter." Claire was quite proud of everything she'd achieved in a relatively short period of time. Her store had only been open for six months, but she was already turning a steady profit.

"Really?" Amanda sniffed, disbelief and derision flavouring her tone. She reached for her chequebook. "How much do you need?"

Claire frowned. "I beg your pardon?"

"Money, Claire, how much money do you need?"

"I don't need any money," she said sharply. "I told you, I'm doing great."

Mouth pinched and eyebrows raised in her standard

I'm-better-than-you-and-I-know-everything   expression, Amanda said, "Then why were you meeting with Luke Hardcastle this week. And don't try spinning some stupid story about him being your landlord again. Utterly ridiculous."

"Luke *is* my new landlord," Claire said. "Although why he's suddenly decided to buy into a commercial venture, I'm sure I don't know. And I was meeting with him to negotiate new leases on behalf of the other tenants."

Amanda looked shocked by Claire's assertiveness. She looked even more shocked when Claire rose from her chair and picked up her handbag, ready to leave.

"I don't know what I was thinking," she muttered to herself before turning on her aunt. "All I wanted to do was say hello, maybe mend some bridges, but you're never going to forgive me, are you?" Then she turned and walked away, hoping her aunt would take the bait.

"Claire Evelyn Morse, stop," Amanda said, her voice carrying every ounce of command it always had. Claire stopped and waited. "Stay for lunch."

Claire turned slowly, Amanda gestured to the empty chair. Taking a moment to pretend to think about it, she cast one final glance towards the exit, then walked as timidly as possible back to the table and sat down.

"Well, it would seem you've found a backbone in the past eighteen months, but just remember who you're talking to, girl. I won't stand for any more of your nonsense."

Claire lowered her eyes, submissive. "Yes, Aunty," she said, the act grating against every last one of her nerves.

"I know Hardcastle is your new landlord," Amanda said. "I simply assumed your business was failing and I needed to be certain you weren't trying to boost your capital selling my trade secrets. But you're right, why would he want that particular piece of real estate? What makes it special?"

"I don't know," Claire lied.

"But I'd bet you could find out," Amanda said. "I find it extremely difficult to believe that a man as importantly wealthy as Hardcastle would stoop so low as to discuss lease terms with the likes of you. He has people to do that for him." A slow, calculating smile spread across her not-unattractive face. "I think he's trying to seduce you."

Claire laughed out loud even as the memory of the previous night flooded through her brain, then she squeezed her thighs together to quash her body's traitorous reactions. "Seduce me? What on earth for? It's well known Luke only dates blondes, preferably models." Trying to ignore the hurt welling in her chest as she remembered him flirting with her assistant manager, she added, "Somehow I don't think I qualify."

"Good point. You are well below his normally high standards. I mean look at you, Claire, honestly. What is with that skirt? And can't you do something better with your hair?"

"Like what?" Claire said, lifting her hand to check everything was still in place.

"Like run a brush through it for starters. And the scarf?" She *tsked*. "You look like you've been disowned by gypsies. Oh, that reminds me...."

Claire clenched her jaw to the point of pain as she forced herself to endure Amanda's never-ending stream of criticism without telling her to go fuck herself, while at the same time fighting off the resurgence of her old—and not so old—insecurities. The feeling that she didn't measure up.

That she'd never be good enough.

Worse still was the knowledge she'd have to relive this vitriol when Luke debriefed her over dinner. She'd have to hear Amanda tell her all over again what a complete and utter disappointment she was.

"Still." Amanda pushed her plate away, her meal half eaten. "He's only recently broken up with... oh, what was her name? Honestly the man changes women like he changes his underwear. I don't know how he keeps track of them all."

"The tabloids probably help," Claire muttered.

Amanda shot her a don't-interrupt-me look. "Anyway, he's probably open to a casual rebound romp. Why not let it be with you?"

Claire stared at her aunt in wide-eyed horror. Her libido screamed in her ear, *"Do it!"*

"Are you out of your mind? Why on earth would I do such a thing?"

The you're-an-idiot look flew her way. "To learn his secrets, of course."

"What secrets? And besides, he would never date me."

"Oh, Claire." Patronising-pouty-face. "You never were very good at this sort of thing, were you? You don't have to date the man to have sex with him. You'd be surprised what a man will tell a woman in bed, much more than he would ever tell her over dinner. And you'd also be proving yourself to me, mending some of those bridges you were talking about."

Claire quickly looked around the restaurant to ensure no one was listening before she said with the appropriate amount of incredulity. "You want me to sleep with him so I can spy on him?"

"Yes."

"But why? You're not even in the same industry. Luke builds luxury apartment buildings and the occasional mansion, you buy out failing companies and sell them off as scrap. What on earth do you want me to spy on him for?"

"That, girl, is none of your concern. And Hardcastle are I are in the same business. The business of making money. Now, I will give you twenty-four hours to decide. Do you want this little family reunion to become permanent, or would you prefer your recent success to be all for nothing and watch your pathetic little bookstore go under in less than a month?"

Claire straightened as her stomach fell to her feet. She swallowed hard. "What are you talking about?"

"It's quite simple really. You will spy on Luke Hardcastle and pass along information to me that I might find useful, and in exchange for proving your loyalty I will release your accounts. Your money will be yours to do with as you wish. But if you don't comply it's bye-bye bookstore."

Claire wanted to throw up. This couldn't be happening. There had to be an out. Like... "What happens if he doesn't want to sleep with me?"

"I suggest you get creative and ensure that doesn't happen." Amanda stood up and tossed her napkin on her plate. "Twenty-four hours, Claire. I'll expect your answer by lunch tomorrow."

Then she sauntered away with a self-satisfied smile on her face.

Claire slowly rose on shaky legs and immediately sat down again, the weight of her aunt's ultimatum pushing her back in her seat.

The redhead hurried over. "Are you all right, miss?"

"Yes, fine. Thank you. Just a cramp in my leg. I don't suppose my aunt paid the bill?"

The waitress shook her head and placed the bill on the table, then whispered conspiratorially, "She never does."

Handing over her credit card, Claire grimaced. "No. Amanda never pays."

Chapter Fifteen

Seeing as the restaurant was right across the road from Hardcastle Tower—and consequently Morse Industries—and because she was avoiding Karen and discussing the whole flirting incident, Claire decided to take the rest of the day off and go shopping. And by shopping she meant drooling over the latest designer linens in Laura Ashley that she couldn't currently afford on her shoe-string budget, and rolling her eyes at the "genuine" antiques a brash young man tried to sell her as she walked past his shop.

Toying with the locket around her neck, Claire contemplated erasing the conversation it held inside its guts. It was humiliating.

But interesting.

To pass the time, she tried to imagine what Luke had done to Amanda to deserve her wrath. After all, she wouldn't want Claire to spy on him for nothing. There had to be an angle, she just didn't see it yet.

Amanda had been absent the day Luke had stormed the offices of Morse Industries, so she'd missed his now infamous tirade. She wasn't the type to care if someone else's feelings had been hurt, so this wasn't about Claire being verbally eviscerated in her stead.

By the time she'd walked back to Hardcastle Tower she was no closer to figuring it out.

Heading across the lobby, head down and thoughts distracted, Claire didn't notice the person exiting the lift and walked smack into them.

"Oh, I'm sor— Oh, it's you," Claire said, her apology replaced with contempt as she saw who she'd bumped in to.

Luke raised one dark eyebrow and smirked at her derisive tone. "I was just about to send out a search party for you," he admonished. "I sent Edward to pick you up from Novelteas and bring you here but he was told you'd taken the afternoon off."

Claire shrugged. "And...?"

"And why didn't you answer your phone?" he said, suddenly frowning at her.

Reaching into her handbag, Claire pulled out her phone and realised she'd forgotten to turn the volume back up after lunch. She had nine missed calls. Six from Luke and three from Karen. Cocking a brow at Luke, she called Karen back.

"Everything all right?" she said.

"Where the bloody hell have you been?" Karen snapped at her. "Some *super*-hot guy named Edward rocked up looking for you, saying he was supposed to drive you into town. I tried calling to find out where you were so he could pick you up and when we couldn't get a hold of you, he rang Luke. Then Luke rang me and I told him—" Karen talked and talked without stopping for breath, hysterical as she retold the tale of "Where The Fuck Is Claire". Claire held the phone away from her ear and continued staring at Luke like it was all his fault—because it was—and he inspected his fingernails and pretended he couldn't hear Karen ranting like a crazy person.

At the end of the call, Claire shook her head and sighed. "My life was so simple before you."

"Let's go home."

Fisting her hand protectively around the locket, she said, "But I thought you wanted to—"

Luke took her elbow and directed her back across the lobby and led her outside. "Not here, Miss Morse."

"Where are we going?"

"I told you. Home," he said, and grabbed her hand to cross the street towards the river.

"Won't we need your car if you're taking me home?" Confusion danced with elation as she registered the heat of his palm, the strength of his fingers wrapped around hers.

"My home," Luke said. "We're taking the ferry."

"Oh. And where are you living these days?"

"South Bank. Just a quick walk through the parklands, up the street and we're home."

As his words registered, Claire glanced at Luke, then smirked and looked away.

"Um... when I said *we're* home, I didn't mean to imply, you know, *our* home," Luke said. It was the first time she'd seen him behave truly awkwardly. It was extremely gratifying to watch.

"Of course not," she said, still smirking. "No one would ever believe you and I.... I mean, I'm not exactly your type, am I?"

Luke cleared his throat and looked away. Claire sighed quietly and tugged her hand out of his. He let her.

When they reached the ferry terminal Luke took a seat on firm ground and pulled out his phone. Claire walked down the gangplank and waited on the pontoon instead. For early spring it was still quite cool, especially in the city where the buildings cast endless shadows over everything. On the water was even cooler. Goosebumps bloomed all over her as a light breeze blew past and ruffled her skirt. She grabbed the sides to stop it from flying up. After the day she'd had the last thing she needed was to flash her undies at everyone in an impromptu Marilyn Monroe impersonation.

She'd only worn a skirt because she knew Amanda didn't approve of jeans. Not that she'd approved of the skirt either. Apparently, stripes were unbecoming on someone of Claire's physique, and according to her aunt, matching navy, red and pink in the one outfit was a cardinal sin. The breeze settled enough that Claire could let go of her skirt and pull on her denim jacket.

"Hello."

Keeping her expression neutral, Claire glanced towards the male stranger and nodded politely.

"My name's Chris. What's yours?"

Claire took a deep breath then slowly let it out. "Not interested," she said.

"Come on now," he cajoled. "Don't be like that. You're too pretty to be standing here all alone."

A hand slid across her back then over her arse. Claire stiffened. The hand squeezed then jiggled her backside. Claire snapped. Twisting towards the stranger, she knocked his hand away and yelled, "Don't touch me!"

Several people milling around them on the pontoon straightened to attention, curious, but not enough to do anything about it. She looked back to land but couldn't see Luke.

"Hey, baby, it's all good," Grabby Hands said, holding his hands up in mock surrender. "See? No harm done. No need to cause a fuss."

Claire felt like her head was ready to explode. This really was just the perfect end to her shitty week. "I'm sorry, but did you just say 'no harm done'? Who the fuck do you think you are that you can just walk up to me, sexually assault me, say 'no harm done' and think we're all good?"

Looking red faced and sweaty, Grabby Hands blustered, "Now hang on, lady! I did not assault you."

"You grabbed my arse. *After* I told you I wasn't interested." Several people had pulled out their mobile phones. She'd probably be a You Tube sensation by morning. "You're lucky I don't pitch you into the river, you fucking pervert."

"Do it," someone shouted.

"Throw him in," another person yelled. "Feed him to the sharks."

Grabby Hands glared at her then hightailed it back up the gangplank to the sound of cheering and applause.

Claire was shaking, anger and adrenaline flooding her veins and heating her cheeks. She needed release. She wanted to hit something. Or someone. Or scream.

"You all right, love?" A young man in jeans and a T-shirt approached her cautiously and said, "I got the whole thing on camera if you wanna go to the cops."

"Who's going to the cops?" Luke. "Claire? What's going on?"

"Is she your girlfriend, mate?"

Ignoring the other guy, Luke gripped Claire's shoulders in strong yet gentle hands. Concern pulled at his features. "What happened?"

The other guy answered. "Some cunt felt her up."

"What?" Claire had seen Luke angry before but the expression on his face in that moment was truly frightening. "Who was it?"

Meeting his gaze head on, she said, "He said his name was Chris."

Luke's eyes narrowed dangerously. "Where is he?"

"Dunno," the other guy said with a laugh. "He took off when ya girlfriend threatened to throw 'im in the drink. Good on ya, by the way. That was awesome."

She tried to smile but couldn't.

"You said you got footage?" Luke said. "Can you email it to me?"

"Sure."

The pontoon bounced from side to side, buffeted by the small waves the ferry made as it cut through the water and slowed to a halt. Claire felt mildly claustrophobic as she watched the crowd of people slowly board the vessel, flinched when she felt someone touch her.

"It's just me, sweetness." Luke's breath was warm against her ear. His voice soothing.

Claire was too upset, too angry and too tired to resist temptation any longer. This time when Luke took her hand, she didn't care what anyone thought.

She wasn't letting go.

Chapter Sixteen

Luke sat beside Claire on the open deck of the ferry and tucked her into his side.

She was quiet, even for her.

The cool air whipped around them as they traversed the river and he rubbed his hand up and down her arm in a vain attempt to keep her warm. He smiled against her hair when she turned her body towards his and slid her hand inside his jacket.

Fucking Chris Marx.

Next time he saw that sonofabitch he was going to knock his fucking block off.

"Excuse me." Luke looked up to see an attractive blonde with too much eye makeup gazing down at him. Claire's arm tightened around his waist.

"Yes?"

"I'm sorry. I never do this, but do I know you? You look very familiar."

Sure I do. Luke knew a line when he heard one, and he'd heard that old chestnut more times than he could count. "Sorry, no. You're probably confusing me with someone else."

"Are you sure?" she said, planting herself in the seat on the other side of him, angling her leg so it was touching his. "You really do look so familiar."

In the past he would've played long. He would've taken her out for a drink, told her she was beautiful, gone back to her place, had unsatisfying sex and snuck out before dawn.

But now...? "Sorry. I just have one of those faces."

She didn't take the hint. "But, really—"

"For fuck's sake," Claire muttered quietly, getting to her feet.

"Claire," Luke said her name like a warning, although what he was warning her against doing, he wasn't quite sure. He certainly hadn't expected her to push his knees together then seat herself in his lap with her back towards the blonde, effectively shutting the clueless twit down. Luke chuckled. "What are you doing?"

"Helping you resist the urge to man-spread," she said, then wrapped her arms around him and rested her head on his shoulder.

"Rude," the blonde muttered, but she finally walked away.

Claire snorted. "Yeah, I'm the rude one," she said. "Does that happen to you often?"

"More than I'd like," he admitted. "Does what happened to you happen often?"

"More than I'd like," she said quietly.

Luke tightened his arms around her. He wasn't just going to knock Chris's block off. He was going to rip him a new arsehole while he was at it.

The ferry docked at the Southbank terminal. Luke led

Claire along the Promenade then across the lawn to Stanley Street Plaza.

The markets were in full swing selling everything from handcrafted soaps and tie-dyed T-shirts to antique teddy bears and fine millinery. The buskers were out in full force, singers and musicians at every turn. And then there were the food vendors scenting the air with everything from baked potatoes and German sausages to French pastries and homemade gelato, not to mention the noodles.

Luke's stomach growled. He stopped to buy them dinner and dessert.

Leaving the markets, they continued along the path under the giant steel Arbour and its canopy of hot pink bougainvillea. Luke looked down at Claire, at their hands joined between them as they walked amongst the joggers and cyclists, the families pushing prams and walking dogs, people living their lives in a world full of uncertainty where the person standing next to you could be gone in the blink of an eye, and he wondered what it would be like to be alone. Truly alone. His family had never been a big one, but they'd been close. Hell, even his dad and stepdad had gotten along well. But they were both gone now. So was his mum.

Lottie was all he had left.

"Look at that sunset."

Lost in thought as he was, it took him a second to realise Claire had stopped walking. She stood behind him staring back at the city, the sky a wash of orange streaked with pink and bleeding into purple and all of it reflected on the surface of the river, setting it aflame with a riot of colour.

As she watched the clouds undulate across the sky, her face was serene, a small smile lifting one corner of her mouth. After all the shit she'd been through she could still smile. *Wow.*

She squeezed his hand.

"Ouch," he said, pulling back.

"Oh, shit. Sorry, I forgot about your hand," she said, taking his hand in hers and inspecting his cut. "It looks like it's healing okay."

It still stung like a sonofabitch but the feel of her warm fingers gently prodding his palm, made it hurt a little less. "I'll live," he said with a shrug. Or maybe he just didn't notice the ache so much when she was near him and his brain had more pleasant things to think about.

Luke's jaw clenched. He wasn't supposed to have romantic thoughts about Claire Morse. He wasn't supposed to hold her hand or crave the scent of her perfume on his clothes or feel just the smallest bit excited by her public displays of possession. He was supposed to hate her, to make her suffer for helping her aunt hurt his sister. But all he'd been able to think about since he saw her enter the Novelteas tearoom was holding her in his arms, kissing her full lips and savouring each and every luscious curve of her body as he made love to her. In his office. In her office. On her kitchen bench. In that sea-foam green cast-iron monstrosity she called a bed.

Anywhere.

He wanted her anywhere and everywhere and it was driving him crazy.

They continued along the path in silence until they reached the edge of the parklands then turned to walk up the street to his apartment building.

"I'm sorry that dickhead frightened you before. I'm more sorry I wasn't there to stop him." He rubbed the back of his neck. "I was on the phone to Lottie."

"Luke, I take the bus to and from work every day. He wasn't the first bloke to ever cop a feel and he won't be the last. But it's been a long week," Claire said, shooting him an accusing glare. "I wasn't frightened so much as pissed off."

"Right," said Luke. "Well, I'm sorry anyway. I never thought he'd hurt you."

"Wait, what?" Claire stopped walking. "You know that idiot?" Anger, sudden and dangerous flashed in her eyes. She yanked her hand free. "What did you do, Luke, send your friend over to give me a scare so you'd look like a gentleman by comparison?"

"Of course not," he shot back. "And he's not my friend, he's a journalist. He approached me at the terminal, tried to strike up a conversation but I blew him off. Chris has always been a tool where women are concerned. I'm not surprised he zeroed in on you, standing alone. I was just worried you might have slapped him into next week and get yourself charged with assault."

Claire smiled tightly. "Thanks for the concern, but I only slap men who are blackmailing me."

Clenching his jaw against a snarky retort, he muttered, "Food's getting cold." Then picked up his pace, making Claire almost have to run to keep up with his very long strides.

They rode the lift in silence to his penthouse apartment, and when he opened the door and ushered Claire inside, he felt surprisingly satisfied by her gasp of awe. He surreptitiously watched her move through the space as he put the gelato in the freezer, grabbed two beers from the fridge and served out the noodles. She bypassed the view of the city, river and parklands and focussed more on the structural details of the room, her expression considering and curious as she ran her hands over the timber, steel and granite that decorated his home.

"What do you think?" he said as she approached the kitchen.

"I think anyone lucky enough to have a gourmet kitchen in their home should learn how to cook."

Handing her a bowl of noodles, he said, "I quite enjoy cooking actually. I just haven't had time lately, what with my busy blackmailing schedule and all."

Her lips twitched with the beginning of a smile, but she shut it down before it could blossom.

Following her to the dining table, he ditched his jacket then asked again, "What do you think of the apartment?" Luke had never cared what previous girlfriends thought of his design acumen, but for some bizarre reason he cared what Claire thought.

Taking his seat and handing her a beer, he blinked as he realised he'd just thought of Claire as his girlfriend.

I'm so screwed.

"I like it," she said. "I'm not sure I could live in it, but I do like it."

Luke frowned. "What do you mean you 'couldn't live in it'?"

"It's too... male," she said, gesturing with her chopsticks. "All the bare metal and shiny black granite. It's very aggressive. In fact, if it wasn't for the timber accents here and there, I'd probably wanna slap it."

Luke choked on his food. He grabbed his beer and swilled the cool liquid down, dislodging the prawn stuck in his throat.

She flashed an unrepentant grin. "Sorry."

"No problem," he rasped.

Still grinning, she asked, "Did you build it, the apartment building?"

Luke nodded. "My company did," he said, finding his

voice again. "I noticed your place needs a lot of work. I'd be happy to help out, if you want."

Claire looked surprised by the offer. "Thanks, but I doubt I could afford your rates."

Luke grinned. "I'm sure we could work out some sort of mutually beneficial payment system."

"I'm not sleeping with you." Frowning, she pushed away her bowl. She'd hardly touched her food.

He mirrored her expression. "You going to eat that?"

She shook her head. "I'm not very hungry."

Luke grabbed the bowl and tucked in, shovelling the noodles into his face as fast as he could chew them. He caught Claire's wide-eyed look of repulsed fascination and slowed down a bit. "Sorry about my manners but I skipped lunch. I'm famished."

"I didn't say anything."

"You didn't have to." He watched her as he ate, watched her fiddle with the locket around her neck as she went back to staring at his decor. "How was lunch?"

"Expensive."

"I offered to pay," he reminded her.

"And I still don't need your charity," she said, then took the locket off and slid it across the table.

Luke pushed the empty bowls away and picked up the locket, turned it over and over in his hand. Weighed his options. He'd learned something today. Something disturbing. Something he wished he'd bothered to learn before he'd set all of this in motion, before he'd crossed a line he wasn't sure he could come back from.

"Do you want me to take you home?"

She shook her head again. "I don't want to be alone."

The slight quaver in her voice made Luke's gut clench. "You ready to listen to this?"

"No, but let's do it anyway."

Leaving Claire to grab dessert, Luke went to his office and grabbed his laptop, then sitting it on his coffee table he geared it up to playback the audio recording. Claire sat beside him on the couch and smoothed out her shirt, straightened her blouse. Her posture was rigid, her face blank and lacking the serenity he'd seen earlier when she'd gazed up at that pink and purple sky.

"You don't have to listen to this if you don't want to," he said, accepting the small bowl of pistachio gelato and the spoon she handed him.

"Yes I do."

"Okay," he said, then with a heavy sigh he hit play, and everything he'd read in that damned investigator's file rang true.

I'm a fucking arsehole.

Chapter Seventeen

Claire listened to the recording and cringed. Someone else being exposed to Amanda in her truest form was almost more than she could bear to witness. Luke's facial expressions ran the whole gamut of emotion from shocked to amused to outraged and everything in between, while she inwardly sighed at the familiarity of it all and the resignation that came from knowing she'd be facing a lot more of it very soon.

By the time the recording ended, Luke was shaking with rage. "Bitch," he muttered under his breath, then refusing to look at her, he added, "On the ferry when you climbed into my lap, was that your way of getting creative?"

Claire snorted. She should've known he'd think that. "No," she said, her anger resurfacing. "That was my way of announcing that I'm tired of being ignored and treated like shit by people who think they're better than me. I'm tired of being bullied and abused and told I'm worthless. I climbed into your lap, Luke, because I wanted to be there. *Me. I* wanted it. And I held your hand because it made me feel safe and I'm tired and I'm pissed off and if that makes me a bitch—"

Luke turned towards her, grabbed her upper arms. He looked... upset. Remorseful even. "Did she hurt you?"

"What?"

"Did Amanda hurt you?"

Ice skittered over her skin and the blood drained from her face. She shivered. *He knows.* Shame replaced her anger as she stammered, "Luke... I...."

In the time it took to blink, Luke pulled her against his chest and tucked her head under his chin. His hands rubbed soothing circles on her back. "I'm sorry. I am so, so sorry, Claire. I never read the whole report. I took from it what I needed, home address, work address, financials, then I shoved it in a drawer and locked it away. I was too blinded by my anger and my arrogance to see the truth. No. Worse than that. I didn't want to know the truth. I didn't want— But she hurt you." He held her away from his body and stared into her eyes, his golden gaze sorrowful as he wiped his thumb across her cheek collecting the silent tears leaking down her face. "Why didn't you tell me that *bitch* hurt you?"

Claire lifted one shoulder in a shrug. Her voice was quiet. "Would it have mattered?"

Luke's jaw dropped. "Would it have...? Jesus Christ," he said, shoving his hands through his hair. "You honestly think— I shoved you back into the hands of your abuser, a woman who starved and beat you. Yes, Claire. It matters." Reaching out, he slammed his laptop shut, then yanked the storage device from the USB port and threw it across the room. "I'm calling it off. All of it. I've already spoken to Lottie and she agrees. It's over."

Shocked didn't even begin to describe what Claire was

feeling. Confused, wary, angry, elated, they all scrambled over the top of one another, jostling for position and determined to win. But in the end one feeling rose higher than the others, pushed them down where they belonged and stood triumphant.

Determination.

Amanda never pays.

After everything she'd been through in the past five days, enduring the criticism and the bitterness and the stomach-churning anxiety... and now it was over? Just like that. Over.

I don't think so.

Firming her jaw and lifting her chin, she said, "No."

Luke frowned. "What?"

"I said no. It's not over."

"Claire." His voice held the note of warning he'd used on the ferry.

"Luke, you've started something you can't control. This isn't over just because you say it is."

"I don't want you anywhere near that woman."

Claire was torn between wanting to kiss the man for his gallantry and slap him again for his crappy timing. *Where was his concern ten years ago?*

She took a breath. "I appreciate your change of heart and that you want to protect me, but you don't get to make that decision. You were right. I do know how she thinks, how she works, which is why I know there's no backing away from this. And quite frankly, I don't want to.

"I was raised to believe the worst of people, to always look for the angle and take advantage of weakness. But eighteen months ago, when I was at my weakest and Angie Campioni caught me dumpster-diving behind her restaurant, she didn't take advantage of me. She took me inside and fed me, listened to my side of the story then took me home with her. Angie reads the news, she knew who I was the moment she saw me, but she didn't hesitate to help me. She taught me to see the best in people, to lift them up when we can and share our good fortunes.

"After twenty years of hell I never wanted to see Amanda again, and sitting through lunch with her today was excruciating in so many ways—"

Luke shifted in his seat. "And again, I'm sorry for that—"

Claire shook her head. "Don't be. Because after lunch when I went for my walk, it occurred to me I've been handed a rare opportunity." Anticipation licked along her veins and lit her up until she positively burned with excitement. "I have the chance to make things right. Not just for Lottie—for *me*. Luke, how can I ever live my life the way I want to if I don't deal with my past? I want to do this. I *need* to do this. So no, this isn't over. Not yet."

Rubbing the back of his neck again, Luke gave her a hesitant look. "Are you sure about this?"

"No," she said, lifting one shoulder in a half-hearted shrug. "But let's do it anyway."

Luke narrowed his watchful, golden eyes and stared at her as though he was trying to read her mind, then nodded. "Okay."

Claire released the breath she didn't realise she'd been holding. "Okay," she echoed, then said, "Oh, and just so we're clear, while we're playing in Amanda's sandbox, you're not protecting me. I'm protecting you."

Chapter Eighteen

"How do you suggest we go about this?"

Claire tapped her finger against her lips, excruciatingly aware of Luke sitting next to her, his hard thigh pressed against her softer one, his fingers tracing circles just above her knee. He was making it very difficult to concentrate on his question.

"That's the part I'm not sure about," she admitted.

"You know, Amanda's idea wasn't half bad," he said. His fingers circled a little higher.

Claire swallowed hard. "Which idea?" she said, suddenly breathless. "The one where she's blackmailing me, or the one where she tells me to sleep with you?"

Luke looked up from under dark lashes and grinned. His fingers edged under her skirt.

"I'm not sleeping with you," she said with a huff.

His grin broadened. His fingers pressed harder against her fleshy inner thigh. "So last night in your kitchen was... what, exactly?"

"I blame the exotic food," she said, concentrating on her breathing. "All that heat... and spice...."

In... out....

"Uh-huh. And sitting in my lap on the ferry? You said you *wanted* to be there."

Crap. Thinking quickly, she said, "And I did. I *wanted* to help a friend get rid of a pest and sitting in your lap was the most effective way of doing that."

Luke's fingers stopped moving. "Friends? Is that what we are, Miss Morse?"

Claire's hands clenched and released as she fought the urge to jump off the couch and run away. Amanda was right. Claire had never been very good at this sort of thing. How could she be when she'd never even had a real boyfriend?

"I'd like to think so. Since you're not blackmailing me anymore."

"Hmm... friends with benefits?" His fingers started moving again, inching closer and closer to her panties.

This time she did jump off the couch. "Ah... maybe we should get back to the matter at hand?"

Luke cocked one dark brow at her. "I thought that's what my hand was doing."

She scowled at him. "How many times do I have to say it?" But it wasn't really Luke she was cross with, it was her. She was confused by all her conflicting emotions, anxious and unsure. She had zero experience dealing with a man like Luke and hated not knowing what to do.

Books could only teach her so much.

Flopping back on the couch, Luke grumbled, "Yeah, yeah, you're not sleeping with me." Then he pinned her with a narrowed gaze. "My question is why? Dating me is the perfect cover for our purpose, I want you, you want me—"

"I never said that."

"You didn't have to. Your tongue down my throat every time we kiss has done all the talking for you."

"I—" Lips pursed, Claire made a growl of frustration.

She couldn't deny it.

She wanted Luke like she'd never wanted any man before in her life, and if she was being completely honest with herself there really was nothing holding her back now. He wasn't blackmailing her anymore. He'd actually apologised for putting her in her current position and even seemed to understand she'd had no choice in the part she'd played in the collapse of Cassidy Holdings. She'd done what she'd done to survive her aunt's wrath. A wrath that had fallen swift and sure when Amanda had discovered Claire's little side project.

Luke rose to his feet then took her gently by the shoulders and made her look at him. "What's wrong, Claire? It's not like we're making a lifelong commitment to one another. It's just sex."

And that right there was why she couldn't—*wouldn't* —do it.

Because it wasn't just sex. Not to her.

"No. It's not," she said, pulling away from him, giving herself some much needed distance from the walking, talking temptation standing before her. "Luke, I don't want to be just another notch on your bedpost, some silly girl the tabloids will trash the minute you get bored with me. How long has it been since you broke up with that other woman? Four, five weeks?" She shook her head. "No. I don't want this. I don't want you to want me just because you're horny and I'm convenient."

His brows shot into his hairline and a smile tugged at his sensual lips. "Convenient? Sweetness, you are a lot of things but convenient isn't one of them."

Suddenly irritated by the use of his endearment, she snapped, "Why do you call me that?"

"What? Sweetness?"

"Yes. I've been anything but sweet to you."

Luke chuckled. "What have you done that I didn't deserve?" He walked to the kitchen and grabbed two more beers from the fridge, handed her one as he returned.

"I...." Claire bit her lip and fiddled with the label on the beer bottle. "I think I've been leading you on. A bit." Too nervous to drink anymore, she put the beer down and drifted towards the window. The sunset had long since dissolved to black and the city lights burned bright against the velvety sky. Only the brightest stars made it past the glare of unnatural light that haloed the city, but she searched for them anyway.

Luke joined her by the window, his hands in his pockets. "You *think* you have?"

His presence was both a comfort and a challenge, daring her to lean into his side and absorb his warmth, his strength, yet winding her anxiety tighter and tighter until she finally snapped.

"I never meant to kiss you back," she blurted. "But once I did, I couldn't stop because you are *really* good at it, and when you took my hand today it didn't feel awkward, and I realised I needed it. I needed your touch to anchor me and settle my nerves and then that fuckwit grabbed my arse and all I wanted was you and then you were there and you were holding me and how *insane* is that because you don't even *like* me and—"

Luke slammed his mouth against hers and swallowed her inane babbling like a man starved for air. His tongue fought hers in a battle of wills and it took her a whole 0.3

seconds to throw the fight and surrender to his superior skills.

A moment later she found herself wedged between his body and the window, the front of her skirt bunched up around her waist. Hot male hardness in front of her, cool smooth glass behind her, he lifted her legs around his hips and ground his thick erection between her thighs, rubbed her clit through the insubstantial layers separating them and hit his mark with devastating ease.

Claire moaned against his mouth as heat spiralled through her, settling low in her belly. Need had her fisting her hands in his dark hair, holding him steady as she nibbled a path along his strong jaw to his ear then sucked his earlobe between her teeth.

"That's it, sweetness," he purred, his deep voice rumbling under her lips as she kissed her way down his neck and dipped her tongue into the hollow at the base of his throat. "And for the record," he said, his breathing laboured. "I do like you. More than I ever thought I could. Definitely more than I should."

Claire yelped in surprise as Luke bit the muscle connecting her neck to her shoulder, just as she'd done to him in her kitchen. Yelping quickly turned to moaning as he continued nibbling and biting and licking and murmuring. Her brain was lost in a fog of lust and she couldn't quite make out what he was saying.

Something about making her feel good. Then something else about hearing her scream.

But then his hand slipped between her thighs and reality exploded all around her. The world slowed down. Her senses sharpened and the fog addling her brain was blown clean away.

He's going to find out.

And she wasn't sure how she felt about that. In her kitchen she'd been terrified. But that all seemed so far away, a distant memory. This right here was happening now and in real time and Claire knew she could stop it if she wanted to. One word from her and Luke would put her down and be none the wiser. He might snap at her again and say something rude. He might even kick her out of his home.

But he would stop.

If she wanted him to....

Or she could let the chips fall where they may.

Her libido voted for the second option.

Closing her eyes against what was to come, she bit her lip and awaited the inevitable. Luke's long fingers slid under the edge of her plain cotton underwear and he groaned.

"I knew it," he said, and she felt his lips form a smile against her throat. "I knew you'd have soft curls hidden under here."

Her brain froze. How was she supposed to respond to that?

"Do you have soft curls under there?" she said, then immediately wished she'd said something, anything else.

Stupid, Claire.

Luke chuckled. "I guess you'll find out soon enough."

Biting her lip, Claire shivered as Luke explored further. He stroked her like he was petting a cat and it felt... *nice.* Very, very nice. The roughness of his fingertips felt so different to her own, sent tiny shocks of sensation right through her body every time he stroked over her clit. Her heart beat so fast she wasn't sure it was good for her, and then he bit her neck right below her earlobe, and she ceased to care.

Her mouth fell open on a moan. "More."

Luke gave her what she wanted, stroked faster, bit harder, probed deeper....

And then he stopped.

Oh, no.

"Claire," he said, the warning back in his voice. "Look at me."

Tears, hot and sudden sprung to fill her eyes, eager to escape their confines and confirm her shame. Lifting her gaze to his, she silently dared him to ask his question.

"Are you a virgin?"

Chapter Nineteen

S o defiant. So proud. Claire stared him down with all the dignity of a queen. But the moment he asked his question her lip began to quiver, and her tears fell.

And Luke felt like a complete shit.

He put her back on her feet and helped her straighten her skirt. She stared up at him, misery leeching into the air around her, but her voice held steady. "Do you want to say it or shall I?"

Treading carefully, he said, "Say what?"

"That you don't *do* virgins, or virgins are more trouble than they're worth, or my all-time favourite, you don't want the *responsibility* of taking my virginity, because apparently only sex gods, Satanic cults and dragons are up for that formidable task."

Luke pinched the bridge of his nose. "Please tell me no one has *actually* said that to you."

Claire folded her arms over her chest and pursed her lips, raised her eyebrows and lifted her chin a little higher. Luke swore. Of course some idiot had said that to her. How else did someone get to be a twenty-nine-year-old virgin?

He rubbed his hand across his forehead, pushed at the sudden ache he felt brewing there. "I don't have a problem with you being virgin, Claire, but a head's up would have been nice."

Suddenly looking very uncomfortable, she shifted her weight from one leg to the other and Luke realised he hadn't treaded carefully so much as stuck his foot in his mouth.

"Come on." He held out his hand, waited patiently until she took it. "So, I guess this explains why you don't want to have sex with me," he said, leading her back to the couch. "At least, I'm hoping that's the only reason."

Her cheeks pinkened and she couldn't hold his gaze. "I never said I don't want to have sex with you."

Luke blinked as he replayed her words in his head. She was right. She'd told him again and again she wasn't *going* to have sex with him, but she'd never said she didn't *want* to.

His brow creased. "So you *do* want to?"

She scowled at him. "Of course I bloody do. Seriously. Have you seen you?" She wriggled in her seat, nervous. "But you were using me and, well, now you're not. It didn't seem to matter so much anymore, you know? And I thought, what could it hurt to give in to temptation but then you said the thing about it being 'just sex'—"

"And then I kissed you again."

"And I really like kissing you," she said, then bowed her head. "I'm not good at this."

Could've fooled me.

She certainly didn't kiss like a virgin. Which suddenly annoyed him for some reason. "You're better at it than you think," he said.

She looked at him strangely. "I'm not sure if that's supposed to be a compliment or an insult."

And Luke realised he wasn't sure either. "I'm sorry, Claire. I made an assumption and I was wrong."

"Considering my age, it's a fair assumption to make."

"No, I mean I'm used to dating women who—"

"Have experience?"

"Who like to play games." Luke shook his head and smiled. "You have no idea how refreshing it is to be with someone like you. Someone genuine."

A shy smile touched her lips. "Thank you."

Tugging on her hand, he coaxed her into his lap and loosely wrapped his arms around her hips, smiled when she slid her arms around his neck and nestled against his shoulder like she had on the ferry.

"How about we try this again. Hi, I'm Luke, I find you insanely attractive and I'd like to have sex with you in every way known to man," he said. "Now you go."

Her warm breath fanned his neck as she laughed. "Hi, Luke. I'm Claire. I'm a... virgin, and I have no idea how to have sex in *any* way known to man." She took a breath and added quietly, "But I'd like to."

"Right now?" he asked, a sly smile stretching lazily across his face even though he knew the answer.

She stiffened in his arms. "I don't know."

He brushed his knuckles over the softness of her cheek, reigned in his hunger when she leant into his touch. "Then you're not ready," he whispered. She opened her mouth to argue but he pressed a finger to her lips. "It's okay. You'll know when you're ready. You'll have no doubts." He traced his fingertip across her plump lower lip. "And I'll be waiting for you."

That shy smile turned cunning. "But are you a sex god, a Satanic cult or a dragon?"

His body shook with laughter. "My ego would like to think I'm one of those things."

Claire chuckled then looked at her watch. "I really should go home."

"Stay the night."

Luke had no idea why he'd said that. He usually couldn't wait to reclaim his space and revel in his solitude in his aggressively male home. But tonight he wanted to sit on his couch and tease and flirt and talk to Claire. When they weren't being combatant, he found she was actually very easy to talk to, and her sharp wit angled more towards humour and less towards eviscerating his vitals.

"I have to open the shop tomorrow," she said.

"Can't someone else do it?"

That earned him another scowl. "No, they can't. Karen and I take it in turns. She opened last Saturday so tomorrow is my turn. I refuse to run Novelteas the way Amanda runs Morse Industries. I don't ask my staff to do anything I'm not willing to do myself, and I don't treat them like shit just so I can sleep in on the weekends."

Luke ran through the variables in his head. "What if I said that by staying here you could open the store *and* have a sleep in?"

Narrowing her eyes, she stared at him for a moment, then said, "I'm listening."

"You open the shop at nine o'clock, right?"

She nodded. "Uh-huh."

"So presumably you get there at eight?"

She nodded again. "Uh-huh."

"Taking into account breakfast, a shower, getting dressed, the fact you rely on public transport to get you to work—and I'm guessing you're one of those people who likes to ensure you're always on time, if not early—I calculate you have to get up at 6:00 a.m. at the latest. If you stay here tonight you can sleep in, you can shower while I make you breakfast and then I'll drive you to work."

She cocked one brow. "The latest I get up is 5:30 a.m. And what about my clothes? And makeup and brushing my teeth and anything else I may need for work?"

"Shit." She had a point. "Well, what do you suggest then?"

Claire tapped her fingertip against her plush lips.

It made him want to kiss her again.

"If you drive me home tonight, then pick me up and drive me to work tomorrow, I can do everything I would normally do *and* have a sleep in because it only takes twenty-five minutes to drive from my house to my shop instead of the hour and a bit by bus." She looked up at him from under her long, dark lashes. "Would that be okay?"

Luke pretended to think about it for roughly three seconds. "Yeah. That would be okay." Then he pushed to his feet, dragging Claire with him. "You know, we still haven't figured out what you're going to tell Amanda."

Claire shrugged her jacket on. "My brain's too fuzzy to think about that tonight. For now, I'll just tell her I'm in. We can work out the details later."

The drive to Claire's house was depressingly short. Time seemed to speed up in her presence and Luke was quickly discovering there were not enough hours in the day. And even though he knew talking would make the time go faster he found himself asking the question that had been burning a hole in his brain since he'd listened to that recording.

"When Amanda said she'd give you access to your money, she was talking about your trust fund, wasn't she?"

"You know about that?" She sounded surprised.

"My investigator's report was thorough."

"Of course it was," she said, sighing. "And yes, she means my trust fund. What else did that report tell you about me?"

Bile rose from Luke's stomach as he recalled the information. Disgust flavoured his tone. "That Amanda has always tried to control you through money. That while she paid you well for your job at Morse Industries, she sunk almost all of it into your trust fund so you'd still be reliant on her for all your day-to-day living expenses. That when you turned eighteen and inherited your house from your father's estate, she convinced you to use it as a rental property instead of letting you move out on your own, and that every cent from your rental income also went into your trust fund." He took a breath and huffed out a laugh. "It also told me you're sitting on a small fortune."

Streetlamps momentarily illuminated Claire's impassive expression. "And did your report tell you I can't touch that fortune until I turn thirty?"

"Yes. It also told me you turn thirty next month, which makes the motive for Amanda's gesture... confusing."

Claire laughed. The warmth of her voice filled the dark confines of the car and slid over him, around him, settled his temper. "Not confusing. Meaningless," she corrected him. "Amanda wants me to do her dirty work but doesn't want to give up anything of value to get me to do it. Giving me access to my trust fund, which she legally has to in a few weeks anyway, costs her nothing."

"A meaningless gesture disguised as altruism," he said, shaking his head. "That's so manipulative."

"Welcome to my world."

Shaking his head at her sarcasm-laced enthusiasm, Luke

realised Claire was right. He'd built an empire on the weight of his word, on honesty and integrity, not manipulation. He was heading into uncharted waters with tactics like these.

"And what about sinking your business? How does she plan on doing that when I own the building?"

"My house," she said, her voice brimming with resignation. "It's like you said the other night, I mortgaged my house to fund my business. And if you know about it, what do you wanna bet Amanda knows about it too?"

Luke's grip tightened on the steering wheel and he shook his head. "No," he said, more forcefully than he'd intended. "We won't be doing that."

"Won't we?"

"You upheld your end of the bargain, now I'll uphold mine. Your mortgage will be paid in full by morning. She won't be able to touch you."

A spluttering sound escaped Claire's mouth but if she managed to form any actual words, Luke couldn't decipher them. She found her voice just as he turned his car down her street.

"I thought you were lying," she blurted. "No. Absolutely not. I am more than capable of paying off my own mortgage, thank you very much."

"I know," he said, pulling into her driveway. "But a deal's a deal and I'm a man of my word. I said if you met with Amanda, I'd pay off your mortgage and that's what I'm going to do. Text me the details before you go to bed. Tonight. I won't take no for an answer, Claire."

Claire's mouth opened and closed, a slight frown pulled at her forehead. A protective instinct rose up in Luke and made him want to reach out and smooth her brow, take her worries away.

She turned to him when he cut the engine. "But... why?"

This time he did reach out and stroked his fingertips over her cheek. "Because we're friends, and I'm not going to let her hurt you anymore."

She grabbed his hand and pulled it away from her face, but she didn't let it go. "No. I'm not comfortable with this. It's asking way too much of you. I'll pay it out when I get my trust fund."

"But that's not for weeks," he said, his frustration with her obstinate pride bleeding through his words. "What are the chances Amanda is willing to wait that long?"

For a moment she looked like she was going to continue arguing with him, then her lips flattened and she huffed out a single word. "Fine."

Luke smirked at her exasperated tone. "Good."

"But I'm paying you back as soon as I get my money."

"Stubborn woman," he said, shaking his head and chuckling.

And it wasn't that he found her fierce independence amusing—after what she'd been through Luke respected her all the more for it—but more the fact he couldn't remember the last time a woman didn't expect him to pay for everything. She'd even argued with him over the twenty dollars he'd spent on dinner.

Need gripped him hard. "You need to get out of the car before I start kissing you again."

She poked her tongue out at him.

His gaze locked on to her soft, pliant lips. "Yeah, that's not helping."

Claire smirked and reached for the door handle, then hesitated. "May I ask you one more thing before I say goodnight?"

"Sure."

"What did you mean when you said I was anything but convenient?"

Luke rolled his lips between his teeth and wondered just how much he should tell her. What would she say, for instance, if he told her that ten years ago instead of getting a coffee anytime he wanted one, he would time his visits to the coffee truck specifically so he could avoid her? Or that he used to sit by his office window and watch for her, mourned the loss of her pretty dress in favour of those hideous grey pants-suits. And that watching her come and go from Morse Industries had become so disruptive to his daily routine he'd moved his office to the other side of the goddamn building to break the habit.

Both of those things had been frustratingly inconvenient.

But neither compared to what happened at lunch.

He cleared his throat. "Remember when I said I skipped lunch today?"

"Yes."

Luke dragged his hand down his face then tilted his head back and let loose a long-suffering sigh. "My morning meeting was supposed to end with a buffet lunch, but instead of joining everyone else in the queue, I stayed in my seat and told them I wasn't hungry."

"Why?"

He turned his head to watch her reaction. "Because the scent of your perfume on my jacket gave me a monster hard-on and that was the first excuse that came to mind."

Claire's eyes widened, her lips pressed together then laughter erupted from her like a geyser—an untameable force of nature, immense and unapologetically loud.

Grinning, he added, "I've never been happier about

rejecting Lottie's suggestion of glass-topped tables in the conference room," which set her off on another fit of hysterical snorts and chortling.

Snortling.

When her laughter finally died down, she toyed with the hem of her skirt. "Can I ask you one more thing?"

"Yes."

"Are you really okay with me being a virgin?"

"More than okay. Knowing no other man has had his hands on you," he said, gently squeezing her thigh. "Knowing my name is the only name you'll scream when I make love to you, I couldn't ask for more than that." He paused for a moment as another thought hit him upside of his head. "Are you okay with giving me your virginity?"

Biting her lip as a shy smile bloomed on her pretty face, she looked up from under her lashes and nodded. "Yes," she whispered, popping the car door open. "More than okay."

Luke took her hand in his and brushed his lips across her knuckles. "Goodnight, sweetness."

Leaning closer, she tilted her head, encouraged him to do likewise, but before their lips could touch, she whispered, "Goodnight... dragon."

Making her escape before he could respond, Claire shut the car door and walked across the yard. A broad grin stretched across Luke's face—*cheeky woman*—and as soon as she disappeared inside her house, he adjusted his aching dick and laughed to himself. At himself.

"What the fuck am I doing?" he said with a shake of his head.

In little less than a week Claire Morse had turned his world on its end, and if she thought him a dragon, then she just might be a dragon-slayer.

Chapter Twenty

Claire awoke to the sound of someone knocking on her front door and an annoying buzzing sound that wouldn't shut up. As wakefulness forced her eyelids to open, she realised the buzzing was her alarm clock and the knocking was probably Luke.

Dragging herself into a seated position she glanced at her clock and swore. She hadn't just slept in. She'd over-slept. Stumbling from bed, she grabbed her dressing gown, hastily dragged it on over her pyjamas then hurried to answer the door.

Luke stood on her doorstep in blue jeans, a black T-shirt and aviators, which he peeled off his face with a flourish as he greeted her. "Good morning, sweet—Jesus, what the hell happened to you?"

Instead of responding with something appropriately snarky, Claire flipped him off then stomped back down the hallway. The sound of Luke's sexy chuckle followed her all the way to the kitchen.

"You're early," she grumbled, scrounging through the fridge for something edible.

She felt him standing behind her. "And a good thing too by the looks of it. Good sleep in, was it?" The humour in his voice grated on her already frazzled nerves.

"It would have been if I'd woken up when my stupid alarm went off, but I didn't and now I'm running late." She spat the words out without stopping for breath and started pulling random ingredients out of the fridge.

Luke's strong arms came around her middle and he pulled her backwards against his chest. "Breath, Claire. Just breathe."

Closing her eyes, Claire sucked down a deep lungful of air then slowly let it out.

"Another one," Luke said, his deep voice a soothing caress across her anxious mind.

She took another breath.

"Better?" he asked.

She nodded and blinked her eyes open again. She did feel better, although she suspected it had more to do with the man standing behind her than the breathing exercise.

Her libido agreed.

It took every ounce of strength Claire owned not to say, "Fuck work," and melt against him. His body heat emanated through her thin dressing gown and made her feel like snuggling by a fire with a hot cup of tea. Or maybe just crawling back into bed with a good book and a naked Luke.

Strong hands turned her to face him then cupped her cheeks. "You are going to have your shower and get dressed and anything else you need to do to get ready, and I will cook you breakfast. Okay?"

Claire knew words were coming out of his mouth and knew they probably made a lot of sense—Luke was nothing if not practical—but she didn't comprehend a single thing he'd said because he was staring down at her with those golden eyes and talking to her in that deep baritone voice and touching her with his sexy man-hands. She leaned into his caress, rubbed her cheek against his palm.

"Claire? Okay?"

"Hmm...? What?"

Luke chuckled again. "You shower. Me cook. Okay?"

Oh, yeah. That made sense. "Okay."

She didn't even try to stifle her yawn as she left him in the kitchen muttering something about his jeans suddenly being too tight. But in the bathroom all remnants of sleep were chased away when she saw herself in the mirror.

"Huh. So that's what he meant," she muttered as she took in the knotted mess of her bed-hair, the misaligned buttons on her pyjamas and the fact her dressing gown was inside out.

Greaaat....

At least she hadn't spilled any food on herself.

Yet.

Discarding her clothes in a heap on the floor, Claire climbed in the shower and got to work. She washed her hair and brushed her teeth, shaved her pits and scrubbed her face, and it was only when she got out of the shower she realised she hadn't grabbed any clothes to put on.

Head rolling back on her shoulders, she let out a groan *—could this morning get any worse?—*then she wrapped one towel around her wet hair like a turban and another around her body as tightly as possible.

Confident Luke wouldn't see her—the bathroom being down the hall from the kitchen—Claire walked down the hallway to her bedroom, but she hadn't anticipated finding Luke in the lounge room with his phone plastered to his ear.

The moment they saw each other the world stopped.

Claire stopped walking.

Luke stopped talking.

They just stared at each other in their shared moment of shock, her eyes wide with embarrassment, his raking over her body as a grin brimming with wickedness slowly spread from ear to ear.

"I gotta go," he said, his gaze colliding with hers as he ended the call.

Claire couldn't move. She kept willing her feet to make a break for it, but the stubborn, useless things stayed planted where they were, refusing to budge. Luke came closer, his body moving with an effortless grace Claire would never master.

Stopping in front of her, he shoved his hands in his pockets. "Not that I don't appreciate the view, but you need to get that sexy arse into gear or we're not going to make it on time."

"I need clothes," she said, her voice breathless as her brain ran through every possible scenario Luke Hardcastle seeing her in nothing but a fluffy pink towel could lead to.

Still grinning, Luke dropped his gaze to the hint of cleavage showing above the fluff and her list of scenarios doubled. "Yes, you do," he said. "And hurry up, I have something to show you."

Claire reached behind her and fumbled for the door handle then almost fell arse over tit when the door popped open. The last thing she saw as she kicked the door closed was Luke rolling his lips between his teeth, presumably to stop himself from laughing out loud.

What. A. Gentleman.

She dressed quickly then rushed through her beauty routine, which on days she was running late basically consisted of slapping on a tonne of moisturiser, applying tinted lip-balm and blow-drying her hair.

When she entered the kitchen, the smell that assaulted her senses was wonderful. So was watching Luke wash and dry her frying pan. *So domesticated.*

"Is this mine?" she said, eyeing the plate he'd left on the bench. He'd made her an egg and bacon toastie.

"Sure is," he said as he put the pan away. "Bloody hell, Claire."

Mouth full of toastie goodness, she said, "What?"

Looking down, she checked she hadn't dripped egg on her blouse.

"A cardigan?" Luke threw down the tea-towel and shook his head. "Of course she wears cardigans," he muttered quietly.

Claire swallowed her food and stood up taller, straighter, tugged at the edge of her pale yellow cardie. "What's wrong with cardigans?"

Luke scowled at her. "Besides the fact you look like every naughty librarian fantasy I've ever had come to life. Absolutely nothing."

What the...? Her eyes flew wide and she hedged to ask, "So you *like* cardigans, then?"

A grin tugged at one corner of his mouth and his eyes sparkled with mischief. "Yes, I like cardigans."

She took another bite of toastie. "Well that's a relief," she said around the food. "Because I own a bunch of them."

Luke groaned. "You're killing me, sweetness."

Claire grinned. "What did you want to show me?"

Picking up his phone, Luke showed her the screen as he pulled up a You Tube video.

"Oh no."

"Oh yes. That kid sent me the footage he had and a link to this video."

A prick of betrayal sent goosebumps skittering over Claire's skin. "*He* posted it?"

"No, the footage isn't his. But look, it's been viewed 327 times and shared six times."

Relief washed over her and she laughed. "Not exactly breaking the internet, am I?"

"You should have kicked him in the balls," Luke said, directing a sudden and fierce glare at the screen as You Tube Claire ranted at You Tube Douchebag.

"I'll remember that the next time someone grabs my arse," she said, then shoved the rest of the toastie in her mouth.

Luke shoved his phone in his pocket and stared down at her, his glare reduced to a frown. "You ready to go?"

"Just need my handbag."

They were halfway to Novelteas before Luke spoke again. "I think I have a plan for dealing with Amanda," he said.

"Does it involve sleeping with you?"

He grinned. "Surprisingly, no."

"Then by all means, do tell."

"Do you think she'd believe I was mentoring you?"

"Mentoring me?"

"Why not? We're friends now. And your business is still new enough that it's not completely outside the realm of possibility."

"But why would I need a mentor when I've been doing fine on my own?" She'd even gotten pissy at Amanda when her aunt had dared insinuate otherwise.

"Hmm... good point," he said. "I guess you'll just have to sleep with me, then."

Claire laughed. "You're incorrigible."

He returned her smile. "No, I just don't think we need

to over-complicate things. More often than not, the simplest solution is the right one."

"Fine," she said, mostly because she was too tired to argue. But also because she'd thought about it for half the night and hadn't come up with any better alternatives. Certainly nothing as simple—or as appealing—as dating Luke. Her best idea had involved hiring him to renovate her house, but then she remembered he had people to do that for him and her plan essentially fell apart. "So, I tell Amanda we're sleeping together. Then what? What do I tell her when she starts demanding useful information? Because she will, and soon."

"We give it to her."

Wait, what? "Not to pick holes in the plan, but wouldn't that be counterproductive?"

"Not if the information she receives is false or out of date."

A slow grin spread across her face. "So, I pretend to mend bridges by giving Amanda dodgy information, and she gives me access to money I'm legally entitled to."

"And while you're mending those proverbial bridges you can get the evidence we need to take her down." Luke pulled up in front of Novelteas and cut the engine.

Claire unfastened her seatbelt and frowned at nothing in particular. "It still feels like I'm the one doing all the heavy lifting," she grumbled.

Luke turned to face her, a frown marring his face, his lips pulled down at the corners. "You are. But I don't know how to do this without you. I tried and I failed," he said, spitting the words out like poison, and Claire could imagine failure was not something Luke was overly familiar with. "All I can do is try to protect you from her the best way I know how. She can't touch your shop because I own it. And she can't touch your house because as of this morning, *you* own it."

Her gaze leapt to his, her breath caught in her lungs and the urge to throw herself at him almost overwhelmed her. When she'd texted him her account details the previous evening, she'd not been completely convinced he would keep his promise.

Luke Hardcastle was slowly but surely restoring her faith in men.

Her hand fluttered to her chest. "You paid my mortgage? You actually did it?"

"I told you, Miss Morse, I am a man of my—"

Claire smashed her lips to his, moaned as he took over and half hauled her into his lap. When she pulled back and started breathing again, she said, "Thank you, Luke. I will pay you back."

"I know you will," he said, a lopsided smile tugging at his mouth. "But FYI, I will be charging you interest payable in the form of kisses, because *goddamn* woman, you can kiss."

Chapter Twenty-One

Claire tried to hide her smile, but Luke hooked a knuckle under her chin and stopped her from shying away. He wanted to kiss her again.

In the back seat of his car.

With no clothes on.

His erection was instant.

As was his recurring irritation over how she got to be so bloody good at kissing in the first place. Obviously someone had taught her some tricks somewhere along the way and he was determined to find out who. So he could crush them.

Her kisses were his now.

"Will I see you later?"

"I hope so," he said, trying not to wriggle in his seat like a toddler. He really needed to adjust his cock. "I'm spending the weekend with Lottie. I try to take her out of palliative care whenever I can, take her shopping or out for a drive. You're welcome to join us for dinner. And by dinner I mean pizza, ice cream and popcorn." When she raised a brow at him, he shrugged. "It's movie night."

"Thanks, but I wouldn't want to intrude," she said.

Guessing at her reasoning, Luke sighed quietly. "Lottie doesn't blame you, you know. For Cassidy Holdings. In fact, she's looking forward to meeting you."

When he'd spoken to his sister earlier, her teasing had been relentless. Then Claire had waltzed past wearing nothing but a fluffy towel and he realised Lottie might be on to something.

For ten years his interest in Claire Morse had been purely fanciful, a torturous daydream he could punish himself with at the end of a hard day or delight in after a big win. But now he'd spent time with her, touched her, kissed her, his interest was changing, growing. Morphing into something bigger than he'd ever believed it could be.

I think I'm falling in love with her.

It was the only explanation that made any sense.

He could barely keep his hands off her, his heart raced every time she walked into the room, and he'd hardly sleep all week because she'd taken up permanent residence in his head, filling his dreams with her luscious curves and sultry voice. He didn't even want to think about the damage being done to his cock.

He hadn't jerked off so much since he was a teenager.

When Claire was around, he was in a near constant state of arousal, he felt jealous and possessive every time he thought of another man touching her and if she thought she was ever using public transport again, she had another think coming. He'd happily buy her a car if it meant she could get from Point A to Point B without being molested. And if she refused the car—which he knew she would—he'd simply task Edward with being her personal chauffeur.

Problem solved.

But the biggest clue his obsession had taken a romantic turn, was the fact he simply enjoyed spending time with her. She was funny and clever and sarcastic and brave, and he wanted to make her his. And it was only then he realised why he'd left his car at home the previous day, why he'd taken the ferry and walked through Southbank. It had nothing to do with how nice the weather was and everything to do with wanting to be seen with her.

Together.

In public.

He only hoped she felt the same.

After the shit he'd put her through it would serve him right if she wanted nothing to do with him. But hope was a sick and twisted mistress.

He would win her over.

"If you're sure it's okay," Claire said, pulling him out of his thoughts.

Luke smoothed his thumb across her mouth, smiled when her lips parted and her eyelids shuttered. "It's more than okay. We'll pick you up after work," he said, shifting in his seat again.

"Okay," she said, shooting him a strange look. "And I'll call you after I speak to Amanda." She cocked her head to one side. "Luke, are you all right?"

Busted. "What?"

"You look like you have ants in your pants. Are you okay?"

Letting his head fall forward, he laughed. "To be honest, sweetness, no I'm not." He watched for her reaction as he adjusted himself. "Whenever you're around, my dick feels like a steel pipe in my pants and until you're *ready* there's not a damn thing I can do about it."

Claire's eyes widened, her jaw dropped and her brows shot upwards. "Oh! Okay." She cleared her throat. "Maybe... um, I could help...?"

Luke went very still. "Are you saying you're ready?"

"No, but, um... I was thinking, you've had your hands down my pants, so it seems only fair I do the same for you. What was it you said the other day, tit for tat?"

Luke's brain imploded and he lost the ability to speak. Never in his life had he been propositioned so artlessly. Or so honestly.

"I mean, I have no idea what to do—I can guess, obviously—but I have no actual experience outside what I've read in books. But I figure *you* could teach me, because even though I'm not quite ready to have sex with you, I *really* want to see you naked."

Fuck me. Luke raked a hand through his hair and blew out a breath. His need was so intense he couldn't even look at her for fear he'd come in his pants. "You need to get out of my car now." From the corner of his eye he saw Claire's back straighten and her face fall. Luke grabbed her wrist as she grabbed for the door handle, held her fast even as she tried to yank her arm free. "Don't ever doubt how much I want you, Miss Morse, but right now you have a job to do and I have sister to collect and if you don't get out of this car, I won't be the only one getting naked."

"Oh!" She sounded as breathless as him and her teeth sank into her bottom lip. "Before I go, did you just call me Miss Morse because of the naughty librarian thing?"

His eyes narrowed. "I admit to nothing."

Claire giggled and Luke let the sound coil around him, comfort him. It would tide him over until he heard her laugh again.

"Have a good day," she said as she climbed out of his

car, and Luke couldn't help but notice the falter in her step as she crossed the footpath to the shop door, as though she too realised she'd just spoken as though they were a real couple.

And hope flared to life in his chest.

The sick bitch.

"You're late. As usual."

"Don't start, Lottie."

Luke nodded his thanks to the orderly who'd waited with his sister then helped her into his car.

"You're looking better today," he said, revving the engine and speeding out of the hospice carpark. "You have more colour in your cheeks than you did on Monday."

"So do you, lover boy."

"Shut up. I told you, Claire and I aren't lovers." *Not yet anyway.*

"You mean Luke Hardcastle, the great and powerful lady-killer, couldn't seal the deal?" Lottie laughed. "I like this chick already."

"A week ago, you wanted me to take her down."

"A week ago, she wasn't giving you a run for your money. And after what you told me about her upbringing...." Lottie shuddered. "I am more than happy to focus all my hatred on her aunt."

"You and me both."

"And Claire really offered to help us?"

"Yes. I think it'll be cathartic for her," he said, driving back towards the city. "You should have heard how Amanda spoke to her. I could barely stomach it for twenty minutes.

Claire lived with it for twenty years. She really is… amazing."

Lottie grinned, smug. "I was right, wasn't I? You're completely smitten with her."

"Smitten?" Luke said the word with disgust. "I'm a grown man. I don't get 'smitten'."

"Really? I think the internet would beg to differ."

He glanced at his sister. "What are you talking about?"

"This," she said, turning her phone towards him so he could see the article displayed on the screen.

Luke released a slow, steady, angry breath. "Shit." He thumped the steering wheel. "Read it to me."

"Are you sure? I don't want your angry driving to kill me before the cancer does."

"Charlotte Alexandra Cassidy," he seethed through gritted teeth. "Read me the goddamn article."

Lottie cleared her throat. *"Raunchy River City Romance.* Jesus, it sounds like the title of a soft-core porno," she said, then read the article out loud.

Luke listened as Claire's comings and goings from Hardcastle Tower were described as *"rendezvouses"*, the proprietor's dinner was *"an evening of casual dining with friends"*, and their snuggly ferry trip and walk through the Southbank markets the previous night was *"a declaration that, for now at least, Brisbane's most eligible bachelor is off the market"*.

"Fucking hell," Luke growled and hit the steering wheel again, then turned down a random side street and parked the car. "Let me see that."

Lottie handed over her phone. "Do you think Claire has seen it yet?"

"Christ, I hope not," he said as he scrolled down the page, stopped to glare at the photos attached to the article.

"Why? I thought you two had come to an arrangement."

"We have in regards to Amanda, but nothing official about, you know, *us*. As a couple. In the romantic sense." At his sister's raised eyebrows, he continued. "The most we've agreed on is we both really like kissing each other."

"Oh, geez," Lottie laughed. "What are you, fifteen?"

"What I am is pissed off. If I find out who took these photos, I'm gunna shove that long-range lens so far up their—"

"Anyhoo...."

"No, Lottie, you don't understand. This bullshit right here," he said, holding up the phone, "This is why Claire turned me down in the first place. She didn't want to become tabloid fodder. She didn't want people to think *exactly* what this article is insinuating. That she's just another notch on my bedpost. Christ," he growled, "as if dealing with Amanda wasn't bad enough, now she has to deal with this shit too."

Staring at the photos again, Luke rubbed the back of his neck. Someone had gotten a shot of them making out in his Penthouse when he'd had her pinned against the floor to ceiling windows with her legs wrapped around him and his hand inside her panties. Thankfully her clothing hid her body and—more to the point—what Luke was doing to her, from the camera. The other photograph showed Claire sitting in his lap on the ferry, her head resting on his shoulder while he kissed her forehead. One of the other passengers must have taken it.

He ran his thumb over the image. It looked so right to him, to be holding her like that. It had felt right too. Comfortable. Easy. Companionable.

Loving.

"You must have done something to change her mind,"

Lottie said, pointing to the first photo. "Because that does not look like a woman turning you down."

After handing back his sister's phone, Luke put his car in gear and drove in the direction of Merthyr Road. "What can I say?" he said with a half-shrug. "I'm a sex god."

He grinned. *Or a dragon.*

Chapter Twenty-Two

Claire's weekend staff arrived just as she was unlocking the door.

"Running late, boss? That's not like you," Brent said with a cheeky grin and a teasing voice.

"Oh, leave her alone. Everyone's entitled to a late start every now and then," Carol said, then *tsked* at Brent. "Some of us more than others."

The lighthearted bickering continued right up until opening time and Claire smirked and chuckled her way through her abbreviated morning routine. But her good mood died a swift death when she opened for business and the first people shoving their way through the door weren't customers.

"Claire, what can you tell me about the rumours that you and Luke Hardcastle are dating?"

"Is it true you're pregnant with his love child and that's why he ended his relationship with Morgan York?"

"Can you confirm the death of Lottie Cassidy and do you blame yourself for her eating disorder in the wake of the Cassidy Holdings fiasco?"

"Do you have anything to say about your recent sexual assault?"

Questions and cameras bombarded her from every angle, blinded her with flashing lights and baffled her with utter bullshit.

And then her phone rang.

Hiding her phone from prying eyes, Claire glanced down and saw Amanda's name displayed prominently on the screen.

Her anxiety threatened to cripple her.

In... out....

Internally cringing at the ear-chewing she knew was coming her way, she hit the end call button, shoved the phone in the back pocket of her jeans and faced off with the gossip mongers clogging up her bookstore.

Lifting her chin and pretending to be a lot less freaked out than she felt, she stared down each of them in turn. "You have until the count of three to get out of my shop before my staff call the police and report you all for disturbing the peace, disrupting my place of employment and trespassing on private property."

"Oh, honey, I'm sorry," Carol said from behind the service counter. "Did you want to wait until *after* the count of three, because I've already called the cops and they're on their way."

Claire bit back a grin as the reporters slowly vacated her shop, grumbling every step of the way, then scowled as they set up camp on the footpath.

Greaaat....

"Boss?" Brent appeared beside her. "I took photos of them all," he said and held up his mobile phone. "I'll put together a quick newsletter and email the rest of Merthyr

Road so they know what's going on and who to refuse service to."

"Thanks." Claire flashed him a grateful smile, one that faded all too quickly. She felt very tired all of a sudden. Tired and crumpled and alone. "I have some phone calls to make. Please let me know when the police get here."

As soon as she was safely ensconced in her office, she locked the door and opened her laptop. A quick search of the online news sites revealed the cause of the brouhaha outside. A quick skim over the article had her clenching her teeth in anger. But it was the name on the by-line that really pissed her off.

Chris Marx.

Squinting at the picture accompanying the name confirmed her suspicions. Chris Marx was the arsehole who'd felt her up at the quays. She braced herself for a scathing read:

BILLIONAIRE PLAYBOY LUKE HARDCASTLE, *owner and CEO of Hardcastle Construction appears to be recovering well from his recent break-up with up-and-coming Aussie couture model, Morgan York. Last night, the man responsible for three quarters of the construction cranes dotting the River City's skyline, was seen with a new woman on his arm—and in his lap. According to eyewitness reports, Mr Hardcastle and his female companion, now known to be Claire Morse, owner of Novelteas Bookstore and Tea Room, and estranged niece of Morse Industries owner and CEO, Amanda Morse, only had eyes for each other. In the words of one observer, "...they looked absolutely smitten with each other and couldn't keep their hands to themselves...."*

The pair have been spotted together several times this

past week including secret rendezvouses at both Hardcastle Tower and Novelteas, and even enjoyed an evening of casual dining with friends. But it was last night's very public display of affection as they strolled through the Southbank parklands together that has everyone talking as it would seem to be a declaration that, for now at least, Brisbane's most eligible bachelor is off the market. But don't worry ladies, considering Mr Hardcastle's track record as a serial monogamist, he's sure to be single again in no time.

STARING at the picture of herself being ravished by Luke in the window of his penthouse filled her with both longing and horror. And as sorely as she was tempted, she knew better than to read the comments section.

Sucking down great gulps of air, Claire tried to settle her temper and rationalise the situation. Only there was nothing rational about having your life turned upside down because any dickweed with a camera apparently had the right to sell pictures of your private life to the highest bidder.

She wanted Luke.

She wanted to feel his muscled arms wrap around her and lean into his strength, hear his deep voice murmur in her ear and tell her everything would be okay.

But it wasn't okay.

How did Chris Marx know who she was or where she'd be? Why did he approach *her* at the quays? And how the fuck did he get a photo of them in Luke's penthouse? No one knew she was going there. Not even her!

Her questions burned an ulcer in her stomach.

And a hole in her heart.

Luke had set her up. It was the only logical explanation.

He'd lied to her and like a love-struck fool she'd believed him. Biting her lip to hold back the sob she desperately wanted to let loose, she felt her nose prickle as tears formed behind her eyes.

Lifting her chin, she said, "It doesn't matter. None of it does."

Fuck Luke Hardcastle!

She was Claire Morse and she was a survivor.

She didn't need Hardcastle's strength.

She had her own.

Picking up her phone, she called Amanda. Her aunt picked up on the first ring. "You did *not* hang up on me!" she snarled.

Claire couldn't sit still. She levered out of her chair and paced the floor of her tiny office. "I'm sorry, Aunty," she said, her voice loaded with the anger coursing through her veins. "I was dealing with a pest problem when you called."

Amanda laughed. "Paparazzi found you already, have they? Must be a slow news week."

"Must be."

"Well, I must say, my girl, I am impressed. When I suggested you sleep with Hardcastle I didn't think you'd jump straight into bed with him. Mind you, he is absolutely gorgeous," Amanda growled in a way Claire guessed was supposed to be sexy. "That man was built to pleasure women. So, how was it?"

"A lady doesn't kiss and tell," Claire said, smiling tightly. "You taught me that."

"Nice to know you paid attention to *something* I taught you."

"I paid attention to everything you taught me, Aunty."

Everything.

"Well just make sure you keep me informed. I think we

should start making our family lunches a weekly thing, don't you?"

Weekly check ins? Why not? "Sure. That sounds great," Claire said, injecting just the right amount of appreciation into her voice without sounding needy. Her aunt hated needy people.

In typical Amanda form, the phone call didn't end with pleasantries. It just ended.

Next she called Luke. He answered on the second ring.

"I'm guessing you've seen the news," he said.

Claire's temper snapped and all that anger coursing through her body was suddenly directed at Luke. "You said he was a journalist, Luke. You forgot to mention the bastard who grabbed my arse was a bottom-feeding gossip columnist."

"Claire, sweetness, it isn't as bad—"

"Isn't as bad as it looks?" she raged, slapping her hand on her desk. "Well it looks pretty *fucking* bad from where I'm standing, Luke. Did the two of you set this up? Set me up? Is this your revenge for my part in the Cassidy Holdings deal?"

"No!"

"I told you, didn't I? I told you I didn't want to be your lover because of shit like this. I've worked too hard to lose everything now through idle gossip and innuendo." Claire took a deep breath, then exhaled slowly as she composed herself. "Look, I'll still help you take Amanda down because I need that as much as you do," she said, her throat swelling with her grief. "But you will *never* touch me again."

"Claire—"

"I'll call you on Monday to discuss our next move. Until then, you stay the fuck away from me."

Jabbing her finger at the phone, she ended the call, then

she closed her laptop and swiped at the tears running down her cheeks, thankful she'd skipped the mascara in her morning routine. *Thank you sleep in.* Outside in the shop she could hear they were busy, so she straightened her clothes, unlocked the door and got down to the business of selling books with a smile firmly and falsely set in place.

Chapter Twenty-Three

When Luke and Lottie arrived at Novelteas, two police cars were parked out front and a half-dozen paparazzi were standing around looking bored. Until they saw Luke and Lottie get out of his car. His sister promptly flipped them off then walked inside like she owned the joint.

"I'll be upstairs," she said. "I've wanted to come here for ages."

Luke nodded at the older woman serving customers at the counter. Her facial expression could best be described as frightening with a dash of murderous intent. And as he moved closer to Claire's office, a tall muscle-bound youth in jeans and a Novelteas T-shirt blocked his path.

"Can I help you, *sir*?"

Luke's patience was disturbingly low and as much as he appreciated Claire's staff looking out for her, he really didn't have the time for this shit.

"Where is she?" he said quietly.

The youth seemed to debate his answer before speaking then tilted his chin towards the stairs. "She's hiding upstairs where the arsehole brigade can't see her, drowning her sorrows in cups of Darjeeling."

"Thank you."

Luke took the stairs two at a time and found Claire sitting at a table with Lottie, staring vacantly at her teacup, her eyes red and her face blotchy. She'd been crying.

He rubbed the back of his neck and swore. A quick scan of the room revealed no other customers. Downstairs had been thin on patrons too. *Fan-fucking-tastic*. The circus out front was scaring off her customers.

And it was his fault.

As he approached the table, he saw Lottie patting Claire's hand and talking to her in hushed tones. Despite the horrible circumstances, the sight caused a smile to tug at his mouth, the thought of his sister and his girlfriend getting along making him incomprehensibly happy.

Snagging a chair from a neighbouring table, he joined the women and sat down. Claire immediately lifted her chin and glared at him. Lottie leaned back and sipped her tea, hiding her amusement behind her teacup.

"You here to gloat at your handiwork?" Claire said, her voice devoid of her usual sass.

"Sweet—" Luke began, but Lottie shook her head and tossed him a warning glance. Right. Save the endearments for when Claire didn't want to cut his balls off. "Claire, I know you told me to stay away but I had to see you."

"Oh, you just *had* to do the complete opposite of what I said?"

"I had to make sure you were okay."

She stared at him like he was an idiot. "Do I look like I'm okay?"

"No, you don't," Lottie said, then she squeezed Claire's hand. "I'll get us some cake."

Claire sniffed and nodded. "Help yourself. It's not like anyone else is here to eat it."

Lottie got to her feet and stared down her nose at him. "*You* don't get any." Then she sauntered off towards the cake cabinet.

Claire watched Lottie leave then lifted her gaze to Luke's. "Why did you do this to me?" she whispered, her eyes filling with tears.

He slid his hand over hers, sighed in relief when she didn't pull away. He stared at their hands as he spoke, memorised the shape of her fingers, the paleness of her skin compared to his tan. Ran his thumb over the ring of silver hearts encircling her index finger. "You're right, I did do this to you. But not in the way you think."

"What I think is you and that arsehole pervert set me up. Why else would you have kissed me the way you did, where you did?"

Luke straightened, Claire's accusations cutting him to the quick. "The only thought going through my head last night was how much I wanted you."

She barked out a disdainful laugh. "You didn't want me. You wanted revenge. You played me and I fell for it. I fell so hard I almost gave you *everything*. So congratulations, Luke. One Morse down, one to go."

Luke listened to Claire's hushed tirade, his gut twisting as he realised she believed what she was saying. She thought Luke was a despicable human being and he had no one to blame but himself. After all, wasn't that the image he'd been trying to portray? A prick, willing to do whatever it took to avenge his sister? And apparently, with the unintentional help of Chris Marx, he'd finally succeeded.

Only he'd changed his mind. After reading that goddamn report he'd decided he didn't want to be that person. Luke wanted to be himself, the good man Claire had said she knew he was. *"You're better than this."*

He shook his head. "I didn't know about the article, Claire. These paparazzi and gossip columnists have spies all over town, calling them with tidbits of information for the sake of a few bucks. The fact Chris Marx knew about our movements prior to last night indicates he's been keeping tabs on us all week. As to who tipped him off or why, I don't know. I just know it wasn't me." He sighed. "That said, I also know the only reason he would've gone after you was because you were with me." He curled his fingers around hers and gently squeezed. "And for that I am sorry."

Claire stared at him for what felt like an eternity, then said, "Amanda rang me this morning."

Luke sat up straighter, his focus sharpened. "What did *she* want?"

"She called to congratulate me on my initiative," she said quietly. "Apparently she didn't think I had it in me to seduce you. Oh, and she wants to have weekly get-togethers so we can plan your demise."

"Ooh, sounds like fun," Lottie interjected as she placed two plates on the table—one filled with finger sandwiches and the other loaded with an assortment of tiny cakes. "Can I come?"

A sudden burst of laughter escaped Claire as she wiped the tears from her cheeks. "Sure," she said with a sniff. "The more the merrier."

Lottie stared at both of them, a wide grin on her face, then said, "Forks! I forgot forks. Back in a sec."

Luke shook his head with affectionate amusement.

Claire gripped his hand, stealing his attention. "Promise me," she whispered, anguish tainting her sweet voice.

"Promise me last night was real. That it wasn't just about revenge."

"Sweetness, I promise," he said, bringing her hand to his lips, kissing her fingers. "Everything I said last night, everything I said this morning, none of it was a lie. I want you, Claire. I want you so much I can hardly breathe. And I know it's going to take time to earn your trust, but if you'll let me, it's time I'm willing to spend."

Her smile was shy, but she didn't try to hide it this time. "Okay," she said, but she didn't sound completely convinced.

Luke swallowed hard, nervous in a way he hadn't been in a very long time. "And will you stay with me tonight?"

She dried her face with a napkin and sniffed. "Why?"

Luke's grin was sly as he lowered his mouth to hers. "Because I really want you to see me naked too."

Chapter Twenty-Four

As the final credits scrolled up the big screen TV, Lottie collected the empty pizza boxes and wished them goodnight.

Claire was tucked against Luke's side where they sat on the floor, his back against the couch, her head on his chest and her arm draped across his middle. Staring down at the top of her head, he watched her hair shift as it caught on his breath and he lifted a hand to smooth it down.

"What are you thinking about?" he whispered.

"How good you smell," she said, burying her face in his T-shirt and breathing deep. "Can I wear your shirt to bed?"

Luke chuckled. "I was hoping you'd wear your cardigan."

Claire leaned back so she could frown up at him. "But the buttons will pop open."

"Exactly," he said, laughing as Claire grabbed a cushion and threw it at him.

He caught it easily then grabbed her around the waist, dragged her to the floor and tickled her ribs. Her laughter was bold and joyful and interspersed with giggles and screams. It ended with Luke on top of her, pinning her to the floor with his weight, her wrists bound in his hands as he ravished her throat with his lips.

She moaned softly. "Luke, should I be jealous?"

A frown pulled at his brow, but he continued kissing her neck, her jaw. "Jealous of whom, sweetness?"

"Her."

Luke lifted his head and smiled when he saw the direction of Claire's gaze. "She was my first love. You can't be jealous of a man's first love," he said, levering to his feet then hauling Claire onto hers.

She cocked a brow at him. "Jessica Rabbit was your first love?"

Standing behind Claire, he wrapped his arms around her waist and rested his chin on her shoulder. Spanning one wall of his home theatre was a collection of posters and movie stills and original animation slides from a bunch of Luke's favourite movies, including a signed pin-up poster of Jessica Rabbit. "She's the perfect woman."

"She's fictional."

"Exactly. Women have book boyfriends so why can't I have a movie girlfriend?"

Claire shook with quiet laughter. "Well now I know why you're so fascinated with my boobs. But that just begs the question, if Jessica Rabbit is your dream girl, why do you always date skinny chicks with flat chests? That makes zero sense."

It makes perfect sense.

"I don't know," Luke lied. "But I tell you what, I'll have a think about it and get back to you."

She half turned in his arms and stared at him with narrowed eyes as though trying to read his mind.

Eventually she gave up and said, "You really like movies, huh?"

Luke debated his response for a moment. "Can you keep a secret?"

"Depends." Claire said. "What's in it for me?"

Luke chuckled. "You can sleep in my T-shirt tonight."

Claire pulled his arms tighter around her. "I can keep a secret."

Luke sighed quietly. "I'm dyslexic."

Spinning around to face him, Claire looked shocked. "No way, really?"

"Mm-hmm. It's why I dropped out of high school and went to work for my dad in construction. I got headaches all the time, and I hated schoolwork. Reading was hard. It never made any sense to me. But movies...? Movies made sense. I don't have to think so hard all the time, I don't have to read anything. Movies give my brain a break."

"But you went back to school, you finished, you went on to university. You hold degrees in structural engineering *and* business management."

Luke wasn't surprised Claire knew about his schooling. It was public record. His dyslexia was not.

"Sure do. Dad told me if I wanted to take over the company then I had to finish my education, so I learned to live with the dyslexia. I learned to work with it instead of letting it control me, learned how to break down words so they made sense. I still have days where I wish I was back pouring concrete or laying bricks because it would be far easier than decoding 300 pages of utter nonsense, but I love my job. I love my company. So, if it takes me a little longer to read things, then so be it."

Reaching up to kiss his cheek, Claire whispered, "You're amazing."

He stared down at her, a grin tugging at one corner of his mouth. "Let's go to bed," he said, then took her hand and led her to his bedroom. Once inside he pulled her into his arms and slashed his mouth over hers, hungry, demanding.

"I love your kisses," Claire whispered across his lips.

"Good, because I love kissing you," he murmured, then slipped his tongue between her teeth and ravished her mouth. Manoeuvring her backwards towards the bed, he pulled away just long enough to ask, "How does a virgin get to be so damned good at kissing anyway?"

Claire veered off course to lick a path up the column of his throat. "I'm a virgin, not a nun," she said, emphasising her point by cupping his dick through his jeans.

Luke groaned as she massaged his balls. *Fuck!* "So, you've had boyfriends, then?" he said, immediately gritting his teeth against the jealousy filling his stomach with bile.

"I've been on dates with people who were boys, but I wouldn't call them my friends."

Luke's gaze narrowed and he grabbed her wrist, moved her hand away from his crotch. "Explain."

With a sigh, she said, "Do you remember what I said in your office Monday evening? About why men speak to me?"

Luke recalled her disappointment when he'd come clean about his reasons for seeing her.

"... the conversation invariably turns to Amanda..."

He finally understood. "Men only asked you out to get to your aunt."

"Yep. So I went on a few dates, even got my hopes up a couple of times, but as soon as they realised the quickest way to get Amanda's attention was to seduce her instead of her niece, I never heard from them again."

"Arseholes."

Claire smirked. "I will admit, I did feel a rather perverse sense of satisfaction watching Amanda chew them up and spit them out," she said. "But enough talking. More kissing."

"As you wish."

Chapter Twenty-Five

The backs of Claire's legs hit the bed and she fell on her arse.

Luke followed her onto the surprisingly soft bedcovers and moved to straddle her body, his knees locking her legs together and his svelte, muscular, god-like arms either side of her ribs, holding his weight off her. "When you said you knew nothing about sex but wanted to learn, what exactly did you have in mind?"

Realising she'd never actually given it much thought, Claire stumbled to answer the question. Over the years she'd read books on the topic of sex—quite a lot of them—and seen many weird, sexy and oddly sensual things illustrated in their pages, but she hadn't made a bucket list or anything. She didn't think she was into anything particularly kinky. Being tied up held zero appeal for her and she'd been punished enough over the years to last her three lifetimes. But she didn't want sex to be boring either.

Luke must have sensed her uncertainty. "May I make a suggestion?"

Claire nodded eagerly. "Yes please."

"Have you ever seen a real, live naked man?" he said, his lips twitching up in one corner.

Her cheeks heated and her eyes widened but not in fear or embarrassment. "I can't say that I have." She swallowed hard, knowing what he was going to say next as surely as she knew how to make the perfect cup of tea.

"Then it's about time you did," he said, his voice dropping lower, his tone more sensual than before. As it had been the previous night, in the window. It reminded her of dark chocolate dipped in thick caramel. "And I think you should be the one to undress me."

Claire's pulse fluttered. "Yes."

Luke pressed a short, sweet kiss to her mouth. "Where do you want to begin? Top... or bottom?"

"Top." Starting with the safer non-sexual option seemed the best move. She'd already seen his chest so it shouldn't hold too many surprises for her.

Luke moved backwards off the bed, held out his hand then hauled her to her feet. "Before we do this, we should probably lay some ground rules."

"Good idea."

He rested his hands on her shoulders. "The first and most important rule is *relax*. Nothing will happen that you don't want to happen."

Claire nodded. "Okay. Good rule."

"Second, I'm not a mind-reader, sweetness. If I'm doing something you don't like, or not doing enough of something you do like, you have to tell me, okay?"

"Yes, okay." She shook the tension from her hands. "Is there a third rule?"

Luke grabbed her hands and cocooned them in his, the heat of his palms instantly soothing her nerves. "Yes. Have fun."

She bit her lip and looked away. "I have about as much experience with fun as I do with sex."

He hooked a knuckle under her chin and lifted her face to his. His mouth a hairsbreadth from hers, he said, "Lets change that, shall we?" Then he was kissing her again, sliding his hands through her hair and holding her where he wanted her while he plundered her mouth.

Claire moaned. "More."

"Put your hands on me," Luke rasped between one kiss and the next.

"They are," she panted, sliding her palms over his chest and around his shoulders.

"No, sweetness. Put your hands on *me*."

It took Claire a moment to understand his meaning but once she did, she slid her hands down his chest, grabbed the hem of his T-shirt and slowly pushed it up. Luke bent down slightly so she could pull it over his head, and when he stood up again the uninterrupted vision of male perfection that greeted her left her mouth dry, her pussy wet and her brain leaking out her ears.

So much for the non-sexual option....

The glimpses she'd gotten in his office, the narrow band of flesh that had teased her from beneath his open shirtfront had been little more than a precursor to this show of raw masculinity.

"Claire, touch me. Please."

With inhuman effort Claire dragged her gaze all the way up to Luke's. His amber eyes reflected the muted light in the bedroom, his face was tight, his expression controlled. He looked like he wanted to devour her whole.

Reaching out with tentative hands, Claire pressed her fingers to his chest. His skin was soft and warm and his chest hair tickled her palms. Sliding down to his stomach, she explored the well-defined ridges of muscle, studied the way they wrapped around his ribs and hips, muscle she'd only ever seen on superheroes in graphic novels.

Feeling bold she leaned closer and flicked the tip of her tongue against his nipple. A shuddering breath escaped him and his chest rose and fell with exaggerated movements. So she did it again, and again, then she latched her lips around the tiny hardened bud and sucked. Hard.

"Jesus!"

Kissing her way across his chest, Claire dropped her hands to the waist of Luke's jeans. The soft, heavy denim fell down his legs with little prompting from either of them and left him standing in nothing but a pair of black boxer-briefs.

His thick erection pushed insistently against the stretch cotton fabric, the head of the beast threatening to poke above the waistband. Claire stared at the thing and moistened her suddenly dry lips. This was the monster she'd felt through his pants only two nights previous. The one that had frightened and excited her. The same monster she'd grabbed earlier when she'd tried to prove she wasn't a total noob. She stared wide-eyed at it, her fingers itching to reach out and stroke its hard length, but she didn't. She didn't move at all.

Luke misinterpreted her hesitation. "We can stop whenever you want to, Claire," he reminded her.

But Claire didn't want to stop. Not when she'd come so far. "Is it wrong that I want to lick it?"

Luke's stomach muscles visibly clenched and a ragged groan rumbled through him. "I know I'm going to regret saying this, but how about we save that for next time?"

Claire flicked her gaze to his and grinned at his pained

expression, then held her bottom lip between her teeth and tentatively reached towards him.

Tucking her thumbs into the elastic waistband, she pushed the briefs down until Luke could kick them off. Then she took a step back and admired her first ever, live in the flesh, healthy, tanned, strong, marvellously and unashamedly erect naked male.

All six feet and four inches of him.

Claire indicated for him to turn around. "Wow," she breathed, her jaw falling—and staying—open. "Please don't take this the wrong way, Luke, but you are stunningly beautiful."

He smiled at her. There was no grin, no smirk, no smugness. He just smiled. And it made her want to do things to him. And herself.

"I know what I want to do," she said, unfastening her jeans and kicking them off.

Luke folded his arms across his chest and raised a brow at her. The pose lacked its usual solemnity, what with the enormous flagpole jutting out from his groin and all.

"And what have you decided we should do?" he said, still smiling as he walked towards her, slid his arms around her.

Pressed his very large, very naked erection against her.

Using her fingertip, she traced a pattern across his chest. "I thought maybe we could... watch each other... ummm... masturbate...?"

His nostrils flared. "Get in the bed."

Luke yanked back the covers and climbed in, leaned against the headboard and patted his hand on the spot beside him.

Sitting in the spot he indicated, Claire suffered an

attack of nervous laughter and covered her face with her hands. "I can't believe we're doing this."

Luke draped an arm across her shoulders and kissed her temple. His own deep chuckle rumbling across her mind and easing her anxiety. "But are you having fun?"

"Yes."

"Good, because I was thinking, if you want, maybe we could make this a regular thing. Have a weekly lesson? Preferably on a night my sister isn't sleeping down the hall."

Claire grinned at the thought of Luke Hardcastle, sex tutor. "I think I'd like that."

"Good." He kissed her temple again. "Now Miss Morse, tell me. When you masturbate, what do you fantasise about?"

Uh-oh....

Chapter Twenty-Six

Luke laced his fingers through Claire's and listened intently as she listed her go-to self-love playlist, grinning like an idiot to discover he was the star of almost all of them. Well, him and Batman. By the time she was done, her cheeks were burning so hot she could have set fire to the sheet she'd pulled over her head to hide under.

Gently tugging the sheet down again, his grin softened as he realised the courage it took for her to spill her sexual fantasies. Fantasies he'd starred in—the man who was black-mailing her little more than twenty-four hours earlier.

If that wasn't humbling, he didn't know what was.

"So, arm porn and utility belts, huh?"

Nibbling on her bottom lip, she nodded, and the uncertainty written across her face almost shattered his own calm façade. Claire wasn't the only one feeling vulnerable tonight.

"Thank you, sweetness," he said, lifting her hand and kissing her fingers.

"For what?"

"Trusting me with your secrets."

"You trusted me with your dyslexia," she said, lifting her shoulder in a half-shrug.

At the time he'd not given it a second thought. "I guess I did, didn't I?" And he wasn't inclined to examine the reason too closely now either.

Time to change the subject. "Do you want to know what I think about?" he said, moving to sit so he was facing her.

She cocked one brow at him in a show of nonchalance, but her breathy voice betrayed her nerves. "I don't know. Do I...?"

Luke stroked his cock. "Your tits. I fantasise about your tits. I have for ages."

Years.

"You have?" she said, an unmistakable hint of surprise in her voice.

Luke nodded eagerly. "Yes."

Claire leaned back against the headboard of his bed and let her legs fall open. Her gaze was glued to his hand, his cock, as she slipped her hand inside her panties.

"Tell me."

He moistened his lips, suddenly nervous. As inexperienced as Claire was, Luke had never done this before, either. It was too intimate to share with just anyone.

But Claire wasn't just anyone.

"There's one where I imagine we're in my office and we're arguing."

"What are we arguing about?"

"I don't know," he said with a laugh. "We just are. But in a desperate bid to win the argument, you cheat and flash your tits at me."

Claire laughed, then gasped, her eyes rolling back a little as she hit her good spot.

"They're so big and soft. Warm," he said. His gaze never left her face. "You know how much I want them. You tell me if I let you win the fight, if I concede to your demands, you'll let me touch them. Taste them. And...."

"And...?"

Luke swallowed hard, hoping to hell he wasn't about to screw everything up. "If I let you win, you'll let me come on your tits."

Her gaze shot to his, the steel-blue of her eyes as dark as storm clouds, hungry, almost predatory. Her mouth hitched up at the corners. "And do you? Let me win?"

Relief flooded through him, his smile was quick and broad. He stroked his cock harder. "Every time."

Claire's body undulated to its own sexy rhythm, her breath sawing in and out of her mouth, punctuated by little sighs and moans that drove him crazy. Her expression grew cautious, curious. "Do you want to come on my tits in real life?"

"Yes," he said, his voice coated thickly in lust. He squeezed his balls. "Do you... think you might let me come on your tits? In real life?"

"Yes," she whispered, the word bursting from her lips like a prayer before it was followed by a much more forceful, "Yes! Yes!" as her back bowed and her heels dug into the mattress and her hand worked like the devil inside her panties.

Luke stroked his cock harder, squeezed his balls tighter —*oh, Jesus fucking Christ*—until his body jerked and his muscles spasmed and he came, shooting his come on his stomach. For a moment neither of them spoke. They just stared at each other, their chests heaving with every breath they sucked down, their wants and needs and longing filling the air between them.

Until a slow smile stretched across Claire's face. "That was incredible."

Luke agreed. "And just so we're clear," he said, sinking back on the bed, panting, grinning. "Yes, you'll let me come on your tits...?"

Claire laughed and collapsed on the mattress beside him, entwined her fingers with his.

Breathless but smiling, she said, "Yes, Mr Hardcastle, I will let you come on my tits. Eventually."

Luke brought Claire's hand to his lips and kissed her fingers, inhaled her feminine scent. "Thank you, sweetness. And if there's anything you'd like me to do for you, just say the word."

"Blowjob."

"What?"

Propping herself on her elbow, Claire said, "That's my word." She stared at his naked body, that plush bottom lip caught between her teeth again. "Like I said, I want to lick it." Walking her fingers slowly down his chest, she tentatively drew them through the sticky mess on his skin. "I want you to teach me how to give a blowjob."

His muscles clenched and his cock twitched with renewed life. "I'm not sure if that's more of a gift for you or me," he said, watching with rapt attention as she licked his come from her fingers.

Fuck that's hot!

Then in a move he would not have expected in a million years, she leaned over him, hesitating for only a moment before swiping her tongue in a broad arc across his stomach.

And Luke almost fell off the bed.

Chapter Twenty-Seven

The next three weeks flew past in a blur.

Claire kept up an impossible pace as she continued to run Novelteas, liaise with Luke's legal department finalising the Merthyr Road lease agreements, pretend to suck up to Amanda with the false information Luke was providing, help Lottie organise a charity ball for the Cancer Foundation and date billionaire playboy Luke Hardcastle.

"You look exhausted."

"Just what every girl wants to hear." Claire sighed wearily as she finished locking up the shop, then practically fell into Luke's car. "I'll be all right. A long soak in a hot bath followed by a light supper and an early night, and I'll be good as new."

"I guess that means you won't be joining me for our candlelit dinner," Luke said. "It's our one-month anniversary."

Claire groaned. "That was tonight? I'm sorry, Luke, I forgot about dinner. Hosting that author signing today was a nightmare. Karen actually overheard the silly woman complaining about the lack of paparazzi, if you can believe it."

Luke chuckled as he pulled out into traffic. "I can believe it."

Taking a deep breath, Claire forced a smile she was certain made her look like a homicidal clown. "Okay, take me home, I'll have a quick shower, I'll put on that dress you like, then romantic dinner here we come."

Luke laughed at her fake enthusiasm. "I have a better idea. Why don't we cancel dinner, you can have your hot bath and I'll make you a light supper?"

"Hmm... bacon toastie?"

"Only if you're a very good girl," he said, reaching over to squeeze her thigh.

Since going public as a couple, the interest in their relationship had waned somewhat. Chris Marx was still a pain in their arses, taking potshots at every opportunity, but for the most part they were left alone to live their lives in peace, which most weeknights consisted of snuggling on the couch, making out like teenagers or Claire reading books while Luke watched tele.

Weekends were spent on day trips to Byron Bay and Montville, eating out at amazing restaurants she'd never known existed, making out like teenagers and agonising over paint chips in the hardware store.

Luke had also kept his word to the businesses on Merthyr Road and dispatched a team of handymen to fix the list of complaints he'd been handed the night of the proprietor's dinner.

Except her sticky front door.

Luke fixed that himself. In a move she was fairly certain was deliberate, he'd rocked up at Novelteas in his King Gees, work boots and a tool belt. He'd been the living embodiment of her fun-time fantasies—especially now she knew exactly what he looked like naked—and she'd gotten absolutely zero work done while he was there. On the upside, with Luke's pop-up workshop set up on the footpath, her walk-in foot traffic increased tenfold that day, more than making up for the paparazzi fiasco.

When Karen had seen him, she'd laughed, saying, "Bloody hell, when I told him to distract you, I didn't think he'd go full 'Construction Man Pin-up' on you."

"What are you talking about? Distract me from what?"

"Last week when you two were trying to keep it under wraps, I knew something was going on. You were distracted all the time. So when he picked you up for dinner Thursday night, I decided to have a friendly chat, told him to find a better way of *distracting* you," she'd said, waggling her eyebrows. "He tried telling me your relationship was purely business, but I totally called him on it. No man looks at a woman the way that man looks at you and has nothing but business on his mind."

"But I saw him flirting with you," she'd blurted, feeling like a total moron the moment the words left her mouth. Karen hadn't noticed.

"He tried to throw me off the scent and convince me I was wrong, but yeah, nah. The moment he saw you walking over he got that goofy grin on his face and I knew he was a goner. I'm telling you, boss. That man is crazy about you."

I'm crazy about him too.

Once inside her house, Claire left Luke in the kitchen while she collected her pyjamas and a light robe and ran a hot bubble bath.

Stripping out of her jeans and T-shirt, she stood in front of the mirror and stared at her naked body. Everything about Claire was big. Big bum, big boobs and a belly in between that would never be flat, but she still had a waist that dipped where it should, and two of the longest legs in town. So what if she had cellulite and stretch marks and a little bit of a muffin top?

She still had days when she found it hard to look at herself though, usually after her meetings with Amanda. Twenty years of being told you're fat and ugly didn't magically vanish just because you were dating a hottie.

For as long as she could remember Amanda had called Claire a freak, had said she was too big, too tall to ever attract a man. That men preferred women like her, slender and petite, women they could toss over their shoulder caveman-style.

Women who made them feel like real men.

And with no one to tell her any different, Claire had believed her.

Until Matt asked her out.

Matt Taylor, the first man to use Claire as a stepping-stone at Morse Industries. Next was Colin Newland then Doug Sands. Young and naïve, she'd fallen for their lines time and again, but with every betrayal of her trust she'd retreated a little more, built her walls a little higher.

Dreamed a little less.

And now Luke was breaking down her walls brick by brick and the thought made her smile. True, he'd started out using her to gain access to Amanda, and also true, it wasn't that long ago she'd wanted to push him in front of a bus, but time and time again he'd proven she could trust him. And time and time again she felt herself falling for him in a way she'd never felt before.

Climbing into the bathtub, she slid beneath the bubbles, and a sigh of pure bliss escaped her as the hot water worked its magic on her tired body and overfull mind. Out in the house she could hear Luke pottering around, a few minutes later she heard music playing.

"Thank you," she called out.

"You're welcome," he shouted back.

Their one-month anniversary, huh? The more she thought about it, the more she knew exactly what to give Luke. A slow smile spread from ear to ear.

She was ready.

Chapter Twenty-Eight

Luke found a tablecloth, wine glasses and some not completely unusable candles and set the table for dinner, then he set up his phone to play some music—an Aussie artist Claire had said she liked—and chuckled when she yelled out her thanks.

The bathroom was located beside the dining room and the sounds of Claire bathing were driving him crazy, filling his head with images of her small, strong hands lathering soap all over her soft curvy body. Worse, he imagined *his* hands lathering soap all over her soft curvy body.

Hello steel pipe. We meet again.

Putting some much-needed distance between himself and the bathroom, he strolled through the house instead, inspecting the renovation work she'd been doing in the lounge room. It took roughly five minutes before he tired of looking at corbels and skirting board samples and headed across the hall.

Towards her bedroom.

Besides the night he came back to retrieve his suit jacket, Luke hadn't been in Claire's bedroom. Every time they'd had a sleep-over, Claire had slept at his place. At first it had been to shield her from more paparazzi bullshit—his building had the superior security—but even as the interest in them died down they'd continued to sleep at his place instead of hers.

The door was ajar. A quick glance down the hall and the sound of splashing water confirmed she wasn't coming out of the bathroom anytime soon. A slight nudge with his toe and the door swung open. Standing in the doorway he took in the scope of the bedroom, one of the only rooms in the house even remotely finished. Her bed frame was a sea foam green cast-iron monster, sturdy, practical and built to withstand a nuclear blast wave.

Which meant it should also withstand vigorous sex.

The rest of the room was tastefully decorated in a mixture of creams, greys and various shades of blue and green. Stacks of books crowded the small table on one side the bed, a vase of soft pink roses and her mobile phone on the other. And on her bed was a handmade quilt designed to look like a bookcase, complete with a sleeping cat on the bottom shelf and a teacup on the top. Even as a man who knew nothing about sewing, he could appreciate the workmanship that went into creating such an exquisite piece. He made a note to ask Claire about it later.

An antique kitchen chair sat in one corner of the room, a pile of discarded clothing stacked on top of it and what looked like black lacy lingerie draped over the back of it.

"Oh, sweetness," he murmured, and rubbed his hand over the erection tenting his trousers. "When do I get to see you in those?"

Leaning in a little farther he inhaled and caught a lungful of Claire's scent, that sweet, sexy aroma that drove him crazy with lust, yet somehow managed to completely relax him.

The sound of a bathtub draining brought Luke back to reality and had him hurrying back to the kitchen to cook the perfect bacon toastie.

Not long after, Claire appeared in the doorway, a light cotton bathrobe wrapped tightly around her body and cinched in at the waist, the belt tied in a bow. Her hair sat piled on top of her head like the laundry on her chair, messy but purposeful, and had some sort of clip holding it in place. He wanted to reach out and let loose her hair, wanted to run his hands through its silky length, wrap it around his fist and guide her mouth to his cock, like he had at their weekly lessons.

And if Luke didn't know better, he'd almost think she was thinking the same thing, the way she fidgeted with her the belt on her robe and her gaze darted to his hard-on.

"Good timing," he said, and held out a chair for her.

"Thanks." Claire took her seat. "This smells fantastic."

"Bacon toasties, as requested. And a glass of bubbly for the lady?" he said, displaying a bottle of mineral water for her perusal like it was the finest champagne.

Claire laughed. "Ooh, *schmancy*. An excellent vintage, I presume."

"Only the best for my woman," Luke said with a grin as he poured.

Despite their joking, the meal was eaten in near silence, neither of them seeming to know what to say. Luke watched the candlelight cast shadow puppets on the walls, little flickering figures that danced around them in time to the music still spilling from his phone.

As she finished her meal, Claire was the first to break the deadlock. "Thank you, Luke," she said.

He half-shrugged then stood to clear the dishes. "It's just a bacon sanga. No big deal."

"Not just for dinner, I mean about everything. Oddly enough if it wasn't for you blackmailing me, we would never have become friends, and if we'd never become friends, we might have never become *more* than friends."

"What are you thinking, sweetness? Because I know you're thinking something."

"I... I'm thinking about going to bed," she said, her voice strange, uneven.

"Right," Luke said, a mixture of confusion and disappointment pulling at his brow. That wasn't the answer he'd expected. Or hoped for. "I'll let you get that early night, then. Just don't forget about tomorrow. We have a big day."

But before he could take two steps down the hall, Claire grabbed his arm. "Luke, I'm thinking about going to bed... with you." She raised her eyebrows like she was trying to communicate with him somehow, some secret code about going to—bed.

Realisation struck and he felt weak at the knees. "Do you mean what I think you mean?"

Claire bit her lip and nodded.

"Say it."

She swallowed hard. "I'm ready."

Luke stared down at her, stroked her cheek. "Are you sure? I don't want you to feel pressured into something you're not ready for."

She slid her arms around his waist and snuggled against his chest. "I trust you. I'm ready."

Reaching atop Claire's head, Luke grabbed the clip holding her hair in place and released it then tossed the clip over his shoulder. Her hair tumbled down around her, the dark waves framing her face like a work of art. Sliding one hand around her waist, the other around her neck, he returned her embrace, held her where he wanted her and tilted her face to his.

A hairsbreadth separated his lips from hers. "If you're sure...."

Claire chuckled against his mouth sending tingling little vibrations through his lips. It felt weird, but pleasantly so. "How many times do I have to say it?"

Scooping her up, he tossed her over his shoulder, and amid a barrage of cursing and laughing and pleas to put her down, he carried her down the hall to her bedroom.

Putting her back on her feet, he smiled as she pushed her hair out of her face then stared up at him, something akin to awe shining in the depths of her steel-blue eyes. "You tossed me over your shoulder. Caveman-style."

Luke frowned. "Was I too rough?" It wouldn't be the first time a woman had complained he'd manhandled her. Sometimes he forgot his own strength.

But Claire shook her head, a broad smile on her pretty face. "I liked it."

Luke relaxed and pulled her to him again. "Good. Because we're just getting started."

Chapter Twenty-Nine

Claire traced the line of Luke's jaw with her fingertip, then dragged it down his throat, slipped it under his shirt collar and tugged. "This. Off."

Without a word he kicked off his shoes and wrenched at his tie, discarding them in seconds. His shirt quickly followed, the buttons flying across the room and pinging off her dressing table mirror as he ripped the fabric from his body, as impatient as she was to get this show on the road.

Luke's gaze never left hers, and she heard more than saw him stripping his lower half—the sound of a belt buckle jingling, the purr of a zipper, the whoosh and thud of trousers falling to the floor.

Stepping back, she allowed her gaze to travel over Luke's magnificent body. It didn't matter how many times she saw him in all his splendour, her heart raced and her mouth ran dry.

He was simply exquisite.

Feeling overdressed, she yanked on the belt of her robe and somehow made the knot tighter. Why was she so nervous? Oh, yeah, because the man she loved was about to take her virginity.

Her breath stalled in her lungs as her brain gave voice to what her heart had known all along.

I'm in love with Luke Hardcastle.

Strong hands settled over hers and stilled her trembling fingers. "Allow me."

Within moments the knot at her waist had been expertly unravelled and her light cotton robe lay in a soft puddle at her feet.

"Fuck," Luke growled, and the slack-jawed expression on his face told her the pale pink satin and lace cami and panties combo she'd chosen to wear were on point. He moistened his lips. "Get on the bed."

Claire didn't need to be told twice.

Throwing back the covers, she wished she'd thought to change the sheets, then dusted off the biscuit crumbs and crawled in.

"Stop!"

On her hands and knees, Claire froze halfway across the bed. "What's wrong?"

Big, warm hands stroked over her arse. "Absolutely nothing. I just wanted more time to appreciate the view."

Laughing, she turned to face him. She knew what he was doing.

The first rule. *Relax.*

Kneeling on the bed, Claire slid her hands over Luke's stomach and chest. His skin was warm, his muscles hard, and as she stroked her fingers up over his broad shoulders and down over his exceptional biceps, she realised how happy she was. Not just because one of the finest specimens of manhood in Australia—and quite possibly the Southern Hemisphere—was standing in her bedroom, nearly naked and rocking a hard-on in his boxer-briefs that would leave lesser men weeping in envy, but because she was in love with an amazing human being.

Luke Hardcastle was an intelligent, kind and thoughtful man, and at that moment, he was all hers.

With little more than a gentle tug she pulled Luke onto the bed, and with the flash of a wicked grin she found herself pinned under his muscled weight.

"I want you, my sweet woman," he growled, nuzzling the sensitive flesh just under her earlobe, nipping and kissing her neck, her jaw until his mouth claimed hers again.

And as always, his hands sought out and quickly found her breasts.

Claire grinned and whimpered and sighed. Luke had a way of touching her that was both sexy and fun and he could turn her on as easily as he made her laugh. And did so frequently.

But this time was different.

This time wasn't just their *first time,* it was also the first time Luke would see Claire completely naked. Sure, they made out like sex starved teenagers every chance they got, but as per their agreement it only ever went so far and no further. It was only during their weekly sex lessons that their clothes came off, and while Luke had been happy enough to strip down to only what God gave him, Claire had been more reserved and kept at least her panties and a T-shirt on at all times.

Luke had respected her decision, said it made the antici-pation greater. Claire hoped he wouldn't be disappointed. Just because he thought she was sexy with her clothes on didn't mean he'd feel the same when they all came off.

Gravity was a bitch.

Rolling to her side, Luke stroked his hand over her belly, fingered the soft satin. "Tonight is all about you, Claire," he said, his voice deeper than usual, quieter. "I want to give you the pleasure you've given me. I want to make your first time memorable for all the right reasons. Will you let me do that for you?"

An overwhelming sense of freedom filled Claire's heart with joy. She didn't hesitate to answer. "Yes," she whispered, her eagerness making her breathless. Her hands fisted in the sheets by her sides. She wanted to reach out and touch him again, stroke the svelte strength of his arms, nibble his earlobe, play with the soft hair on his chest, or better yet, follow the thin trail of it that disappeared below the waistband of his boxer-briefs to the thick erection beneath.

Luke smiled and his face was almost boyish, bashful. "I love your body," he said, sliding his palm over one satin covered breast then the other. "It's so warm and soft, so sensitive, so responsive."

Luke pinched her nipple and she almost arched off the bed. "Luke!"

"That's it, sweetness," he said, gently tugging until her cries became moans. "I'll have you screaming my name all night long."

Chapter Thirty

Moving over her, Luke slowly kissed a path leading down, settled his head against the swell of her breasts and showered them with attention. It had been almost a month since the first time he'd had Claire in his bed, and in all that time he hadn't once seen her naked tits.

The anticipation was killing him, but he'd promised himself he wouldn't rush.

The satin separating his hand from her flesh had been warmed by her body. It was soft and slippery and slid over her skin so easily it would've been nothing to slide it all the way up and reveal her breasts to his hungry gaze. Or....

"Are you particularly attached to these pyjamas?" he said, straddling her body.

Claire's brow pulled down. "No, not particular—"

Riiiiip....

Luke tore the satin right down the middle and her breasts spilled free.

Stunned into silence, Claire stared up at him with an

odd look on her face. He couldn't quite tell if she was incredibly turned on, horrified or needed to pee.

Until she said, "Fuck me. Please, Luke, fuck me now."

Definitely turned on.

He waggled a finger at her and *tsked*. "Good things come to those who wait."

"Yeah, all I heard was blah, blah, come, blah, blah, blah."

Luke burst out laughing. "Horny little shopgirl," he said, then he lowered his head to finally, blessedly take her nipple in his mouth.

Listening to Claire suck in a breath as his lips made contact with the sensitive little bud, then slowly let it shudder back out was the most erotic thing Luke had ever heard. He wanted to record the sound and play it back, over and over on his way to work, wanted to plug in his headphones and listen to it when he went to the gym. Fuck, he wanted to make it her ringtone and insist she call him every day.

That tiny sighing breath was the new soundtrack of his life.

And he wanted more.

Cupping both breasts in his hands, he delighted in the feel of her skin, as soft and warm as the rest of her. And while he suckled one nipple, he tortured the other, plucking and pinching and twisting in a calculated rhythm that would heighten her pleasure, and therefore his.

Claire's fingers dug into his thighs and he could feel her legs twisting as she writhed beneath him. "More, oh God, more."

Luke had never made a woman orgasm from nipple play alone but thought Claire might come close. She was so free with her reactions, so honest in her responses.

"Mmm... harder...."

So open to experiencing pleasure.

His cock twitched, eager and ready, and Luke pulled away.

"No! More."

Claire's demands were accompanied by her sharp little fingernails digging into his thighs causing him to grunt in pain.

"You'll get more, sweetness, but if you don't sheath those claws the 'more' you get will be a lot less pleasurable." And he pinched her nipple harder until she cried out in agony. "Understand?" She nodded. "Say it."

"Yes, Luke, I understand."

"Good girl."

Giving her aching bud one last gentle suck—and almost coming in his pants as she whimpered—he kissed his way lower. Starting between her breasts, he skimmed his lips slowly south, over her stomach and around her navel, all the way down to the top of her panties. Then tucking his thumbs under the satin and elastic he shuffled his way down her legs tugging her panties down with him.

The soft curls he'd felt the night he'd discovered her secret were finally revealed to him, and as he dropped the scrap of satin and lace on the floor, he leaned down to inhale her scent. Clean and fresh, she smelled faintly of flowers and woman.

He had to taste her.

The moment his tongue made contact with her clit, Claire gasped. Her pelvis lifted off the bed and Luke used the movement to slide his hands under her arse and hold her steady while he ate his fill.

She tunnelled her fingers through his hair and whimpered. Luke loved the sound, wanted more. Took more. He licked her clit with hard flicks of his tongue then sucked the nub until she cried out for more. He teased and tasted and slid one finger inside her until he felt the barrier he'd felt before, only instead of shock and wonder, this time all he felt was eager.

To be Claire's first lover was a prize he'd never known he'd wanted, but to be her last would be even better. He knew it was selfish of him—he'd had his fair share of lovers while she'd had none—but the thought of another man putting his hands on her made him want to hit something.

She was his woman.

His lover.

His.

"Yes... more... please...." Claire writhed beneath him and her breathing quickened. He sucked her clit harder, thrust his finger a little deeper. She was so wet, so tight, and as she came apart and screamed his name her body clamped down around him. He watched her ride the waves of her orgasm, saw her first man-made O-face and felt so completely in love with her he almost let it slip out.

Not yet.

Not until he knew she was as addicted to him as he was to her.

When the last of the tremors had left her and her eyes were shuttered and her smile was the goofiest he'd ever seen it, Luke slipped off his briefs and lay down beside her.

"How do you feel?"

"Can you ask me again, but call me Miss Morse?"

Luke chuckled. His woman was an odd one but *fuck* if he didn't love her for it. "How do you feel, Miss Morse?"

"I feel amazing, Mr Hardcastle, thank you for asking."

Luke kissed her shoulder, slid his hand down her body

and savoured every inch of her ample flesh. "Are you ready for more?"

Turning to face him, all joking gone from her face, she stroked her fingers along his jaw. "Yes. I want you."

Luke pulled away only long enough to sheath himself with a condom then he was on top of Claire again. He hadn't lain with a virgin since he was one himself, but he remembered the girl's fear well enough. Nuzzling Claire's throat, he whispered breathy nothings in her ear, kissed her cheek, tasted her mouth, reassured her with every loving caress of his lips that he would be gentle with her.

He would make love with her.

Luke's erection was hot and hard as it waited, poised and ready to begin its intrusion inside her. She tried to relax, to lose herself in Luke's hot kisses and scorching touch but as he slid inside her she couldn't help but clench up.

"Relax, Claire," he cooed. "Breathe for me." She started breathing in slow steady breaths and Luke timed his thrusting to match. He pulled back and slid in, again and again and she could feel him stretching her, pushing against her barrier. She could feel the heat and the pressure of his cock trying to invade her body.

"Are you ready?" Luke whispered by her ear.

"I'm ready," Claire said, planting her feet on the bed with her knees bent, and her favourite naked person on top of her, sinking deep inside her.

All the way inside her.

Biting her lip to stifle her cry, white hot pain shot through every nerve in her body. But then it stopped, and she realised Luke had too.

"Take a moment. Breathe. When you're ready, I'll move again."

Claire stared into Luke's dark golden eyes and saw the strain on his face. Was he in pain too? "Are you okay?"

He spoke through gritted teeth, his breathing was harsh. "Christ, you're tight. But it feels so fucking good inside you. I have to move, Claire. I have to fuck you."

Biting her lip, she nodded. *"Please."*

A wave of relief washed over his features and he rocked his hips, slowly at first, gently, giving her time to adjust to his body, to his size.

He really was a big man.

Sighing in unison with Luke's rhythmic thrusts, she got quite a shock when he lifted one leg around his hip and sank in a little deeper. Curious to know what would happen if she copied the action with her other leg, her head fell back and she moaned as the most glorious pleasure lit through her.

Claire had been ready to accept she probably wouldn't have an orgasm her first time. She'd read it was common not to. But she also recognised the telltale signs of a climax building inside her. Only this wasn't like any orgasm she'd ever felt before. This felt different, fuller. More. This felt like all the joy in her body was trying to explode out of her all at once and anyone caught in the blast radius was in for a fucking surprise.

Joygasm!

"Am I hurting you?" Luke's eyes had darkened, and his thrusting was less even than it had been. A slight frown pulled at his brow.

Claire was quick to reassure him. "Not hurting. It feels... so...."

"Good?" He looked so hopeful.

"Yes. Yes, good." She gasped. "*Sooo* good."

Her orgasm chose that exact moment to send her temporarily blind, tearing through her like wildfire, lighting her up in places she'd never known existed. "Luke!"

"Claire!" Luke's body jerked and shuddered against her, his breathing was fast and heavy. "*Faaark.*" Then he collapsed in a sweaty heap on top of her.

Claire wasn't sure how long they lay there like that, but it was Luke who broke the silence, his voice the rich purr of a self-satisfied male. "You're all mine now," he said, then brushed his lips against her temple, rolled to her side and gathered her up in his arms.

How was she supposed to respond to that? She knew what she wanted to say, that she'd been an idiot to deny him her body all this time, that she was his whenever he wanted her, that she loved him.

That she hoped he loved her back.

Her head gave her heart a little rope.

"I was always yours," she whispered.

Just enough rope to hang itself with.

Chapter Thirty-One

"Hardcastle," Luke growled, blindly answering the phone beside the bed.

"Luke?"

"Lottie? What the.... What time is it?"

"I have a better question for you. Why are you answering Claire's phone?"

Luke's eyes flew open and he swore softly. He'd forgotten where he was, forgotten he was sleeping in Claire's bed instead of his own.

Answering the phone had been an automatic reaction.

Glancing beside him he smiled, content as he saw his lover still curled up beside him, her hair strewn across the pillows, her creamy breasts exposed above the sheet.

And completely undisturbed by the phone call.

"But to answer your question," Lottie continued. "It's ten to nine. You two were supposed to pick me up twenty minutes ago. I called Claire looking for you. Your phone is going straight to voicemail."

Luke swore again. "Sorry. The battery's probably dead."

"So, was it a late night or an early morning?" she said, happily laughing at him.

"Shut up."

"Fine. When can I expect you?"

Luke looked at Claire beside him and his body swelled with burgeoning need. "We'll pick you up at ten for brunch."

"See you then, lover boy."

Scowling at his sister's teasing, he hung up the phone. Claire shifted beside him, the sheet falling away to reveal more soft creamy flesh, warm and inviting.

Luke selected a rose from the vase on the bedside table, then propped himself up against the bedhead. He had a glorious view of Claire's body, the cotton sheets outlining that of her figure not already exposed.

Damn she's got long legs.

Starting at her shoulder, he dragged the rose petals over her skin, traced the swell of her breasts, watched her nipples pucker into tasty little buds. Over her subtle swell of her belly, her hip, then over the backs of her fingers and along the length of her arm. He'd almost made it back to her shoulder before her eyelids fluttered open.

He bent to kiss her mouth. "Good morning."

"Yes, it is," she said, smiling up at him.

Their lips met and Luke lingered, wanting to take the kiss deeper, but he didn't dare. They were late enough as it was. With a dramatic sigh he pulled back.

"What's wrong?" Claire's eyes widened.

"We have a problem," Luke said seriously. "After last night... the sex... your body.... How can I be expected to keep my hands off you now?" Then he demonstrated his point by tossing the rose away and grabbing her boobs.

Her fearful expression replaced by a withering glare, then followed by a snort of laughter, Claire swatted at Luke's hands until he let her go. Then she got to her knees and straddled his lap, wrapped her fingers around his already hard and raring-to-go cock.

Luke shook his head. "Do you see what you do to me?"

"Yep." Claire smirked at his dick then looked up from under her lashes. "Do you want to see what else I can do to you?"

Groaning with sexual frustration, he said, "My dear, I would love nothing more than to be at the mercy of your tight, wet pussy. Unfortunately, we have shit to do. It's time to get up."

Her groan of disappointment was a soothing caress to his male ego. "What time is it?"

"Around nine."

Claire swore. "Lottie's going to kill us," she said. "How do we explain why we're so late?"

"Tell her the truth. We overslept because we're exhausted after indulging in amazing sex. All. Night. Long," he said, then stole another kiss.

Claire cheeks pinkened. "We can't tell her that. What will she think?"

Luke wasn't sure what his sister thought, besides the fact she seemed to find the whole thing rather amusing, which he found confusing at best, suspicious at worst.

"Lottie already knows," he said, examining his tattered business shirt. "I don't suppose you have any of my T-shirts here?" He moved to the chair in the corner and started looking through the clothes piled on top of it.

"What?"

"T-shirts?"

"Before that. Lottie knows?"

"She rang looking for us. You didn't wake up," he said, finding and yanking his favourite Star Wars T-shirt of the pile. *I'd wondered where you'd got to.* He slipped the shirt over his head. "I forgot where I was and answered the phone. Force of habit." At Claire's sudden stiffening he added, "Answering the phone I mean, not forgetting where I am. And Claire, we've been dating for weeks. Everyone already thinks we're having sex."

"Yes, but thinking it and knowing it are two very different things. Ladies don't kiss and tell."

Luke grinned and cocked a brow. "I'm no lady, and I didn't tell her anything. I just answered the phone." Pulling her into his arms, he gave her arse a playful squeeze and pushed his fresh erection against the apex of her thighs. "Now, whaddaya say we get out of here before she feels the need to call us again?"

As they drove through the city to the hospice, Luke couldn't help stealing glances at the woman who sat beside him. The woman who was smiling serenely and blushed every time he caught her eye. Reaching over, he laid his hand on her thigh, smiled when she threaded her fingers through his.

Claire Morse was so very beautiful to him.

So vulnerable, so desirable.

His.

When Lottie had asked Luke to embark on the endeavour of exposing Amanda Morse and her means of success, he'd been delighted some of his rancour had finally rubbed off on his little sister, that she'd finally seen just how much she'd been screwed over by the underhanded bitch. And her suggestion to use Claire to aid in their mission had seemed like a good idea at the time.

His investigator had discovered Claire was the main number cruncher on the Cassidy Holdings deal. She'd been the one to tell Amanda how much profit could be made by cutting up his sister's company and selling it off bit by bit. And that tidbit of information had sealed her fate along with her aunt's, as far as Luke was concerned.

It also closed the book on any fantasies he still harboured about the only woman who consistently made his head turn no matter how hard or how often he fought the attraction.

But now....

He was tired of fighting.

Claire had no choice in the things she'd done for her aunt. It was basic survival. Do as you're told and you won't get hurt. She'd apologised, anyway, for her part in the whole damned mess. And both he and Lottie had been satisfied with that.

Over the month, she'd also filled in the gaps in his report, like what her actual job at Morse Industries was, the names of the men who had tried to use her, and how she'd ended up in Amanda's care in the first place. The report said her parents had died in a car accident, but the truth was far more tragic. Her mother had indeed been killed in a car accident. Her father survived, though severely injured. Unable to endure the chronic pain he'd been left with and unwilling to live without the love of his life, he'd killed himself. An overdose of painkillers. Claire had found him on the couch the next morning, stone cold and still.

A week later she was living with Amanda.

And when he asked what it was like growing up with her aunt, she'd said, "My father's corpse was warmer than that woman."

One thing he still found baffling was what Claire did to

make Amanda cut her off and kick her out. The official report said she was fired for misconduct, but that excuse covered a multitude of sins, and Claire wasn't confessing to anything. No matter how many times he asked.

What did she do?

Chapter Thirty-Two

After brunch, Claire and Lottie got down to the very serious business of shoe shopping. Luke bowed out after the second store—lightweight—but the women had made it their mission to visit every shoe store in the Queen Street Mall.

And there were more than a few.

"I just can't find the right pair of shoes to match my ball gown," Lottie declared to every shop assistant they encountered. "Help me!"

By the time they reached the dress fitting Lottie needed the shoes for, she still hadn't found the *perfect pair*.

Claire liked Lottie. She was the type of person anyone would assume was a right ditz on first meeting her, but she hadn't become the youngest CEO in Brisbane by chance.

Charlotte Cassidy was a certified genius with an off-the-scale IQ.

She was naturally vibrant, bubbly and outgoing and made connections with people within seconds of meeting them. She was exceedingly funny, her humour leaning towards the dark side, and she was unafraid to speak her mind no matter who she upset or how much trouble she got in.

Claire had to admire that. She'd never been able to stand up to people. She was Amanda's perfect little yes-man.

Until the day she wasn't.

And what a spectacular failure that had been. Instead of earning her aunt's respect for standing up for herself and what she cared about, she'd incurred her wrath and found herself staying in the local homeless shelters faster than one could say "fiscal downturn", scrounging for food and sleeping with one eye open, more terrified than she'd ever been in her life.

"When in doubt, wear flats," said Nina Barbeau, Lottie's friend and fashion designer extraordinaire. "Flats go great with everything. The hard part is finding the right colour."

"What about you Claire? Have you decided on a dress yet?"

Lottie's question reeled in Claire's wondering thoughts and she looked up to see her still standing on the dressmaker's pedestal, having her hem pinned. The Regency style gown suited her long, slender frame, and the pale gold satin and embroidered chiffon made her appear almost regal. Her short dark hair added an air of nonchalance not many could pull off.

"You look amazing," Claire said.

"Thank you," Nina and Lottie replied at the same time, then laughed.

She turned her attention to the flip book in her lap. Claire hadn't seen anything she thought she'd look good in and was beginning to feel like a complete heel.

Ever since that ridiculous article outing Luke and

Claire as a couple, Lottie had been so patient with her. She'd helped her navigate the ins and outs of dealing with the paparazzi and had even helped debrief her after her meetings with Amanda, making jokes at her aunt's expense, making her cups of tea and devouring half her cake cabinet.

Claire had still been wary of her new friend though, as they'd hunted through shoe shop after shoe shop, the issue of Luke answering her phone hanging thickly in the air between them.

Eventually she'd just blurted out, "Are you mad about me and Luke? With, you know, him answering my phone this morning."

She felt like such an idiot asking these things—an almost thirty-year-old should know this shit, right?—but she had no experience to guide her.

No good experiences anyway.

"Why would I be mad?" Lottie had replied. "You make my brother happy."

It struck Claire as truly amazing how five little words could make her feel so wonderful.

"You make my brother happy."

With that thought in mind she flicked the pages of the album back and forth a few more times, then shook her head. The dresses in the pictures all looked so delicate and fine, much too fine for her big frame. It wasn't as though she'd never been to a formal event before, she'd been to many, but Amanda had always chosen her outfits.

Uncomfortable, unflattering, uninspired creations that essentially covered her from top to toe and gave away nothing of the woman underneath.

"Can't I just re-wear the dress I'm wearing to the party tonight?" she muttered, closing the album.

"That's a cocktail dress. The charity dinner is more formal. You need a ball gown."

Not wanting to spew her insecurities all over the place, but also not wanting to insult Nina, Claire tried to be diplomatic. "I'm not sure these designs would suit me," she said.

"Rubbish," Lottie said, hopping down from the pedestal.

Averting her gaze while her friend slipped out of her dress and into her jeans, Claire shook her head. "I'm not a model, Lottie. I'm not one of those girls who could wear a potato sack and make it something *très chic*. Stick me in a potato sack and I look like a sack of potatoes."

Lottie let loose and exaggerated sigh. "Nina, I think we need a fashion intervention here."

"Lottie, I couldn't agree more," the designer said. "Miss Morse, if you would please strip for me."

"What?" Claire pushed herself as far back into her chair as possible. She'd only gotten naked in front of her lover for the first time less than twenty-four hours ago and these women wanted her to get *whaaat*? "Ah, no. I'm good thanks." But suddenly Nina had one hand and Lottie had the other and they were hauling her to her feet.

"Strip," Lottie and Nina commanded together.

"Come on, love, we're all girls here," Nina said. Claire just stared at them, cheeks blazing and eyes wide. "This is couture, love. I need to see how your body sits naturally, how it moves, so I can tailor the dress to fit your body the best way possible and emphasise your assets. You can leave your undies on. We're not total savages."

She gritted her teeth. "Fine."

Five minutes later Claire stepped inside a mirrored cocoon that showed off every lump, bump and dimple on her body, feeling more like a freak every moment she stood there, and more embarrassed than she'd ever been in her life.

"Bra off too," Nina said gently.

Clenching her jaw, Claire slipped her bra off and slung it over the top of the mirror. She fisted her hands by her side, fighting the urge to cover her breasts. Nina stood in front of her with her hands on her hips and scoured Claire's nakedness with an intensity that made her feel like a bug under a microscope.

"Well now, let me just say for starters... great tits," she said, giving Claire two thumbs up. "Fabulous legs, long and shapely." She indicated for Claire to turn around slowly. "Good round bum. Geez, there's nothing scrawny on you, is there, love? Hmm... back in a sec."

Nina quickly returned with three dresses of various styles and colours.

"Now, don't worry about the sizes, I can adjust everything to fit."

They held the first dress up in front of her, a sea green gown with a short train, lace detail and halter neck. Nina and Lottie ummed and ahhed then screwed up their noses and shook their heads.

The second dress was a disaster from the start. Claire didn't *do* frills. And as much as she loved the colour purple, that particular shade made her look like a giant bruise.

The third dress was a more than a little snug, but it was her favourite of the three.

Lottie liked it too.

A red satin sheath nipped in at the waist with a long split in front that showed off her legs when she walked.

"It's perfect," Claire said. "Why wasn't this in your album?"

"It's new," Nina said, dress pins sticking out of the

corner of her mouth. "I had planned on adding a red velvet belt with a Swarovski crystal brooch stitched into it."

"I think Claire's right, Nina. It's perfect as it is."

The designer looked over the top of her glasses at both of them, her gaze curious. "Why?"

Claire and Lottie exchanged a look, then said together, "Jessica Rabbit."

"What?"

"Luke has a thing for Jessica Rabbit." Claire grinned.

"Yep. He always has. Reckons she's the perfect woman."

Nina looked up at Claire as she pinned the hem. "Well then, I can see why he likes the look of you. And with your china fine complexion and dark hair, Manhattan Red is definitely your colour. By the time we're done, you'll look stunning."

Stunning? Me? Claire turned to face the full-length mirrors again and hardly recognised herself.

Stunning. Me!

"Luke won't be able to keep his hands off you," Lottie said. "In fact, we may have to keep you covered up until we get to the ball, just to be sure you arrive unscathed."

Claire laughed. She was happy, truly happy and it made her stand a little taller, feel a little less scared.

"I have a question," Nina said, resuming her pinning. "If Luke's dream girl is the very definition of voluptuous, why does he date all of those flat chested, bony-arsed stick insects?"

That was a very good question.

And Claire didn't have a single answer.

Chapter Thirty-Three

T he party was a promotional affair, a product
launch for a local winery. The *Kookaburra
Queen*, the paddle steamer that traversed the Brisbane River, was the evening's venue and photographers and
journalists lined the red carpet leading to the gangway.
Reluctantly, Luke stopped with Claire and Lottie to pose
for photos then ushered the women on board.

Luke was immediately greeted by the emcee and introduced to the vintner, Nate Bellows. A man no older than
Luke, Bellows had an easy manner and tanned skin that
proved he worked outside an office.

The men shook hands as Luke introduced Claire and
Lottie. He didn't miss the other man's eyes lingering on
Lottie for longer than was considered polite.

Bellows cleared his throat and held out his hand, beck-
oning a willowy blonde to his side. "I believe you know
Morgan York," he said. Luke's ex wrapped her arms around
Nate's neck and whispered in his ear.

Luke tightened his grip on Claire's waist, pulled her

closer. Although whether it was to protect himself or her, he didn't know.

"Luke Hardcastle," Morgan purred. "It's so good to see you again. And you must be... Blair, is it?"

"Claire," Luke corrected with forced politeness.

"Of course. And you must be Luke's sister," she said, taking Lottie's hand in hers as though she were handling the most fragile thing in the world. "It is so good to see you up and about."

Luke opened his mouth to say something but a warning look from Lottie kept his temper in check.

Silence ensued.

Discomfit followed.

Bellows cleared his throat again and excused himself to greet more guests. Morgan trailed after him but cast Luke a coy smile over her shoulder.

Claire shifted by his side, tilting her head as she watched Morgan walk away. "Wow. And I thought I had insecurity issues."

Luke looked down at her, momentarily stunned, before laughing out loud.

"You're amazing," he murmured as he wrapped his arms around her and shuffled her towards a table laden with *hors d'oeuvres*.

Picking up a fat prawn, he dipped it in sauce then put it to Claire's lips. He groaned as her teeth sank into the juicy morsel. Sauce covered her bottom lip.

Leaning forward, Luke said, "Allow me."

Turning her face away from prying eyes, he lowered his mouth to hers and sucked her lip between his own, then kissed her long and deep. "By the way," he whispered when they came up for air. "When we get home, I'm going to rip this dress off you with my teeth."

Then he pulled back to enjoy Claire's blush, slipped his arm around her waist and began the arduous task of circulating in the crowd.

The party progressed as parties do. Food was eaten, wine was drunk, and gossip was shared. Claire was never far from Luke's sight. Even while he danced with Lottie or chatted with business associates or leaned against the deck railing while he got some fresh air and pretended to watch the city lights dance on the surface of the river.

He couldn't keep his eyes off her.

"I love your rebound girl," a familiar voice sounded at his elbow.

Luke turned to see Morgan York by his side, her short blonde curls bobbing in the gentle breeze, the scent of expensive perfume wafting from her throat.

"No, really I do," she continued as though they were sharing a private joke. "Lifeless hair, dull eyes, huge arse... I can see why she caught your eye."

Luke thought better of responding and simply walked away.

He didn't get far.

"You can stop torturing yourself. You can have me back anytime, you know. Just say the word, Luke, and I'm yours."

"For fuck's sake." Luke turned back to Morgan with a pained expression. "Please tell me you're not using Bellows to get back with me? I made it quite clear months ago, we're not compatible and I'm not interested in continuing our little... whatever that was."

Morgan slid her hands up Luke's chest and adjusted his tie. "And now I'm calling your bluff," she said with a self-assurance that bordered on cocky.

She tried to press her body against Luke's, but he stepped back and removed her hands from his clothing.

"No bluff, Morgan. It's over. It was over before it began."

"Nate is very successful you know. He has boutique vineyards here in Queensland and in Western Australia. And he's gorgeous. Even your rebound girl hasn't been able to take her eyes off him. Aren't you even a little jealous?" she asked, mischief twinkling in her clear blue eyes.

Not of you *and Bellows.* Luke shoved his hands in his pockets. "Nope."

Mischief turned to malice in the blink of an eye. "You can't just toss me aside like last month's fashion rag, Luke. We had something special. What could fatso over there possibly give you that I can't?"

Besides the most erotic night of my life?

Luke shoved the thought down before he said something cruel. "I've neither the time nor the patience to put up with your childish tantrums. We both know what you're after, Morgan, and it isn't me."

"But—"

"But nothing. You will stay away from me and my sister, and you will most definitely stay away from Claire."

Morgan's only reply was to flash Luke a picture-perfect smile before turning on her heel and stalking away.

He watched her disappear into the crowd before turning to stare at the water. His hands clenched the railing so tightly his knuckles blanched and the tiny scar on the palm of his hand ached. The last thing he needed was his gold-digging ex causing trouble.

Luke couldn't even remember why he'd asked Morgan out. She was beautiful, there was no doubt about that, but she was also greedy, spiteful and mean, and her friends were much the same. But at the time he'd not cared. For eighteen months—for ten years—he'd not cared what type of woman he dated as long as they weren't Claire Morse.

I'm an idiot.

Instead of trying to eradicate her image from his mind with tawdry women and meaningless sex, he should have been storming Morse Industries and sweeping her off her feet. Rescuing her from her shitty life and abusive aunt.

But he had her now. His sexy, sassy, cardigan wearing, tea drinking, independent thinking, shy, fire-spitting Claire. The beautiful, stubborn woman who didn't expect him to pay for everything and even argued with him over the price of pizza. Who wasn't scared of drinking tea with full cream milk and sugar or eating pasta covered in creamy sauces, and wasn't afraid to tell Luke off, to say 'no' to him.

Claire, who wanted more than anything else his friendship.

Luke walked in from the balcony, his mood settling the moment he saw his lover. She was standing with Nate Bellows, her pretty face animated as they chatted away, her eyes alight with humour.

She beckoned him to her without saying a word.

The paddle steamer slowed as it hit the halfway point and turned back towards Southbank. The party was slowing down too, the guests gathering around tables, talking and laughing, or slow dancing on the open dance floor. Claire was sipping wine, imitating Bellows as he swirled the golden liquid in the glass and held it up to the light.

He couldn't wait to get her home, to fold her into his arms and make love to her again.

But just as that happy thought made his cock jump to attention, Morgan sauntered over and joined Nate and Claire. Draping herself over Bellows like a strangler vine, she took a sip from his glass and made pouty faces as Nate continued conversing with Claire.

Slowly he made his way over to the trio, smiling to himself as he compared the women.

Morgan, for all her travelling and hobnobbing and apparent sophistication, lacked maturity. And while her face was considered one of the most beautiful in the world, the rest of her reminded Luke of a porcelain doll. Cold to touch, prone to damage if handled too roughly and empty on the inside.

They'd had sex only once in the three weeks they were together and as far as Luke was concerned, it'd been one time too many. The sight of her bony hips and barely-there breasts had turned him off entirely, and his size compared to hers was exaggerated by their nakedness, but they'd had sex anyway, as uninspired and unsatisfying as it was.

Not like last night.

Sex with Morgan had been harsh, painful even. For both of them.

Sex with Claire had been a lesson in sensuality.

Her soft, plush body had accommodated his, had wrapped him up in her tight, wet embrace and wrung him dry with the most intense orgasm in living memory. And when he'd lain on top of her, delighting in feel of her body still clenched around his cock, in the smell of sweat and sex and roses, she'd held him close. She'd not insisted he was squashing her, had actually laughed when he'd suggested it.

To a man who didn't know better, Claire looked plain next to a top fashion model like Morgan, but the way her eyes would change from a pale silvery blue to a dark steel depending on her mood, and the way her lips formed such a perfect pout that begged to be touched and kissed, just like the rest of her with those delectable curves begged to be touched and kissed, made her far more desirable than any woman he'd ever met.

Locking his gaze to hers, he took her hand and kissed her knuckles.

"You have to try this," Claire said, her cheeks darkening.

Without a word Luke took the glass from her fingers and sipped the chardonnay. He sampled the flavour of the wine, savoured the crisp fruity notes and let the chilled liquid slide down his throat.

"Magnificent," he said, his eyes still locked with hers.

Morgan barked out a laugh.

Claire lowered her gaze, but Luke raised her face again and winked, bringing a shy smile to her lips.

"You make good wine," he directed at Bellows.

"Thank you. I was just telling Claire you two should visit my Mount Cotton set-up sometime. And Lottie too, of course," he added with a subtle hint of inquiry.

Luke raised an eyebrow at the mention of his sister.

"I've just opened a restaurant there, with plans to open at my other winery next year," he said, smiling with honest good humour.

"Yes, I understand you have another vineyard in Western Australia?"

"That's right, down around the Margaret River region."

Luke slipped his arm around Claire's shoulders. "We may have to visit. I was going to lure Claire away to Perth with me in a couple of weeks. I don't see why we couldn't extend our trip to include a tour of the Margaret River. Maybe even stop by the famous Chocolate Factory...?" he added with a sly grin and a raised brow.

"Maybe," Claire said, returning Luke's grin as he bent to kiss her mouth.

"*Blergh*. All those calories," Morgan blurted out. "Don't you care about your health."

Claire turned away from his kiss. "I.... Excuse me," she said softly.

Luke tightened his grip on her shoulders, but she shrugged him off and walked away. Morgan threw Luke a gloating look and walked off in the opposite direction.

"I'm sorry about Morgan," Bellows offered, sounding as awkward as he looked.

Luke's mouth pulled down at the corners. "So was I."

Chapter Thirty-Four

Claire found the bathroom and leaned against the bench, stared in the mirror and desperately tried not to cry. She'd been doing so well. Not once in the last month had she argued with Luke when he said she looked pretty in that dress or lovely with her hair down or even more beautiful naked....

Who the hell was Morgan York to tell Claire she was fat?

Okay, so she didn't actually say the 'F' word, but it was implied for all to hear.

For Luke to hear.

And it reminded Claire of that other 'F' word she used to hear a lot.

Freak.

As a girl she'd been tall and awkward and a little on the chubby side. She'd never felt comfortable in her own skin. As a woman she'd learned to accept her height and curves as indelible fact and, eventually, to be proud of them, but over the past month—and certainly in the last twenty-four hours —she'd gained a whole new perspective on the subject.

It turned out size was relative. And when you found the person you were meant to be with, they didn't care what shape you were or how much you weighed, they showered you in compliments and kisses simply because you were theirs.

Claire had been sailing on a high ever since Luke tossed her over his shoulder caveman-style and had his wicked way with her.

And in less than two minutes that walking bobble-head had destroyed her self-esteem and Claire found herself floundering back at square one.

Logically she knew Morgan's comments were coming from a place of jealousy and insecurity, but when those comments were being delivered by a woman who looked like the fucking embodiment of Aphrodite herself, it was a pretty quick trip back to the corner of Freak Street and Fat Avenue.

Morgan had made Claire look foolish in front of Luke. Worse, Claire had let her. She'd just walked away without so much as an angry glare in her general direction. Chris Marx had put his hands on her and she'd threatened to throw him in the river. Morgan York insults her and what does she do?

Hide in the bathroom.

"Claire?"

Luke's voice preceded a gentle rapping on the bathroom door and a quiet creaking as it slowly opened. His head appeared around the edge of the door. "Are you alone?"

Claire double checked the stalls. "All clear."

"Are you all right?" He drew her into his arms and held her against his chest and she couldn't stop her tears from leaking out. Luke's arms tightened around her. "Don't let that spiteful brat spoil our evening."

Snuggling against Luke's chest, Claire inhaled his scent and let it wrap around her. She leaned into his strength and heat, listened to his heartbeat and let it sooth her nerves.

"It's not just her," she said, taking a deep breath. "I've been hearing whispers all night. I've tried to ignore them as best I can, but Morgan was the last straw."

"Whispers? About what?"

"About us. How you're using me for rebound sex, and I'm using you for your money. How you must be either blind or desperate or both to be sleeping with a fat... *slut* like me."

"Morgan." Luke spat the woman's name out then cupped Claire's face in his big hands so she couldn't look away. "We can discount the first two comments to begin with. We both know I'm using you for revenge and you're the one using *me* for sex."

He said this with such a straight face that Claire burst out laughing.

"Much better," he said, wiping an errant tear from her cheek. "And as for that last comment, I am neither blind nor desperate, and you, sweetness, are the most beautiful woman I've ever known."

Luke's words wrapped Claire in a world of confusion. She wanted to believe him, wanted to shrug and shake it off and be the confident woman she'd been at the beginning of the evening, before Morgan's little barbs started sticking in her flesh and stinging her pride.

But the simple fact of the matter was, Morgan's words sounded so much more familiar to her than Luke's.

All her life she was told how unwanted she was for one reason or another, and apparently it was going to take more than a few weeks of being told otherwise to change her psyche's mind.

Luke sighed. "You don't believe me, do you?" He sounded angry.

Claire opened her mouth to answer but no words came out. She shook her head.

He hooked a knuckle under her chin. "Is it because Amanda took every ounce of self-worth you ever had and ground it into dust? Is it because that self-serving, sanctimonious miserable bitch forced all of her own insecurities down your throat, raising you to believe you're not worth a damn just so she could feel good about herself?"

Claire opened her mouth again but closed it when she felt the tears filling her eyes. Her chest felt tight and her stomach churned but she nodded, acknowledging her shame.

"You are a beautiful, passionate woman, Claire Morse. And I'm going to tell you that as often as I have to. Until you believe me."

She searched Luke's eyes, looking for the truth in his words. "Why?"

"Because you *are* worth a damn. No matter what anyone else tells you, you're worth a damn to me."

Without another word Luke slashed his mouth over hers, telling her with that simple action he believed every word he'd said.

Luke believed she was beautiful.

He believed she was sexy.

He believed she was passionate.

Then she believed it too.

Leaning into the kiss, Claire deepened it, entwined her tongue with his. Luke growled against her mouth as he backed her up against the bench and lifted her onto its edge. He slid his hands under her skirt and up her thighs, spreading them wide, nestling himself between them, then curled his fingers around the edge of her panties. A quick yank and a quiet rip and he had an all access pass to Claireville.

"I'll buy you more," he said, shoving the torn lace in his pocket.

Next he attacked her dress, his lean fingers making short work of the zipper at Claire's back. "Oh, sweetness," he groaned, tugging her dress down to reveal the black lace basque she'd finally had the guts to wear, and no longer had the panties to match.

Claire clawed at Luke's chest. She wanted to rip his shirt from his body the way he'd done in her bedroom and send his buttons shooting off all over the place. She wanted to rip open his pants and let loose the huge erection she could feel pressed against her.

Reaching between them, Claire cupped his rock-hard dick. "I want you inside me," she said, then gasped as he slid two fingers into her hot, wet centre.

"This will be quick and dirty, sweetness," he murmured by her ear. "But when we get home, when we have more time, I'm going to show you exactly how beautiful you are."

Claire bit her lip to stifle her moans and Luke pistoned into her with the same determination he'd used to seduce her the night before. Bringing her easily to orgasm, he muffled her cries of ecstasy with his mouth as she bucked uncontrollably against his hand.

With one arm around her waist, Luke held her as her pleasure subsided, but before her trembling ceased completely, he bent his head to tease her nipples from their lacy prison. Latching his hot lips around one tightly puck-ered bud, Luke sucked hard, and Claire had to roll her lips between her teeth to stop from crying out.

The purr of a zipper brought her back to the now as

Luke exposed himself to her appreciative gaze and eager caress. Reaching into his jacket pocket, he pulled out a condom and within moments he'd sheathed himself, gripped her hips and yanked her forward. Claire watched, mesmerised as Luke fisted his hand around the base of his cock and slowly guided it forward, filling her up inch by inch until he was seated deep inside her.

"Christ, you're tight," he groaned, wrapping his arms around her again, holding her close. "Tight. Wet. *Fuck!*"

His mouth crashed against hers in awkward, jerky movements, mimicking their bodies as he slammed himself inside her. Claire slid her hands under his jacket and raked her nails down his back, drawing him closer still.

But it wasn't enough.

She wanted all of him. His mind, his heart, his soul...

But she would settle for his body.

For now.

Luke kissed a trail across her cheek, flicked his tongue around the shell of her ear then nibbled a path down her throat. Claire had read books about erogenous zones, knew all the ins and outs of heightened sexual responses and what to expect, but she was quickly learning there was no substitute for hands on experience. And Luke was a very hands on teacher, touching her in ways that made every inch of her come to life with unrepentant desire, desire that was demanding release and making her want to scream with the frustration of keeping quiet.

Tunnelling her fingers through Luke's hair, she pulled his mouth back to hers, the heat of his twisting tongue the only thing capable of ensuring her silence.

But all too soon the tension of her building climax made her whimper and writhe. The hurried yet powerful thrusts of her lover's hips, the thought they might be discovered at any moment, the heat of his breath against her neck and face...

It was all too much.

"Luke..." His name burst out of her on a gasp of breath as her body began spasming, clenching down on him, wringing every bit of pleasure she could out of him. Then Luke tightened his grip and his body jerked, his face buried in the crook of her neck to stifle his own cry of fulfilment.

Resting his head against on her shoulder, Claire held him there with shaking hands.

Slowly the blood stopped pounding in her ears and her breathing calmed to normal. Luke lifted his head and Claire stroked his cheek, then snaked her hand around his neck and pulled him back for one last lingering kiss.

Helping her to her feet, he said, "Are you sore?" At seeing her confusion, he continued. "You only lost your virginity twenty-four hours ago, this was the fifth time we've had sex in that time, and I know I'm... a bit *bigger* than most men. I just want to make sure I'm not hurting you. That's the last thing I want."

Claire realised what he was asking. "Oh. Um, yeah. I'm a little bit sore, but I've read that's normal, so I'm not worried about it. And the payoff is kinda worth it," she said, smiling up at him. He grinned in return.

"Turn around. I'll zip you up."

Claire checked her hair and makeup in the mirror while Luke tucked her boobs away and zipped up her dress, then she realised in wide eyed horror Luke had been facing the mirror the entire time.

He'd not only participated in their tryst but watched it too.

At first the thought mortified her, then she saw his

reflection grinning wickedly at her and she couldn't help laughing, at herself, at him.

At the torn panties sticking out of his pocket.

Luke nuzzled the back of her neck and slid his hands under her skirt again, squeezing her naked arse with one while slipping a long lean finger through her slick curls to rub at her clit with the other.

Claire slapped his hands away even as she giggled, thankful the skirt of her dress came down to her knees.

All she had to do now was avoid sitting down.

And strong updrafts.

Chapter Thirty-Five

Luke woke up alone.

He didn't like it.

Feeling the sheets on her side of the bed he found them warm. Wherever she was she hadn't been gone long.

His body ached with need. His heart with want. He wanted Claire, needed her deep, soft, tight body. He wanted her back in bed, under him, on top of him. As long as she was naked and in his arms he didn't care. He just wanted her. In his life.

Forever.

Throwing back the covers, he moved to sit on the edge of the bed, leaned his arms on his knees and rested his head in his hands.

Life was so much simpler without women.

If they weren't trying to steal his money, they stole his heart. And so far, there was only one woman who couldn't care less about the size of his bank account, who knew there was more to life than money.

Claire valued friendship and honesty. She trusted him.

Even after everything he'd put her through, she trusted him. And there was nothing Luke wouldn't do to keep that trust.

Almost nothing.

He wouldn't give up his plans for revenge, not only because Amanda Morse deserved to be knocked off her perch, deserved to be revealed and reviled for the mendacious bitch she was, but as long as he sought that plan of action he knew he could keep Claire by his side, in his bed.

Once all of this was over, once Claire got the evidence Luke needed, he wasn't all together sure he wouldn't lose her. He wasn't blackmailing her anymore, and she'd offered to help but that didn't mean when all was said and done, she'd stick around.

Claire was an independent woman now. She had her business and her house and her life, the life she'd built for herself through sheer bloody-mindedness. Why would she give that up for a man? For him? And he would never ask her to, not knowing what he did about her upbringing.

She finally had her freedom and he'd never take it away from her again.

Getting to his feet, Luke stretched his muscles, but he needed more than that to ease the tension riding his spine. He hadn't liked waking up alone, his body tightly wound with need, and he knew of only three things that helped relieve that tension. He couldn't face a cold shower, Claire had already left the bed so that left push-ups.

If he'd been single or gone to bed alone it wouldn't have been a problem. Luke would happily push out a quick twenty just to wake himself up before facing another punishing day in the corporate world.

Hell, he'd done push-ups almost every morning since he was thirteen just to try and bulk up his already freakishly tall frame. But he'd discovered they had other benefits when he was sixteen and started dating girls, before he'd discovered sex was a much more satisfying way of relieving tension.

Going to sleep with a beautiful woman in his arms meant his body expected a beautiful woman to be beside him when he woke up, and that meant his arousal was more demanding and edgy than usual. But even if he pushed out a solid fifty, he doubted it would take the edge off this morning. Still, he tried.

Slowly rising from the floor, he listened hard. No noise. Lottie must still be asleep. So where was Claire? Pulling on an old pair of board shorts he went in search of her and found her doing yoga in the large open living space, her feet together, legs straight, hands on the floor, her glorious arse pointed squarely at him.

And *oooh* the urge to slap that arse... *Jesus....*

He just stood in the hallway and watched her, mesmerised by her indecently short candy-striped boxer shorts and tight pink curve hugging singlet as she moved from one impossibly twisted position to the next.

He thought about doing more push-ups but really didn't think they'd help at this point. Slowly he stalked towards Claire. She turned at the sound of creaking floorboards, greeted him with a blinding smile.

"Good—"

Luke stole her greeting with a frenzied kiss, his tongue lashing, his lips crushing, his need all consuming. But the sound of a throat clearing, cut through to his lust-addled brain and he knew it wasn't him, and it wasn't Claire, so....

Turning towards the dining table he saw his sister eating cereal and reading the morning paper.

So much for Lottie sleeping in.

His sister's eyes danced with good humour and when

she turned the newspaper around, he could see why. The social pages were filled with pictures of people at various events from Saturday night, including Nate Bellows' wine launch.

Luke took the page from her and stared at the photos, grinning at the one of him and Claire in a passionate embrace, oblivious to the camera, their lips locked, his hands groping her arse, a filmy scrap of lace protruding from his pocket. The photo was captioned, *"Luke Hardcastle and Claire Morse, a couple steamier than the balmy Brisbane nights."*

There was also an interesting shot of Nate and Morgan. While Morgan was clinging to Nate for dear life, the wine maker's eyes seemed bashfully engaged elsewhere.

"Poor bloke," Luke grunted, "I hope he's as sensible as he seems and gets rid of that gold-digging twit quickly."

"Oh, he is," Lottie said, looking smug. "And he has."

"How do you know?" Luke asked with a frown.

Claire sidled up to him and slid her arms around his middle. He draped his arm around her shoulders and pressed a kiss to her temple, loving the natural easiness they'd fallen into over the past few weeks.

"Because after you two, uh... *disappeared*... Nate followed Morgan outside to have a few quiet words, only they didn't stay very quiet. He called her greedy and childish and she called him an old leather handbag. Then he told her it was over, and she told him to jump overboard. And then Morgan teetered away on those *ridiculously* high heels of hers and began drinking anything she could lay her hands on, and Nate asked me to dance. Oh, and he's escorting me to the ball, FYI."

"I see," Luke said, that last tidbit of information sinking in. "And does he know about...?"

Lottie stiffened and shot him one of those little glares she reserved just for him. "Yes, he does. Oddly enough he likes me anyway."

Luke nodded but said no more on the subject. Lottie was a big girl, and as much as he wanted to wrap her up in cotton wool and hide her away from the world, he knew better than to try.

The last time he'd tried telling her who she could and couldn't date, she'd switched out his hair product with hair removal cream. More than fifteen years had passed since then, but the memory still stung.

"So, we have a few hours to kill before the barbeque at the Campioni's. Who's up for a swim?"

Chapter Thirty-Six

Friday night seemed like a lifetime ago.

Claire sat in silence as Luke drove her home, feeling drained and emotional. Restless.

Luke was quiet too. He'd spent most of the afternoon watching his sister while wearing a guarded expression on his face.

She broke the silence with an educated guess. "Are you mad about Lottie and Nate?"

"Not mad," he said, sighing. "Concerned. What is she thinking starting a new relationship with someone?"

"She's probably thinking she's not dead yet and Nate is hot." Luke glared at her. Claire shrugged. "What? He is. And you can't tell Lottie not to do things just because she's sick."

"No one's ever been able to tell Lottie what to do. That's not what this is about."

"Then what?"

"She's all I have left!" he said and smacked his hand against the steering wheel. "And every time she overtaxes herself, she weakens just that little bit more, steps a little closer to death's door, and call me selfish if you like but I want my little sister to stick around for as long as possible."

Claire sat very still as silence shrouded them once more, as Luke reminded her that all of this, everything they'd done in the last month, everything they would do until they took Amanda down, was temporary.

Lottie was all he had left.

As much as she'd avoided thinking about it, Claire had always known it would end this way. But hearing him dismiss her so out of hand still hurt. A lot.

And, yeah, maybe she'd tried to forget Luke Hardcastle didn't exactly have a sterling reputation where relationships were concerned, and maybe she'd sort of shoved to the back of her mind the fact she was the complete opposite of every woman he'd dated in the last ten years.

And maybe she'd even been one of those total morons who thought they'd be the one to change his ways and he'd fall head over heels in love with her and they'd settle down and live happily ever after....

Except Claire didn't get happily ever afters.

She never had.

She never would.

So, she did what she'd always done. Lifted her chin and soldiered on.

Survived.

"I've never had a family of my own," she said. "Not really, so I don't know how it feels to lose the people you love one by one, but I do know when you find people who make you feel like you belong and go out of their way to help you, who make you feel safe and actually give a damn —" She clenched her jaw to rein in her tears as she heard herself repeat what Luke had said to her. "Those people are your family too. It doesn't have to end with Lottie."

His only response was to reach for her hand and press a kiss to her knuckles.

When they arrived at Claire's house, he helped her carry several containers of barbeque leftovers inside and stacked them in the fridge, then asked if he could stay the night, as if he wasn't sure she'd say yes.

As if she'd say anything else. She was selfish and greedy and pathetic and wanted to spend every available second with him while she could. "Of course you can stay."

He slipped his arms around her waist and bent his head to kiss her, but just as their lips met, his phone rang. "Shit." He looked at the screen and swore again then hit the answer button. "Hardcastle."

Claire tried to slip away and give him some privacy, but Luke grabbed the back of her T-shirt—the back of *his* T-shirt—and yanked her backwards against him. The first thing she noticed was the huge erection stabbing her in the butt, and despite herself, she grinned.

Turning to face him, she dragged her fingernails down his chest to the waistband of his jeans, made short work of the button and fly. Luke pretended to scowl at her, shook his head and pointed to his phone.

Tapping her finger against her chin, she pretended to think about it for a moment, then pushed his jeans down and followed them to her knees. Luke stared down at her with a pained expression but as she freed his cock from his briefs, his gaze darkened, his pupils dilated, and an overwhelming sense of power sizzled through her.

The first swipe of her tongue made Luke gasp, the second had him rolling his lips between his teeth, but the moment she wrapped her mouth around the head of his shaft his hand fisted in her hair and his hips began thrusting. Slowly and with purpose.

The feel of his hand guiding her, the sound of his breathing, ragged with the effort of keeping quiet, spurred Claire on to take the lead. To relax and have some fun.

She might not have him forever, but she could have him right now.

Cupping his balls in one hand and grasping his cock with the other, she ignored all the rules and the tips and the tricks and she worked his flesh with everything she had.

Luke's jaw tightened. "I'll check my schedule when I'm in the office tomorrow, but it shouldn't be a problem. Yep. Sorry, mate but I have to go. I was in the middle of something when you rang. Yeah. Yep. Jesus! No, I'm fine, just a cramp in my leg. Okay. See ya."

——————— ———————

Luke couldn't hang up fast enough.

When Claire had sunk to her knees and pulled out his cock, he didn't think she'd actually go through with it—sucking him off while he was on the phone? It wasn't her.

Clearly, he was wrong.

Not only was she sucking him off, but he was ready to explode. "Claire... sweetness...."

She sucked harder and his fists tightened in her hair, holding her steady as he thrust into her mouth. Eyes closed, head falling back, his pleasure built and built, until....

Faaark.

As his breathing calmed to normal, he helped Claire to her feet and pulled up his jeans. Then mentally slapped himself as he realised the probable cause of her impromptu blowjob. Scooping her up in his arms, Luke headed for the bathroom.

"What are you doing?"

"Taking care of you," he said softly, putting her back on her feet.

The only other room in the house to have been fully renovated, the bathroom was of a modest size and tastefully decorated in black and white. In the centre of the room stood a beautifully restored cast-iron claw-foot bathtub, big enough for two.

Once he got the water running and added some bath salts, he started stripping Claire. She'd already kicked her shoes off so that just left his Van Halen T-Shirt and denim shorts. The shirt was the first to go.

"I can undress myself," she said, avoiding eye contact.

"But I like undressing you. It's like unwrapping my favourite present."

She snorted. "Does that line usually work on women?"

"You tell me. I've never said it to anyone but you."

Slowly Luke stripped her of clothing until she stood there, naked. Beautiful. His. His own clothes followed with much more haste. Taking her hand, he helped her into the bathtub then he climbed in behind her.

It was a tight fit in the tub. Obviously the two people who were supposed to occupy it were much smaller than Luke and Claire. He rested his feet on the outer rim to give her more room to move.

"I'm sorry, Claire," he said, massaging her shoulders and neck.

She made a delicious moaning sound he wanted to hear more often. "For what?"

"For saying Lottie was all I had left." The instant he

said the words, she stiffened, and he knew he was right. He'd hurt her. "It's been just the two of us for a while now, and even before our parents died, we were always close. Letting someone else in isn't easy for me, and hearing Lottie talk about Nate... I don't know. It felt like I was losing her. Sooner than I have to. But you're right. People don't need to be related to be family and Lottie isn't all I have left. Because I have you."

Water splashed over the sides of the tub as Claire tried to turn around. She got about halfway and stopped but it was enough for her to look him in the eyes.

"What do you mean, you have me?" Her steel coloured eyes were wide and hopeful, yet not. "Our relationship isn't real," she said, shaking her head. "It's all for Amanda. It's all for show. I mean, yes, we've been having some fun along the way. But we're consenting adults. Friends with benefits, that's what you called it."

Luke sighed and stroked her hair. "I keep forgetting how inexperienced you are."

"Meaning," she said, her eyes narrowing dangerously.

"Meaning I was teasing you. Claire, sweetness, this became a real relationship the moment I stopped black-mailing you. At least it did for me."

"But Friday night was the first time we had actual sex."

Luke chuckled. "Sex has nothing to do with relation-ships. It's just the icing on the cake. And yes, it has been a lot of fun, but getting to know you, spending time with you, talking to you, learning all about you and telling you about me.... I think you'll agree it's a very old-fashioned way of doing things. But everything about you, Claire Morse, is a little old fashioned," he said, indicating the ancient bathtub and antique pedestal basin.

"I like older things," she said, her tone defensive. "They're more homey."

"Does that include me?" he asked, one brow raised.

"I'm not sure I'd call you homey."

"Oh? Then what am I?"

Her smile was blinding. "Mine."

Chapter Thirty-Seven

The day of the charity ball arrived.

Luke checked his watch and huffed an impatient sigh. "And they tell me I'm always late," he grumbled.

Nate Bellows waited with him. At Lottie's insistence, they'd spent the day together and Luke had used the opportunity to remind the man that Lottie was his only sister, and if anyone were stupid enough to break her heart the authorities would never find his body. Such were the advantages to owning a construction company that poured several metric tonnes of concrete every week.

The winemaker surprised him by nodding in agreement and saying, "Fair enough."

Lottie was the first to emerge from her room, gliding across the floor in a dress that could best be described as a golden breeze, and looking so much like their mother his heart hurt.

He was about to say something, but Nate got there first. "You look like a goddess," he said, his voice awestruck.

Lottie smoothed her hands down his jacket lapels then

leaned up to kiss him. "Thank you. You're looking pretty fabulous yourself."

Checking his watch again, Luke called out, "Come on, Claire. We're going to be late."

"What else is new?" Claire said. "I don't think I've been on time to anything since I met you."

Luke spun around in time to watch his lover enter the room and all speech deserted him. Just when he'd thought they couldn't be more right for each other, she had to prove him wrong. They weren't just right for each other. They were meant to be. And Luke had known it, had felt it the very first day they'd met when he'd almost worn five coffees, before his temper and his arrogance had gotten in the way and wasted the next ten years of his life.

His real girlfriend was dressed like his movie girlfriend. No, actually, the dress Claire wore would put Jessica Rabbit to shame. It was the perfect mash-up of fiction and reality and she was the sexiest woman he'd ever fucking seen.

Taking a moment to absorb the vision before him, Luke admired the way the red satin dress left nothing to the imagination, clinging to every single one of Claire's luscious curves. A long split revealed one shapely leg after the other as she glided towards him on red satin stilettos that inched her over six feet tall. Her long dark hair had been styled in soft waves, and her sensual pout was painted as red as her dress.

But something was missing.

"Wow. I think I broke him," Claire said.

"Not broken," Luke said. "Just calculating the fallout if we didn't go tonight."

"You even *think* about ditching after all the work Claire and I have put into this and you are dead to me." Lottie glared at him like only Lottie could.

"Fine, we'll go. But first...."

Luke pulled a king's ransom worth of diamond jewellery out of his pocket.

"Are you on your way home from a heist?" Claire said, her eyes wide as he beckoned her closer. "Where did you get those?"

Luke grinned. "You know that antique jewellery place you refuse to go into because you can't afford to buy anything?"

"Yeah."

"It turns out, I can afford to buy everything. But I restrained myself and bought you these," he said, handing her a pair of Art Deco drop earrings. "And these," he added, fastening wide matching bracelets around her wrists.

"Luke, they're beautiful. Thank you."

Pulling her into his arms, he said, "Will it ruin your make-up if I kiss you?"

She smiled. "I can always fix it if it does."

Luke took her mouth in a passionate yet brief kiss, then said, "I need to grab something."

"Is it my arse," Claire whispered when Luke stole another kiss.

He grinned against her mouth. "No, but I like where your head's at. Back in a sec."

——— ———

When they arrived at the ball, they were confronted by a media storm. The red carpet was lined with reporters and photographers and filled with their fellow guests. Overwhelmed by the spectacle, Claire stuck to Luke's side like glue and let him guide her through the worst of it until they were safely inside.

If inside the ballroom could be considered safe.

Even upon entry Claire could hear Amanda laughing like a jackal, fawning over a young man too stupid to know a succubus when he saw one.

And then there were the models.

One table had been bought by the Mod Dolls Modelling Agency, the people who represented Morgan York. And several other of Luke's ex-girlfriends. Who all just happened to be in attendance.

Greaaat....

Claire gave them a healthy dose of side-eye as she and Luke coasted past their table, but she'd have to be blind not to notice Morgan amongst the crowd. She looked stunning.

Old insecurities crept sideways through her brain, tried to steal her good mood and self-esteem, but just as she lifted a hand to fiddle with her hair, Luke dragged her into the staging area to the side of the main ballroom. Ignoring the comings and goings of the wait staff, he pressed her against the wall and slashed his mouth over hers.

And Claire forgot all about feeling nervous and insecure.

Luke's offer to ditch had been tempting. Dressed in a black dinner suit with a crisp white shirt and white bowtie he looked good enough to eat. And his scent was driving her wild.

All of him was driving her wild.

Slipping one hand inside the split in her dress, he hoisted her leg around his hip. His erection fit perfectly in the notch between her thighs.

Claire gasped. "People are watching us."

"Don't care. I want you. Now," he breathed hotly against her neck.

"Luke, we can't."

"Sure, we can," he said. "There's a hotel right next door. Let's be bad and rent a room. No one will miss us."

"Your apartment is ten minutes down the road," she said.

"More like thirty by the time Edward brings the car around. I don't think I can wait that long," he groaned, pressing his forehead to hers. "This dress is disturbingly arousing, and I have a hunch you're wearing equally inspirational panties. I want to strip you down to nothing but those diamonds and eat your pussy til you scream."

Claire was so turned on, wanted to escape with Luke so much it almost physically hurt to turn him down. "We can't. Lottie's counting on us."

Growling his frustration, Luke slowly released her leg and helped to straighten her dress, then leaned his forehead against hers again until their breathing calmed and his erection subsided.

When they were in the clear he held out his arm. "Shall we?"

It didn't take long for Claire and Luke to be separated, and once they were, it took even less time for the vultures to circle.

Amanda was the first to swoop.

"My, my, haven't we been decked out to the nines this evening. What's all that bling worth do you think? Two, three hundred thousand? A cool half million?"

Claire didn't miss the acidic note of resentment in her aunt's voice, so she smiled as smugly as possible and fingered the diamonds. "I honestly didn't think to ask."

"It must be nice... but, no, I shouldn't say anything."

Trying her hardest not to roll her eyes, Claire said, "Yes you should, Aunty. What were you going to say?"

"Well, it's just with all the money he throws at you, the

dresses, the jewellery, *your house*.... It's just nice to see you've finally stepped up."

"Stepped up?"

Amanda snagged a glass of champagne from a passing waiter. "Yes, after all the fuss you made over the man when you left Morse Industries, about morals and codes of ethics, et cetera, it's just good to see you've realised what absolutely horseshit it all was."

"And how exactly did you come to that conclusion?"

"Because you're taking him for all he's worth, darling. The ice dripping from your every limb tonight proves that, and I must say well done. I mean it Claire. I'm almost proud of you. Gold-digging whores the world over will be clamouring to learn your secrets. Tell me—"

"Claire, here you are." Lottie grabbed her arm. "I'm so sorry to interrupt but I need you. It's an emergency."

"Excuse me, Aunty."

"You're welcome," Lottie said when they were out of earshot. "You looked like you needed rescuing. Are you all right?"

"My only living relative just congratulated me on successfully becoming a gold-digging whore. I think it's safe to say I'm *not* all right."

"Your face was turning as red as your dress. You looked about ready to explode."

Claire took a deep breath then slowly let it out. "I think that's what she had in mind."

"Maybe you should go find Luke. From what I saw of him earlier, I think he could use your company too. Maybe I should've left you two at home."

Luke lost sight of Claire just as she was accosted by Amanda. Every instinct in him said he should keep an eye on her, but it just wasn't possible in the crush of the crowd. To pass the time until he could be with Claire again, he made the effort to socialise and spoke with a number of people from the Cancer Foundation and chatted quietly with one of Lottie's doctors. But just as he was accepting a glass of champagne, he found himself facing two men he didn't know.

"Matt Taylor," the first man said. "Head of Acquisitions at Morse Industries."

"Doug Sands. Accounting."

"Luke Hardcastle," said Luke coolly, recognising their names immediately. They were two of the men who hurt Claire. He shook their hands more firmly than necessary.

"Oh, we know who *you* are," said Taylor. "And we wanted to ask you, how did you do it?"

Luke regarded Matt Taylor with unabashed disdain. The man was at least four inches shorter than Luke and very thin. His suit hung on him like it was still on the coat hanger.

This guy thought he was man enough for Claire?

"Do what, exactly?"

"Transform Claire Morse from virgin to vixen," chimed in the other one. "Who knew she could look like that?" Then he whistled through his teeth.

Narrowing his eyes on Doug Sands, Luke took his measure. This one reminded him of a bulldog—short, brawny and tactless.

"I don't discuss my private life with strangers," Luke said, but he couldn't seem to escape the asinine pair.

Taylor chuckled. "Ten bucks says she's giving you the run-around too."

Sands piped up. "Can't say I'm surprised. I dated her for a month and all I got was a fucking case of blue balls. Bitch can kiss though. I'll give her that."

"I tried every trick in the book for two whole weeks," Taylor continued. "Never made it past first base. If I'd known she could look like that, though, I might have persevered."

The sound of breaking glass was the only warning they got before Luke let loose his temper. "One more word about Miss Morse, just one, and I'll personally throw you out on your arses. Stay the fuck away from her or you'll deal with me."

Folding his arms across his chest, he used his superior height and size to his advantage. Luke was a big man with a bad temper. He didn't lose it often, but when he did it was spectacular. The smaller men cringed, then scurried away like rats under Luke's blazing glare.

Looking down at his feet he saw the champagne flute smashed on the floor. Looking at his hand he saw he was bleeding.

Claire's gunna be mad I cut my hand again.

Grabbing a passing waitress, he told her about the broken glass, then asked for directions to a first aid kit. And after assuring her he was quite capable of applying a Band-Aid all by himself, Luke patched up his hand.

"Hardcastle, I've been looking for you."

"Chris Marx." Luke sighed heavily and closed the first aid kit with a bang. "This night just gets better and better."

Chapter Thirty-Eight

Claire wandered the ballroom for what felt like an age before finally spotting Luke. He was disappearing into the staging area again. And he didn't look happy.

Maybe I should take him home.

Turn that frown upside-down.

In nothing but diamonds....

With that delicious thought sparking all sorts of naughty scenarios in her mind, she followed him to the staging area, but stopped just short of entering when she heard raised voices.

"Stay away from Claire," Luke said. "I won't have her upset. Not tonight."

"Man's gotta make a living somehow. Especially since you cost me my last job."

"When your job is spreading rumours and lies and passing it off as entertainment, I can't imagine your employers put much faith in things like loyalty. You got yourself fired, Marx."

The other man was Chris Marx? A slow smile spread

across Claire's face at the thought of that perverted gossiping arsehole being on the receiving end of one of Luke's tirades. She settled in for the show.

"I grabbed a chick's arse. No one would have cared if she wasn't your alleged girlfriend."

"Alleged?"

"Oh, come off it, Hardcastle. One, she's the niece of the woman who destroyed your sister's company. Two, by pure coincidence you just happen to start dating her at the same time she reconciles with her aunt. Three, I only knew where to find you because someone sent me anonymous emails telling me where to look. Sound familiar?"

Wait, what? Claire's good humour slipped, and her heart beat faster than a hummingbird's wing. That's how Marx knew she'd be at the ferry with Luke?

Someone tipped him off.

Luke swore to her it wasn't him but who else could it have been? No one else knew where they'd be or where they were going.

Not even me.

"Fuck you. This conversation is over."

"I'm right, though, aren't I? It's all a big scam. Some sort of payback for what happened to your sister."

Time slowed to a crawl as Claire waited for Luke's response. She had to strain her ears to hear him say, "Let's say you're right, what's in it for you?"

Her heart cracked. *No.*

Her nose burned as tears threatened and she clenched her jaw against the sensation. Now wasn't the time to be weak.

"Money," Marx said.

Luke laughed without humour. "It always comes down to *fucking* money."

"Look, I don't really care why you're doing what you're doing, but if you want me to keep it out of the news then you'll pay me for the privilege."

"I see," Luke said, his tone contemplative. "How much?"

Marx laughed, an unpleasant sound that made Claire's hair stand on end. "To keep it out of the news, or to keep it quiet from Miss Morse? Yeah, I've seen the doe-eyed way she looks at you. She doesn't have a fucking clue, does she?"

"How much?" Luke said, his voice tight.

Blood pounded in Claire's ears as her life, her heart fell apart, and before she could think better of it, she turned the corner, revealing herself. "Yes Mr Marx, how much?"

"Claire," Luke took a step towards her, but she took a step away. "This isn't what you think."

"What I think, Mr Hardcastle, is that you two deserve each other," she said, proud of herself when her voice didn't betray her grief. "What I think is it's time to put this whole mess to bed once and for all, and if either of you know what's good for you, you'll stay the fuck out of my way."

Turning on her heel she marched back out to the ballroom, only clutching at the ache in her chest when she was certain Luke wasn't following her.

He'd gotten his revenge after all.

But not completely.

There was still one Morse standing, and Claire would be damned if she was going down alone. Taking a deep breath, she surveyed the crowd. Laughing, happy people stood in every direction, mocking her in her despair.

But then she saw her.

Amanda Morse.

As she stormed towards her aunt, anger the likes of which she'd never felt before rose up inside her like a volcano, rich and volatile and resplendent in its destructiveness.

Amanda never pays.

But that was about to change.

Claire had never broken her non-disclosure agreement, not just because she was afraid of her aunt's retribution—which she knew would be swift and severe—but because without an actual confession from Amanda any information would be hearsay and therefore inadmissible in court. If she wanted her aunt to pay, she had to make her confess. And the only way Claire knew how to do that, was to make her angry too.

"You pathetic old hag."

"I beg your pardon," Amanda spluttered at Claire's opening volley.

"You heard me, Aunty."

Amanda raised a hand to her chest, attempted to stare Claire down. "How dare you speak to me like that you ungrateful—"

"Ungrateful?" Claire spat, her voice growing purposefully louder every moment she faced her aunt down. "And what exactly should I be *grateful* for, Amanda? The never-ending stream of insults you threw at me every chance you got? Telling me over and over how stupid and fat and ugly I was? Or do you mean the impossible standards you set so you could watch me fail? So you could prove you were smarter than me, better than me? Or maybe you feel I should thank you for the makeup lessons, when you taught me how to hide the bruises you gave me. Is that what I should be grateful for?"

Amanda straightened to her full height, narrowed her eyes, modulated her voice. "I took you in when you had nothing. I gave you everything."

"*Saint Amanda*," Claire sneered, planting her hands on her hips. "You only took me in because the courts forced you."

Her aunt folded her arms over her chest and shot her a withering glare. "And didn't that turn out well?"

"Very well. You got a slave and I got a first-class ticket to hell."

"Oh, boohoo. You lived in luxury."

"I lived in a prison. Don't touch. Don't talk."

"Children should be seen and not heard," Amanda said with her usual indifference.

"That's rich. A whole week would pass and the only communication between us would be via post-it notes on the fridge. You were never home to see or hear me."

"Most kids would see that as a blessing."

"I was nine," Claire raged.

"What you were was a waste of space," Amanda said, matching her tone and volume. "I took you in to my home, I educated you at the best schools money could buy and what did it get me? A useless, good-for-nothing traitor. You were more interested in mooning over the competition than running Morse Industries. Or did you think I didn't know about your pathetic little crush on Luke Hardcastle, even before you stabbed me in the back."

"I didn't stab you in the back, Amanda. I stood up for what was right. Because I couldn't stomach it anymore. These were people's lives you were ruining, and you didn't care."

"Don't be so naïve."

"Naïve?" Claire scoffed. "Isn't that why you chose *me* to study Luke and look for weaknesses, because you thought me too naïve to understand what you were doing? What did Luke ever do to you anyway, Amanda? Besides refusing to sell you his father's legacy at bargain basement prices, I mean."

"Oh, get off your high horse, Claire. I will not be spoken down to by the likes of you."

"The likes of me?"

"You're his whore! A gold-digging slut he keeps around for his amusement."

Claire's mouth twitched up in one corner and she raised a brow. "What's wrong, Amanda? Jealous?" Her aunt's eyes widened, flickered with fear. *Gotcha.* Claire pushed the advantage. "That's it, isn't it? You're jealous. But what of I wonder? Maybe because I'm actually making something of myself despite your best efforts to see me fail, or does it just come down to the fact that a man, *this* man," she said jabbing a finger at Luke. "Wants *me* more than you?"

Amanda's voice sharpened. "Stop talking right now."

"No. I won't. Because I'm not afraid of you anymore. You'd heard Hardcastle Construction was going through a change of management and assumed the worst. It never occurred to you it was just Luke's dad passing the baton to Luke."

"Shut. Up."

"But it wasn't just the sale Luke refused, was it?" Understanding dawned. "He refused *you*, didn't he? You made him one of your 'special offers' and he laughed you out of the building. He insulted you, and we all know what happens when Amanda Morse doesn't get her way."

"You're dangerously close to a lawsuit, girl," Amanda snarled.

But Claire was on a roll. She'd kept her aunt's secrets for long enough and if spilling the ones she knew helped reveal the few she didn't, then it was worth it. She could return to her little life with a clear conscience, lick her wounds and begin again.

"You harassed Luke to the point he got a restraining order against you, and when you couldn't go after him anymore, you went after his family. You attacked his weakness."

"Claire." The this-is-your-last-warning look fired her way.

"You went after Cassidy Holdings, went out of your way to influence the market where you could and when Lottie's dad got sick and their share prices dropped, that's when you swooped in for the kill. Only Lottie got there first, didn't she?"

"Jumped up little shit. Youngest female CEO my arse!" Amanda jabbed her finger into her own chest. "I was two years younger when I started Morse Industries."

Claire continued as though Amanda hadn't spoken. "Lottie was good at her job. She turned the company around, made them profitable again. Cassidy Holdings share prices went back up and it was going to cost a lot more to buy them out and dismantle them. And that really pissed you off. But you found a solution to that problem too, didn't you?"

Amanda's bubbling rage boiled over. "Damn straight I did! That little upstarts cancer was the best thing that ever happened to me. I knew share prices would plummet if the company's CEO was in doubt, especially for the second time in as many years. I wanted to shout it from the rooftops, but why should I when I have contacts at every news outlet in town?"

"You disgust me," Claire said.

"The feeling is mutual, I assure you. It's no wonder I kicked you out. You always cared more about protecting

Hardcastle's family than you did your own. I wasn't even surprised when security intercepted that email you tried to send him, warning him of what was coming. I get more loyalty from his goddamn secretary than I ever got from you."

And there it was.

The secret they'd all been waiting to hear.

"Sandra?"

"Who do you think told me about Cassidy's cancer, you twit. I have spies in every one of my competitor's camps. And if you think for a moment that I won't sue the shit out of you for breaking your NDA then you have another thing coming. That tidy little trust fund of yours will be mine by Christmas. You can count on it."

Amanda continued ranting but Claire had heard enough. She turned and surveyed the silent crowd surrounding them, eyes wide and mouths hanging open like a hundred goldfish, except she was the one in the glass bowl. Then ignoring the sound of a hundred cameras sounding for all the world like a hundred guns being fired at her public execution, she stood before Luke, her chin raised with the last scrap of dignity she possessed.

"There's your evidence," she whispered. "And I hope you bloody-well choke on it."

Tired and miserable and certain she'd lost everything she'd ever cared about, Claire shoved her way through the crowd and ran out to the terrace, found a private place away from prying eyes and let her tears come.

Chapter Thirty-Nine

Luke glared at Amanda with sheer, unadulterated hatred.

All of this bullshit had been because she couldn't take 'no' for an answer?

Jesus fucking Christ.

Well at least he knew now *how* she did it. And by tomorrow morning the rest of the country would too. Every news castor, newspaper, radio station and online news source in town had someone here tonight, and Amanda Morse admitting to her underhanded business tactics in front of rolling cameras was definitely going to come back to bite her in the arse.

Luke had been unaware of Amanda's dealings with his stepfather, and Claire had actually broken her non-disclosure agreement to tell him. Not only that, but she'd been fired for trying to protect Lottie, a woman she'd never met.

"I was always yours."

Did he dare to hope, did Claire love him?

Why would she do all of this otherwise?

Luke's gut clenched as he remembered the look on her face when she'd confronted him and Marx.

Devastated. Betrayed. Determined.

Brave.

He had to find her, but first he had to protect her.

Luke towered over Amanda, his arms fold across his chest. "You should have left well enough alone."

"You shouldn't have said no," she said.

Luke snorted humourlessly. "There is no scenario in this world when I would ever say yes to a woman like you. You will stay the fuck away from Claire or I will come after you with everything I have. And if you've been keeping up your research then you should already know that's a shit-load more than I had ten years ago. Do not test me, Amanda. You will lose."

Then he turned his back on her and left the ballroom in search of Claire.

It didn't take him long to find an Amazonian woman in a tight red dress trying to hide in a sheltered corner of the terrace. He just wished he hadn't found her crying, her body shaking, racked by sobs, her eyes red, her face blotchy from her tears.

He approached with caution, draped his jacket around her shoulders. "Sweetness? Can I talk to you?"

"Fuck off, Hardcastle," she said, sliding her arms through the sleeves and fastening the buttons.

"Well, you're talking to me. That's a start."

Steel-blue daggers turned in his direction. "What do you want? What more could you possibly want from me? You've taken almost *everything* I have, and now Amanda's coming for the rest."

Body shuddering as the next wave of anxiety washed over her, Luke pulled into his arms and wrapped them tightly around her. "Breathe, Claire. Remember to breathe." And he felt her hands fist in his shirt as she took deep breaths. He rubbed circles on her back. "Good girl. That's my good girl. And Amanda isn't coming for anything. I've seen to that."

Claire pushed him back enough to raise her head. "What do you mean you've seen to it?"

"I mean if she knows what's good for her, she'll do as she's told and stay away from you."

She wriggled out of his arms and stepped away from him. "And I'm just supposed to trust you, am I? After you lied to me, after you swore to me that what we had was real and—" Her words ended on a sob.

"It is real, sweet—"

"Don't. Just... don't. How am I supposed to trust anything you say after what I overheard in there?" she said, flinging her arm towards the ballroom. "You told that arse-hole where we'd be."

His frustration was palpable. "No, I didn't. And I don't have a fucking clue what he's talking about. I don't know how to say it any plainer. I have never sent Chris Marx an email."

"Then why were you paying him off?"

"I wasn't paying him shit. I was trying to goad the fuckwit into a fight so I could punch him in the face," he said, holding up his right hand so she could see the bruises already forming on his knuckles.

"You hit him?" she said, frowning. "Why?"

He stroked her cheek. "Because he hurt you."

Luke waited patiently as Claire sniffed and sized him up, narrowed her eyes as she stared at his hand then watched his face and searched for the lie. Eventually, she said, "Well if you didn't send the emails, then who did?"

"Yeah, that would be me." Lottie and Nate appeared from the direction of the ballroom. "I sent Chris Marx the emails divulging your *affair*."

Luke stared at his sister as though she'd grown another head. "What? But you... Lottie, *why?*" What possible reason could she have for doing such a thing?

Hands akimbo, she said, "Because you're an idiot too stubborn to go after the only woman you've ever truly wanted to be with. Have you told her yet?"

Luke rubbed the back of his neck. "I... um...."

"No, I didn't think so."

"Told me what?" Claire said, her mistrust of him clear for all to see. He hated the look on her face. Hated even more the fact he'd put it there.

"Why I date skinny blondes," Luke said, sighing heavily and dragging his hand down his face. "It's because they're the opposite of you."

Her bottom lip wobbled, and her eyes filled with fresh tears.

"It's not what you think," he said quickly. "I was infatuated with you. I've wanted you since that day at the coffee truck."

Her brow scrunched, her voice wavered. "But you yelled at me. All that time I thought you hated me. I thought I was some kind of sicko for crushing on you because you hated me."

Luke couldn't help the smile that sprung to his lips. "You really did have a crush on me?"

Claire nodded, the action reluctant. "Because you were kind. Before you yelled at me, you were kind to me. It probably didn't seem like much to you, but it meant the world to me."

"Jesus. I really am an arsehole." Luke pulled her into his

arms again, relaxed when she returned his embrace. "I'm ashamed to admit it now, but back then the thought you might be just like Amanda kept me away. It was easier to hold on to the fantasy of you than it was to discover what I assumed was the truth. But then the fantasy became too much of a distraction and I did everything I could think of to get you out of my system. So even though I'm attracted to curvy brunettes, I dated women who were your complete opposite. Skinny blondes."

Claire stared up at Luke like he was a complete moron. "Why didn't you just date curvy brunettes?"

"Because they wouldn't be you," he said softly, stroking her hair. "And that wouldn't be fair to them or me."

Claire wiped her eyes and took a breath, then looked at the situation as only Claire could. "So what you're saying is, I wasn't the only sicko with a weird crush?"

Luke laughed and held her close. "Exactly."

"But I'm also saying I love you, Miss Morse. And...." He pulled back and patted down his jacket. "Hang on a tic...." He reached inside the inner pocket and retrieved what he was looking for, then got down on one knee. "Will you marry me, sweetness?"

Claire blinked several times, her gaze jumping from the ring in his hand to his face and back again as though she wasn't sure what she was seeing was real. Luke frowned at the ring, another piece he bought from the shop she refused to set foot in.

"Don't you like it? You can choose a different one if you—"

"Yes."

His eyes narrowed. "Yes, you don't like the ring...?" Luke wanted to be sure which question had garnered the answer.

"Yes, I'll marry you," she said with a laugh. "Mr Hardcastle. Because I love you too."

Luke slid the ring on her finger, got to his feet and kissed her. "I was going to ask you next week at your birthday dinner, but when I saw you in this dress.... I thought my heart might explode if I didn't propose to you tonight. I love you so much, Claire," he whispered against her lips, then took her mouth in a searing kiss.

A distant voice spilled from the open ballroom doors, recalling them to their surroundings. The event's emcee was announcing the evening meal and asking everyone to take their seats.

"Come on, let's go rub Amanda's nose in it," Luke said.

"Might be a bit late," Nate said. "We saw her running for cover after your... ah, whatever that was. What was that all about anyway?"

"Love," sighed Lottie.

"I thought it was about revenge," Luke said, feeling as confused as Nate looked.

"Yeah, nah, not so much."

Luke stopped and pinned Lottie with an irritated stare. "Then what the hell did we do all this for?"

"Well, I had to bring you two together somehow and agreeing to your quest for revenge seemed like the easiest way to accomplish that."

"You mean everything Luke and I have done to get Amanda's admission of guilt was just a ruse to get us together? Even before you tipped off that horrid gossip monger?"

Lottie grinned unapologetically then shrugged. "He loves you. He always has. And I don't know how much time I have. I couldn't bear the thought of Luke being on his own, so I did what was necessary."

Nate hugged Lottie tightly. "My little love goddess."

Back in the warmth of the ballroom they found their table and sat down. Well, Luke sat down then hauled Claire into his lap. "From now on, sweetness, neither of us will be alone. Never again. You're my family now, and I'm yours. Forever."

"Forever," she agreed as she snuggled against his shoulder. "I think I'd like that."

Epilogue

F*ive months later...*

"I love you, Mrs Hardcastle."

"I love you too, Mr Hardcastle," Claire murmured against her husband's mouth even as she wriggled against the steel construction crane he called a cock.

It probably wasn't the smartest idea, teasing Luke that way when they were in the middle of their first dance together as husband and wife, all eyes on them as they spun across the floor, but she couldn't help herself. Knowing he wanted sex as much as she did brought out her naughty side.

He only had himself to blame.

Not that Luke seemed to mind being teased. He grinned, even as he groaned and grabbed her arse, pulled her tighter against his thick erection. "*Fuck*, sweetness, I can't wait to get you out of here and on my jet."

She grinned back. "On your *jet*, huh? Is that what we're calling it these days?"

Luke laughed, then pressed the sweetest kiss to her lips. "Cheeky woman," he murmured, then pressed his cheek to hers and kept dancing.

By the end of the song, the dance floor was full of wedding guests and idle chatter and Claire's mind drifted, the gentle swaying of her husband's—God, she loved calling him that—body against hers and the strength of his arms wrapped around her making her feel safe enough to explore her thoughts in peace.

Her life had changed so much in the last few months, and all for the better.

Sandra, Luke's ex-assistant, had been unceremoniously fired. Lottie and Karen had actually taken lawn chairs and popcorn to Luke's office so they could watch the awful woman's departure from the building. Claire had declined to join them, certain she'd be unable to resist the urge to slap the little twit for hurting her family. Last they'd heard she was working in a cafe in Melbourne.

Chris Marx tried suing Luke for punching him in the face, until Luke's team of lawyers reminded the douchebag that they had video evidence of him sexually assaulting Claire at the quays. Not to mention allegations of blackmail, coercion and invasion of privacy. He dropped the suit so fast it was laughable.

And then there was Amanda.

The morning after the ball, the local news was dominated by their fight and the revelations that had come from it. She'd been audited a week later, and arrested a month after that, charged with manipulation of the market, corporate espionage and intimidation. And pending further evidence, she could be facing insider trading charges too.

She'd been let go on bail, pending her trial, but her accounts had been frozen, her passport seized and no one was taking her calls anymore.

Amanda Morse was done.

Luke's legal team had managed to get Claire's trust fund released though, which meant she'd been able to pay Luke back for her house, and hired a team of renovators to finish fixing up the old girl. She'd even had security cameras installed, because Amanda had continued making threats, especially after losing access to her money.

When it all got to be too much, Luke moved Claire into his penthouse, and Claire now rented the house to Karen. Which reminded her....

"So, how much do you want to bet Karen and Edward hook up while we're gone?"

Luke chuckled and smiled down at her. "You're so certain they will?"

She cocked one brow. "Are you not?"

Luke's eyes narrowed in a look Claire knew well, calculating and devious. "One thousand dollars. That's my bet."

Claire sighed and threw him a look of mock-pity. "Like stealing candy from a baby."

"Speaking of babies," Luke said, guiding Claire back to the bridal table. "Let's not overdo it on the dance floor. I need you to save your energy for later."

"I'm pregnant, not an invalid," she murmured so no one would overhear them. They hadn't gone public with their happy news just yet. "I can dance *and* have sex."

"And I look forward to seeing your moves in action," he said, one corner of his sensuous mouth lifting in another grin. "Just as soon as I get you on my... *jet.*"

"You're incorrigible," she laughed, then tugged him

close again and smothered his grin with one of her own, kissed her husband long and deep.

"I love you," he whispered against her lips when they finally came up for air. "Both of you," he added, sliding his big, strong hand across her belly.

"I love you, too," Claire replied, adding her hand to Luke's. "Both of you."

"Forever?" he asked, leaning his forehead against hers.

"Forever," she agreed, knowing she meant it with every fibre of her soul.

I hope you enjoyed Claire and Luke's story.

Please consider sharing the love by leaving a review for other readers to find. It doesn't need to be very long, and every review is greatly appreciated.

#sharethelove

Ready for more sexy bachelors?

The Roller Derby Darling and The Delinquent
is next!

Edward Berringer is a chauffeur, a soon-to-be business
owner, and oh, yeah, he's an ex-con.

With the promise of financial backing for his vintage auto
garage on the line, Edward has no time for dating, but when
months of flirting with Karen Walker finally culminates in a
scorching hot kiss, he'll make the fucking time. After all, the
manager of his favourite bookshop is everything he wants in
a woman: smart, sassy, and a total badass. Who also
happens to come from a family of cops. *Awkward.*

He knows he should probably stay away from her—and her
overprotective brothers—but then again, he's never been
one to play by the rules.

Especially when love is involved.

More from Jennie Kew

Carved In Stone

Battery Operated Boyfriend

Tying The Knot

Quirky: The Complete Q Collection

Acknowledgements

To my family for all their encouragement, their love and understanding, thank you for being you and for putting up with me being me, especially when deadlines are involved.

A special thank you to my crit partners, my cheer squad, my sisters-in-arms, Bec McMaster and Kylie Griffin. You always challenge me to be a better writer and I really couldn't do this without you. Thank you for keeping me sane...*ish*.

And finally to my readers, thank you for taking this journey with me, and for allowing me to share with you all the people and places who occupy my head and my heart. I hope you enjoy reading about them as much as I enjoy writing about them.

Meet the Author

Jennie has always enjoyed reading but never had aspirations of becoming a published author. At least not until a dance with death made her ask herself what she really wanted out of life, and she's been writing ever since.

When not writing stories about her imaginary friends, Jennie can usually be found reading a book, watching a movie or building stuff out of Lego. She lives in regional New South Wales with her husband, her husband's magnificent beard, and their small menagerie of furry companions.

www.jenniekew.com

Glossary

As all of my books are set in Australia and use a lot of Australian terms and slang, I've created this guide for my readers to keep you on track when you come across any Aussie-isms in my books.

A bit of all right: If someone is 'a bit of all right' they're considered to be very attractive.

Ambo: Short for ambulance, the term has come to mean anyone associated with any of the public or private ambulance services, their drivers and paramedics.

Arse: Aussie spelling of ass, aka buttocks, bottom, booty and bum.

Arvo and *Sarvo*: 'Afternoon' and 'this afternoon'.

Copper: Police, cops.

Fashion Rag/Local Rag: Fashion magazine, any locally produced magazines or newspapers.

Fierie/s: Firefighter/s.

Fuck-knuckle: An idiot.

G'day: Pronounced 'gidday', this official Australian greeting is a contraction of the words 'good' and 'day'.

Kiwi: Pronounced 'kee-wee', anyone born in New Zealand.

Larrikin: An unruly, boisterous but generally good natured person, usually male.

Mate: Unlike paranormal or sci-fi erotic romances where your 'mate' is the person you're fated to be with for the rest of your life, in Australian culture 'mate' could mean anyone from your best friend to some random bloke you just met.

Pav: Pavlova, a dessert made from baked meringue, topped with cream and fresh fruit, particularly popular around Christmas. We nicked it from the Kiwis.

Phwoar: An estimation of the sound one makes when a bit of all right enters your vicinity. See also, 'panting' and 'drooling'.

RFS: Rural Fire Service.

Sanga: Sandwich.

She'll be right, mate: Usually given as a response when someone is offering aid of some kind, it means 'Everything will be fine but thanks for asking'.

Togs: A swimsuit.

Tradie: Any tradesman.

Uni: Pronounced 'you-nee', University aka College.

Yeah, nah and *Nah, yeah*: Whichever word the phrase ends on, is the affirmative answer, therefore 'Yeah, nah' means 'No', and 'Nah, yeah' means 'Yes'.